MADAME
AURORA

MADAME AURORA

BY

SARAH ALDRIDGE

THE NAIAD PRESS INC.

1983

Printed in the United States of America
First Edition

Cover design by Susannah Kelly

Typesetting by Sandi Stancil

Library of Congress Cataloging in Publication Data

Aldridge, Sarah.
      Madame Aurora.

        I. Title.
PS3551.L345M3 1983   813'.54   83-8204
ISBN 0-930044-44-4

To

TW

From women's eyes this doctrine I derive:
They sparkle still the right Promethean fire;
They are the books, the arts, the academes,
That show, contain, and nourish all the world.

Love's Labour's Lost, Act IV, sc. 3

WORKS by Sarah Aldridge

THE LATECOMER	1974
TOTTIE	1975
CYTHEREA'S BREATH	1976
ALL TRUE LOVERS	1979
THE NESTING PLACE	1982
MADAME AURORA	1983

I

CHAPTER ONE

Hannah sat by the window, listening to the din. It was midnight and the church bells, the whistles, the horns, the yells, even the sound of someone beating on the bottom of a tin washtub below in the dark, were greeting the new year. 1897. Three more years to the end of the century. Or four, if you took the other side of the dispute about when the new century would begin.

She hoped that the racket, muted a little by the closed pane, would not wake Elizabeth. This was the first night that Elizabeth had slept peacefully, not murmuring and tossing, since the onset of her illness. Hannah, restless with the thoughts that crowded her mind, sat without a light, waiting to see if she would stir.

In the last few days, with each passing hour, it had become clearer to her that she must do something or they would soon be out on the street with nothing to eat. Never had their supply of money been so low. Elizabeth's illness was the last straw. Fortunately she had found a woman doctor who agreed to postpone payment till things were better. But how could they get better if she was unable to earn sufficient money?

It had been easier when they were younger, she and Elizabeth. She had always been able to find work to tide them over the less prosperous patches. Here in Washington, whenever they came for a sojourn so that Elizabeth might do research in the Library of Congress, she had often found temporary work, taking advantage of the fact that the Federal Government was a large employer of women. That was something that had begun with the Civil War, with the shortage of men at a time of an expanding bureaucracy. Over the years she had worked as a sorter of bills in the Treasury Department, as a letter scribe in the New Department of Agriculture, as a clerk in the Pension Office- most of it poorly paid work usually carried out in cramped and badly ventilated, ill-lit quarters but at least it provided a steady income for the many women who needed to earn their own bread. Now, however, though she knew herself to be still strong and capable, nobody wanted to hire an old woman for any but the most menial, low-paid drudgery. And as long as Elizabeth was too ill to fend for herself, she could not go out slaving all day for a pittance and leave her to the care of some ignorant slattern, for that was the only sort of person she would be able to hire.

A sound from the bed roused her and she went over and lit the gas flame, turning it low so as not to disturb Elizabeth. She looked down at the gaunt white face on the pillow. Elizabeth stirred and moved her lips. Understanding what she wanted, Hannah lifted her head and gave her a drink of water. Then touching her forehead she assured herself that the fever had not returned. Yes, with careful nursing Elizabeth had a good chance to recover. She certainly could not leave her.

At the moment when she straightened up beside the bed she came abruptly to a decision. There was one way in which she could provide for them. Often in the past her mind had wandered in that direction and she turned deliberately away from the thought. But now she contemplated the idea steadfastly. She must get Elizabeth out of this mean room and into more suitable quarters. She must find the money not only to feed them both but to provide the luxuries Elizabeth should have. There was only one way open to her and she must take it. As soon as Elizabeth was well enough to discuss the matter, she would tell her about it. But now she must act.

She would become Madame Aurora, spiritual advisor.

She smiled to herself. Even the name had come easily to her. She noted that she was not at all concerned about the venture or doubtful of its success. The way opened. This was the path she should follow. The propitious moment had come. She must use her gifts.

What troubled her was that she would be acting without Elizabeth's knowledge and concurrence. Elizabeth had never approved of the use of her gifts, especially for money. Since their first coming together, Elizabeth had demurred at the idea of recognizing manifestations of the supernatural. She had never questioned Hannah's good faith. She simply refused to accept the existence of phenomena that were beyond human hearing, sight, understanding. But nevertheless over the years she had come to an unacknowledged, halfway belief in the validity of Hannah's apparent ability to foresee, to experience contact with others too remote in time and space for the intervention of the usual means of communication.

Yes, she was troubled by the fact that for the first time in their thirty years together she was undertaking something vital to them both without Elizabeth's knowledge and consent. Through the years she had scrupled to ignore Elizabeth's disapproval and had refrained from making use of her gifts except in cases when they had come spontaneously into play. Now, however, she must act on her own. It was foolish, she assured herself, to hesitate now. If Elizabeth were able to judge the circumstances, she certainly would agree to what Hannah proposed to do, on the principle, at least, that beggars could not be choosers. Nevertheless, she shrank a little from taking the first step, because it encroached on that precious terrain of absolute unity of thought and feeling, that magical ground on which she and Elizabeth had stood, alone together, over so many years.

But it had to be done. She bent over the bed and kissed Elizabeth. Then she turned down the gas as low as it would go and lay down on the bed beside her to take a little nap.

∿ ∿ ∿ ∿ ∿

When she woke her mind reverted to her decision. She knew just what steps she was going to take. The City of Washington, she was aware from old acquaintance, was a fertile field for anyone who professed the gift of clairvoyance, prophecy, spiritualistic powers. Her habit of noticing what went on about her and her retentive memory had over the years furnished her with a fund of information about the life of the city, the kind of people who were apt to come there with each change in the administration of the national government. All sorts of mediums, seers, even gypsy fortune tellers flourished in the shadow of the Capitol building. No doubt the special uncertainties of life in the political world sharpened the wish of many for a glimpse into the future. She could do much better—she was certain of that—than this rabble of self-styled spiritual guides. She felt her own ability. She had a very good idea of the degree of psychic power that was hers and how effectively she could use it if she chose to.

Her first act was to rent the front room on the ground floor of the lodging house in which she and Elizabeth were living. She placed a discreet sign in the heavily curtained window— Madame Aurora, spiritual advisor. She regretted that she could go no further afield than this shabby street, dirty and littered, where the well-to-do would not care to come. Nevertheless, her sign was soon noticed, by modest people, some troubled, some curious. It was a beginning. She would have to use it as a stepping stone to something better.

She also placed a small advertisement in *The Washington Post*, saying that Madame Aurora had now established her residence in the Nation's Capital and was prepared to give spiritual counsel to any who wished reliable and genuine guidance in their personal and financial affairs. The few lines of print took almost the last penny she had. Reading them, she thought of Elizabeth. She glanced across the room at her, now sitting and dozing in the chair by the window. This venture must succeed.

She was not really surprised by the response she began to have almost at once. People had always sought her as a confidante, ready to believe that she could foresee what the future might hold for them. Her feeling, readily communicated to them, was usually compassionate for these seekers after spiritual comfort. Even people of greater than average sophistication endured moments of psychic distress, of feeling forlorn, of doubt about themselves, the meaning and worth of their lives. Her capacity for listening with sympathy, for giving encouragement, her ability to sketch some hopefulness in someone's future, seemed to reassure them. Many people in the past had attached themselves to her with fondness, seeing her as a dear friend, their shield against despair, a comforter in matters too private to be discussed even with their intimates.

And then there were the curious, those who were disposed to believe in the supernatural and wished to test her powers, those who wanted to be taken behind the veil of earthly things into a world of marvels beyond the reaches of the physical senses. Even men in the financial world and politicians found their way to her.

But she wanted a wider scope and she hit upon the idea of having gatherings—she made it plain that these were not seances, that she had no dealings with mysterious rappings, ghostly presences, voices from the dead—of people who wished to learn from her the laws that she believed governed the universe. That universe, she taught, was made up of the world as experienced by humans—a minor part, she declared, of the whole—and the vast unknown that lay beyond the perceptions of the average person. Everyone, she told her rapt listeners, had the capacity to penetrate the thick layer of the physical world that shrouded them, was capable of seeing into the astral light that dazzled the mind beyond the reaches of our physical senses. She would teach those who were eager and dedicated. For this purpose she was even willing to go to the house of anyone who wished to gather a group of friends together to hear her.

It was in this way that she met Mrs. Head, in the drawing-room of a house in a neighborhood favored by well-to-do Congressional families. She had spotted her at once, from the sweet eagerness with which she fixed her eyes on her face. She was a pretty, fashionably dressed woman in middle age, with the well-kept hands and delicate skin that spoke of a life of luxury. She was, in fact, Hannah soon discovered, the wife of Colonel W. T. Head, the silver magnate, whose wealth was believed to be incalculable and who had come to Washington to spend his last days. So Mrs. Head could be supposed to be a woman without worldly anxieties. But to Hannah's observant eye she appeared to be a woman who sought some solace that money could not buy. Among the group of curious people listening to this new seer she was especially attentive, as if she closed out the presence of the others and was aware only of the woman who spoke. The next time Hannah addressed a gathering she was again present and after the meeting seemed about to join those who pressed around the seer with questions. But when Hannah with bland impartiality turned her way, she took fright and drew back. I shall see her again, thought Hannah.

She did not expect her to come to her shabby consulting

room. Such a woman would not venture into such an unfamiliar, rather forbidding neighborhood. Instead, within a day or so, she sent a message, asking Madame Aurora as a great favor to call on her at her house on Sixteenth Street.

∿ ∿ ∿ ∿ ∿

The April afternoon was mild, hazy with the coming warmth of the Washington summer. Sixteenth Street was empty of traffic and silent except for the small crescendos of sound from the sparrows in the big elms. Hannah, walking purposefully around Scott Circle, did not glance at the general in bronze on his horse, staring down towards the White House. Her attention was on what lay ahead of her.

She was a vigorous woman and the colorful flowing skirts she wore emphasized her portliness. She wore a dark shawl over her head and shoulders, pushed back from her face. The hand with which she held its ends together at her breast was a weathered brown and pudgy, with a ring with a large dark opaque stone.

When she came to the enormous stone house whose facade jutted out toward the street she glanced briefly but intently at its upper stories, battlemented, with clusters of chimneys of irregular height and round-arched windows. Then with scarcely a pause she walked through the wide arch of the driveway up to the front door set inside another smaller arch faced with white stone. There was the scent of horses and hay coming from the end of the drive beyond the kitchen door, visible behind a vineclad abutment. The coachhouse and the stable must be down there.

The black servant who opened the door looked her up and down with a disparaging eye. She faced him down with a bold stare and said, "Mrs. Head is awaiting me."

Reluctantly he led her across a wide dark hall, deeply carpeted and furnished with carved mahogany tall-backed chairs and a bronze statue of two beasts in mortal combat, to the door of the drawingroom. It was a very large room lit by numerous tall windows so heavily curtained that the light was dim and gave an illusion of coolness.

Mrs. Head was hurrying across the room to greet her. "Oh,

Madame Aurora, how do you do? I am so pleased that you could come to see me!"

Her nervousness echoed in her voice. Hannah bowed slightly without speaking.

"Won't you come and sit down?" Mrs. Head led her to the great fireplace, shut off by a large summer screen. She gestured to a massive high-backed chair and sat down in another like it. Hannah, gathering her full skirts, fitted herself into its arms.

Mrs. Head rushed in nervously. "I know that you rarely pay personal calls. I quite appreciate your kindness in coming to see me. It would be quite impossible for me to come to your house, so that I can only meet you in gatherings at my friends' houses. What I want to talk about I cannot say before even close friends."

"So I understood," said Hannah. Her voice was deep for a woman. "Yes, it is true that I do not usually visit in this way. But there are occasions when I feel I must seek those who need me." She leaned forward a little as she spoke, her light, brilliant eyes fixed on the woman opposite her.

Mrs. Head gave a high, tremulous, involuntary laugh. "Oh, I do feel I need you! There is really no one else I can turn to! I have been to a number of your gatherings. It was at Mrs. Ewing's that I first heard you. Your renown has spread very quickly. I have never been to a medium before —"

Hannah raised a hand to stop her. Her eyes flashed briefly. "I object to the use of that word. It has too much the flavor of fraud about it. I do not deal in contrivances to deceive the credulous. A true understanding of the occult involves a combination of a sensitive spirit and unusual qualities of mind."

Mrs. Head's pretty face flushed in alarm at this reprimand. "Oh, I merely meant —! I did not mean to offend you. I did not use the word derogatorily. I suppose I would not have been persuaded to come to your gatherings if I had really thought of you as a medium —"

"I am a spiritual advisor." Hannah's tone of voice was positive. "My spirit is a storehouse upon which I can draw for assistance in confronting the problems of the world we know through our senses. I have nothing to do with the tricks that some use to deceive the credulous — such as purporting to communicate with the dead, setting down ghostly writings. It has been my observation that such experiences are contrivances to deceive the griefstricken, the fearful. In my lifetime there have been many exposures of such unworthy deceptions."

Mrs. Head's innocent brown eyes were opened wide. "But you do believe that we can communicate with living persons at a distance and with those who have passed on, through spiritual means? I understood this to be your belief from what I heard at your gatherings. You have certainly been able to foretell events to take place in the future."

Hannah did not answer at once but sat gravely thoughtful. Finally she said, "There are those—I am one of them—who have a special sensitivity to the spiritual world that surrounds us, beyond the ken of worldly means. This sensitivity provides me with information not obtainable by physical sight and hearing and touch. However, even I am helpless to aid those who do not trust me, who are not in sympathetic understanding with me, who wish to set traps to catch me out in what they believe to be contrivances on my part."

"Oh, yes!" Mrs. Head was suddenly eager. "I understand your rejection of such people. But I am not one of them. I feel you can help me in a very intimate matter. I have every confidence in you. I do indeed trust you."

Madame Aurora looked at her inquiringly. Again Mrs. Head laughed, compulsively, nervously. "How shall I begin? How can I explain? It seems such a difficult thing to set before you. You will think me a mercenary woman, a —"

"Simply tell me what is in your heart. I know that you are troubled by a flaw in your life. I have known that since I first observed you at Mrs. Ewing's house. In the past you have taken an action that was contrary to your deepest instincts. It was a reasonable action, one that others applauded and which you have since sought to justify to yourself. But you are not at ease because you cannot erase from your spirit the fact that you acted as you did and that you violated your own inner peace by doing so."

Mrs. Head stared at her aghast. "Oh, Madame Aurora, how can you know this? I have never spoken of it to anyone—of my feelings, I mean. It is only lately that I have begun to feel so weighed down by this. Up till now I have been able to put it out of my mind—justify myself to myself, as you say. But now I feel so lost, so uneasy—yet I cannot blame anyone but myself." She hesitated. "Even now I cannot bring myself to tell you what it is."

"There is no need for you to do so. I understand your problem. The solution is for you to examine the matter in a calm, dispassionate manner, and apply the principles of spiritual knowledge, which you have begun to learn from me, and realize that the concept of blame, of punishment, of retribution is false."

Mrs. Head's eyes filled with tears. "Dear Madame Aurora! How comforting you are! I would never be able to unburden myself even so far with anyone else. Will you continue to come here and teach me, alone? I am too shy, too fearful, to speak of personal things in a group." She paused for a moment. "You must know that, as a woman of considerable wealth, I must be careful how I appear to people. I do not like to be cynical but it is true that the possession of large means does change the way in which people see you."

"I am well aware of that, my dear lady. Yes, I can make an exception in your case. I believe you need the help I can give you."

In the following weeks Hannah paid several more visits to the huge house, built like a fortress and furnished in an exaggerated imitation of great castles and palaces in Europe. It was a strange setting, she thought, for a woman of such restraint in manner, such delicacy of spirit, such sensitivity to other people's good opinion, as Mrs. Head.

When she mentioned this to Elizabeth, Elizabeth said with a quizzical smile, "A bird in a gilded cage. A bird whose wings flutter in the hope of escape."

Aware that this was Elizabeth's way of teasing her about her new career, she ignored the twinkle in Elizabeth's eye and replied, "I am quite sure that Mrs. Head has no wish to escape from her gilded cage. If she has any anxiety, it would be the opposite."

"Well, my love, then you must find out what it is you are to comfort her for."

Journeying once more by trolley and on foot to Mrs. Head, she pondered. When she had finally told Elizabeth that she was now Madame Aurora, that she had taken the bold step of venturing her gifts among worldly people, Elizabeth had merely said, "Indeed." Elizabeth did not like it. But Elizabeth was always fair and to a degree curious about new ventures. She would wait to see what came forth.

Walking up Sixteenth Street once more she thought, Obviously it was not Mrs. Head's taste that was reflected in this towering monument to riches. It was the Colonel who was portrayed here in this house. Its flamboyance, its larger than life proportions, its aggressive splendor spoke of him, of his desire thus to create a memorial to his own achievements, to the tremendous power he had conjured out of nothing.

Or, rather, out of silver. She knew his history as well as anyone who read the newspapers. His origins were obscure—some hamlet in rural New England, perhaps. Before the Civil War he had gone West with thousands of other seekers after gold. In the new territory that was to become the State of Colorado he had been among those who had found and prospered from silver mining. After the Civil War he had gone to South America, to Chile and Bolivia and Peru and had again prospered in mining. But not only that. Through unscrupulous means, so many believed, he had built out of this prosperity an immense fortune, a pyramid of power, profiting from the political battles that divided opinion on the subject of silver as the standard of national wealth. He was a ruthless man who would let nobody and nothing stand in the way of his ambition. He had, said his enemies, of whom there were many, no allegiance to family, God or country, only to his own aggrandisement.

A strange husband, she thought, for Mrs. Head.

On each succeeding visit it became more apparent to her that Mrs. Head's immediate concern—whatever might be the basis for her spiritual lack of ease—had something to do with her husband. She knew, by watching her, that it was taking Mrs. Head a little while to steel herself to broach the subject.

Finally, with an impatience she could no longer deny, she decided to break through the barrier of Mrs. Head's reluctance. She said, "Mrs. Head, you are distracted by something that prevents you from giving full attention to our discussion. I believe you are troubled about something that has to do with your husband."

Mrs. Head looked at her with mingled surprise and relief. "Oh, how you see into me! There is something that worries me." She considered for a moment. "Madame Aurora, would you see my husband? Would you visit him in his rooms and give him the benefit of your counsel?"

Hannah frowned. "I do not visit anyone who does not ask for my assistance. It would be useless."

"Oh, I know! But I know also that he would never invite you. Yet I feel that he needs your comfort. He is troubled—by memories—perhaps by uneasiness about the hereafter. He is elderly, you know, many years older than I. He is ill—he has had a stroke. I believe he feels lonely—a loneliness I cannot dispel —"

"Many people, as they draw near their earthly end, wish for reassurance about themselves, about the after-life, even though in their earlier years they have given such things little heed."

"Yes." Mrs. Head hesitated. "I am sure you know that the Colonel has had a very varied life. I myself am not acquainted with the details of much of it—though of course there is a great deal of slander in what some people say about him. Great wealth arouses envy, as I am sure you know."

The note of defensiveness in her voice caught Hannah's ear. Her own interest rose. She was curious about the Colonel. She must see him, of course, if she was to understand what troubled his wife. But she assumed a measured reluctance. "As you know, I do not press myself upon those who do not come to me freely, seeking my help. Those who do not open themselves to me cannot receive my help."

Mrs. Head sighed. "There is a matter on which I do need help and I am sure you could provide it. A practical matter."

Hannah waited for her to go on.

"I must tell you that I am very anxious about my own future in case of his death. It is dreadful to be concerned with mercenary matters at such a time. But I cannot pretend to ignore them. Madame Aurora, I have no idea what provision my husband has made for me when he dies. I do not know what I can expect—how I shall live —"

She came to a trembling halt. Hannah, astonished, glanced quickly around the imposing room, at the massive furnishings, at the paintings crowding the walls. "But surely the Colonel will have taken the proper steps to insure your protection and comfort. Need you doubt this?"

Mrs. Head's unhappiness showed in her face but she did not answer.

"Have you never discussed the matter with him? Have you never asked him what his wishes are, as far as you are concerned?"

The small pretty woman seemed to recoil at such forthrightness. "Oh, I have never spoken of such things with him, never! It would not do for me to broach such a subject with him. He would be offended at the idea that I should be thinking of his death. Besides, I have no notion of business." She gave her nervous little laugh. "What woman does?"

Many women did, thought Hannah. But aloud she said, "he must have advisors—lawyers, business associates."

"Oh, yes! Mr. Carson—Hugh Carson. He is quite a young man but the Colonel seems to have every confidence in him."

"Then probably he knows what the Colonel's plans are."

"But he would not tell me!"

Hannah heard the note of desperation in her voice. "Then what do you expect that I could do to help you?"

Mrs. Head hesitated. "I don't know, really. It just seems to me that perhaps if he talked to you, he would be more candid."

"Why should that be?"

Mrs. Head's embarrassment almost overwhelmed her. "Because you have such an influence over people—over anyone who hears you speak. I have noticed that people confide in you. They feel such trust in you. Why, look at me! I have never spoken to anyone else about this!" Again she laughed.

"I see. But how should I have an opportunity to converse with him? It does not seem likely that he would invite me to see him."

"I think I could arrange that. I mentioned that he is a little worried about himself—what the future holds for him. He has had a stroke but he has recovered his faculties very well, though he cannot walk. His mind is not affected and one scarcely notices that he has difficulty in speaking. He is confined to a wheelchair and that, I think, affects his spirits. I have told him about you—how everyone succumbs to your magnetism, what an extraordinary power you have to throw light in dark corners. He has admitted that he would like to meet you."

Hannah debated with herself. How much did what Mrs. Head say really reflect the Colonel and how much her own eagerness to bring this about? She was aware that Mrs. Head's eyes were fixed on her beseechingly. Finally she asked, "Are you quite sure he will receive me?"

"Oh, yes! Oh, do see him!" As Hannah still hesitated she got up from her chair and came toward her with an outstretched hand. "May I take you to him now?"

CHAPTER TWO

The two women mounted the baronial staircase and walked along a wide corridor lighted by tall windows before which were large baskets on stands filled with ferns. When they reached the end of it Mrs. Head opened a dark polished door and motioned for Hannah to follow her into the room.

Like the one downstairs it was a very large room filled with massive furniture and walls covered with satin brocade. Only a little daylight came in through the heavily curtained and draped windows. Over close to one window Madame Aurora saw the silhouette of someone in a wheelchair. Mrs. Head hurried away from her, speaking rapidly in her light, high-pitched voice.

A male voice rumbled, "What did you say?"

"I have brought Madame Aurora, William. You remember, you said you wanted to see her."

"I don't remember any such thing."

"Oh, William! You did say you would like to see her!"

During their exchange the man in the wheelchair had been looking beyond her. "Well, you've got her here now. So I might as well talk to her."

Mrs. Head turned back to Hannah with a smile. She whispered as she passed her on the way out of the room, "He is quite pleased. It is better if I go away."

Hannah stepped across the Turkey carpet towards the man. His chair was placed close to the window where the daylight fell the strongest but against the light she could not see the expression on his face.

He said peremptorily, "Sit down, won't you?" and pointed to a chair nearby.

As she lowered her bulk into it, he said as abruptly, turning his head, "You can clear out, Davis." It was only then that she was aware that a young man had been sitting in a straight chair against the wall. His attendant, she guessed, as the young man, with stolid indifference, got up and went out of the room.

From where she sat she had a better view of the Colonel. He was spare, with a gaunt, lined face and brilliant dark eyes that showed no sign of age or failing health. He wore a moustache as white as his hair. It drooped at the corners of his mouth and like his fingers was deeply stained with nicotine. There was a heavy scent of old cigar and pipe smoke in the room.

He did not wait for her to speak. "So you're Madame Whats-hername. You don't have to worry because I've sent that young jackass away. If I have a fit, you can call somebody. I don't like eavesdroppers."

"I am not alarmed."

He studied her a moment. "You're no spring chicken, are you? Well, that's a good thing. Wouldn't have much confidence in you, if you were."

She returned his stare impassively, aware that he sought to make her ill-at-ease. She judged that this manner of his came from a lifelong habit of setting his visitor at a disadvantage. "Mrs. Head has told me that you wish to consult me."

"Consult you? So that's what she told you? I doubt that you're likely to have any information or advice that would be any use to me. You're one of these fortune tellers, aren't you, like those gypsies that come around once in a while. You look like one."

His eyes were alight with malice as he watched to see what effect his deliberate disparagement would have on her.

Hannah was bland. "In that case, you had better make clear what you wish to see me about, for I have other pressing engagements to meet."

"Oh, you do?" He snapped up her rebuke half in pleasure at having aroused some annoyance in her, half in outrage at the idea that she would claim concerns of greater importance than waiting on him.

"Yes, I do. My advice is highly valued by many people of some importance."

He swore under his breath and said, "A lot of poppycock. Don't take much to fool most people."

Hannah gathered up her full skirts with one hand, ready to

get up from her chair. "In that case, I shall take leave of you. Mrs. Head was obviously mistaken about your wish to see me."

He was startled. "Hey, what are you doing? I didn't say you could leave."

It was her turn to snap. "I do not need your permission. I shall say goodday to you."

She stood up but he put out a hand to grip her arm. "Now, come on. Don't take on like that. Now that you're here, I'd like to talk to you. I'd like to find out if you're like all the rest of them, just a fraud. I'm not thick-headed, though I'm not the man I used to be. I can still tell the genuine article from the other thing. Sit down. I can't talk to you like that."

Reluctantly she sat down. "So you did say that you wanted me to come to you." She spoke softly.

He chewed on the end of his moustache for a moment. "I'm an old man. There's no use trying to deny that. I've got to think of what's lying in store for me. But I'm still in charge, you understand. Nobody is going to be mixing in my affairs." He grew belligerant as his line of thought reasserted itself. "Don't get any ideas about getting around me. No matter what my wife says. I'm not that far gone yet."

"I do not know why you should think that I have any interest in your business concerns."

"Oh, you don't? Just remember, I've had plenty of experience in dealing with people who want something out of me—and that means everybody."

"Your wife?"

His eyes were keen. "She's going to get what she's entitled to. Did she send you here to find out?"

"Then you think I am here as a spy?"

They stared at each other for several moments. Then he suddenly grinned, his false teeth giving an extra menace to his expression.

"Don't like the sound of that, do you? Just wanted to let you know that I'm not fooled by women's wiles. How much is my wife paying you for your services?"

Hannah bit her tongue to hold back her retort. After a moment she said, "It is indeed sad that you cannot trust your wife. She seems to have only your wellbeing in mind."

He demanded angrily, "What has that got to do with it? She's an intelligent woman. She knows how to look out for herself—all women do. They can lead men by the nose, if men let them. But I don't. Never have. I can see a step ahead of the best of them. My wife is going to know just as much as I decide she's going to know. I can still match my wits against anybody. I don't intend to lose, you understand."

He smiled at her sardonically. She sat back in her chair.

"You enjoy a battle of wits. That is within your aura, which is one of power. That power is diminishing as your life flows towards its end. You are aware of this and you seek to revive it, to prevent its ebbing. You are thwarted because you have no one with whom to engage in trials of strength in order to preserve your own—strength of will, of cunning."

She saw his anger rising as she spoke. Furious, he shouted, "God damn you! You can't talk to me like that, to my face! You aren't going to bury me with your talk." In his rage he thrashed about in his chair and pounded on the arm with one hand. The other lay limp in his lap and Hannah focussed her eyes on it. She was silent as he cursed and raved, waiting for the burst of fury to subside. The sweat sprang out on his forehead and he shook as his strength waned. She continued to wait silently, pretending indifference, to disguise the anxiety with which she listened to his jerky, heavy breathing. Presently, noticing a carafe of water on the small table near him, she poured out a glass and held it for him to drink. He gulped it eagerly.

She asked, "Do you want me to call your attendant?"

He shook his head vehemently. When he could speak normally he demanded, "What would you have done if I'd had a fit? It would be your fault."

"I would have summoned assistance, of course. I am not responsible for your bad temper."

"My bad temper! Goddamn it, woman! You're enough to drive me out of my wits. What if I'd had a fit and it had taken me off?"

"That would have been unfortunate, perhaps. But the moment of your departure from this plane of existence is fixed in your destiny. The circumstances are immaterial."

"Oh, they are! You're a cool one, I'll say. Doesn't faze you, huh?"

"I see no reason why I should feel remorse for something not of my doing."

He grimaced. "I never was one for all this remorse business, anyhow. So you know when I am going to die?"

"No, of course I do not. I have had no message from beyond concerning you."

He looked alarmed. "Message? What are you saying? Who is going to send you a message about me?"

She recognized the fearfulness in his demand. She deliberated a moment, to increase the tension of the moment. "There are unseen powers that can sometimes—and only to those endowed with sufficient sensitivity—provide little glimpses into the great cosmos, little glimpses that illuminate the destiny of individuals —a particular individual —"

"You mean, you're claiming to be a clairvoyant. I never had any opinion of mediums. Frauds, that's what they are, damn frauds."

There was a certain crispness in Hannah's voice. "Those are your characterizations. Those whom you call mediums—indeed, many who call themselves mediums—are not persons who can work in the astral light. They are not vouchsafed the necessary degree of sensitivity. They have not the developed capacity to reach beyond the confines of this terrestrial globe —"

The Colonel was grinning again. "Damn words. Do you talk to spirits? What do you know about me? Can you tell me anything about myself?"

Malice gleamed in his eyes. Hannah took her time in replying. "You've always been a man who made his own terms—with your associates, your friends, your enemies. You have seized wealth where opportunity offered, regardless of the claims of others. You have made many enemies in the course of your struggles to seize this wealth, some of them bitter enemies. You have outlived most of them, the men you wrested silver mines, power, from. You have never stayed your course for the sake of anyone else's claims. You have never felt the softer emotions— of love, trust, compassion. But now you fear the consequences of what you have done, now that you are old and disabled —"

The Colonel yelled in a sudden return of anger, "That's a lie! I'm not afraid of anything! I don't regret anything I've done. Love—remorse! A lot of poppycock! Just let anybody cross my path that thinks they can thwart me —" His voice faltered and for a moment Hannah thought there would be a recurrence of the rage of a few moments ago. But he stopped and seemed to control himself, saying then in a calmer mood. "You're right—they're all dead. And I'm not afraid of their ghosts, either. None of them." He paused and seemed to look into the past. "I wasn't afraid of them when they were alive. Why should I fear them now?"

Hannah said softly, "Why, indeed."

He looked at her with suspicion, which changed to a grudging respect. "But you're pretty good. You're not afraid to call a spade a spade, are you? Yes, I've been a tough customer all my life. A man's got to be a man, none of this feeling sorry for people, just come out on top of the heap. Guts—that's what you need."

A slight sound at the door called Hannah's attention. Mrs. Head came into the room, her skirt swishing softly over the carpet.

"William, dear." Her soft voice caught the Colonel's ear and he turned to glare at her. "I do think you are getting tired. It is time for your nap. You know what Dr. Knox said. You must not —"

" 'You must not' ", he mimicked her. "Nobody's going to tell me what to do. But his voice had weakened and he did no more than mumble when Hannah stood up and followed Mrs. Head out of the room. As she was about to pass through the doorway he roused enough to bellow after her, "Come back here again. I've got some more questions for you."

"Yes, of course. When you are more rested," said Hannah soothingly.

Standing outside the door with Mrs. Head, she waited for the other woman to speak. She suspected that the Colonel's shouts had penetrated even the thick walls of his room and had been heard by his wife.

Mrs. Head said apologetically, "I am afraid he became agitated —"

Hannah made a deprecating gesture. "Such a man, under his restraints, must feel often impatient."

"Then you will return to visit him again?"

"Why, of course, since he has invited me."

Mrs. Head clasped her hands impulsively. "Dear Madame Aurora! I shall be eternally grateful!"

Hannah, with an embarrassment she tried to hide, murmured, "Oh, no! Oh, no!"

∿ ∿ ∿ ∿ ∿

The ride back on the trolley gave her time to marshall her thoughts. Especially she pondered what she should say to Elizabeth. To some extent, she supposed, this would depend on how attentive Elizabeth was. It was sometimes difficult to capture Elizabeth's attention. She often thought this a blessing. Lately she had been glad many times that Elizabeth, immersed in the twelfth century, paid little heed to what she had to say.

Their money affairs were certainly in better condition than they had been at the beginning of the year. Her creation of Madame Aurora had brought them a slowly increasing income. Now she saw opening before her the opportunity for something much more lucrative. She wondered how much she should say of it to Elizabeth, though she longed to tell her every detail and receive from her the moral support she needed.

She got off the trolley at Seventh Street and Pennsylvania Avenue and crossed over to the Center Market. She must get them something for dinner. She walked slowly along the aisles between the stalls of vegetables, fruit, cheese, chickens, seeking something especially tempting that they could afford. She felt a twinge of guilt occasionally that she denied Elizabeth little luxuries that were obtainable with the money in her pocket. But they must hoard up a little nest egg against emergencies. It was too late in the day to get fish. She would have to come early in the morning for that and then they would have to have it at once for there was no way in which they could keep it on ice. Finally she chose a small chicken the farm woman had already dressed.

From the market she found her way southward to the shabby

street of ill-kept houses where she and Elizabeth lodged. Noisy children played on the dirty sidewalk. A peddler's wagon clattered by behind a tired horse. She paused when she came to the short flight of steps to the house in the middle of the block. Automatically, she glanced at the small sign in the curtained front window: Madame Aurora. She adjusted her shawl over her shoulders as if it was uncomfortable but she knew that it was not the source of her discontent. Elizabeth should not have to live in such a place. At the thought, the underlying resentment rose in her once again. The path of their lives had been downward for the last ten years. Why should it be that women—single women without close family ties, able and intelligent women, like themselves—should have so few options in earning a livelihood? And now, as old women —

As she was about to step through the half-open street door she glanced briefly at the one door at the foot of the stairs. There was a white card barely visible under it and she stooped to pick it up. S. Wilmot was engraved on one side, with the word Broker under the name. On the other were the words in handwriting: May I have an interview? I shall call at seven in case. She mused for a moment. A broker. Someone recommended to her by someone who had already been to see her. At least it meant a fee.

She climbed the stairs, grimacing at the stale, musty smell of the old, unkempt house. No, no. Elizabeth should not have to live in such squalor. She reached the landing at the top of the stairs, lit by one dirty window, and walked over to the double doors of what had once been the parlor of the house and was now the room in which she and Elizabeth lived. She unlocked it and stepped inside.

The woman sitting at a table by the window did not turn at the sound of her entrance. Even seated she was plainly a tall woman, slender, her white hair drawn back in a loose bun at the nape of her neck. She was intent upon a sheet of paper on which she was writing, holding it down firmly with one long-fingered hand as her pen moved rapidly across it. Hannah threw off her shawl and stepped over to her and put her hand on her shoulder.

Elizabeth sat back without a start and looked up at her with a smile. "Ah, you're back, my love. Why, it is evening!"

"I was longer than I expected to be." She moved across the room to lay down her bundles. "I brought a chicken for our dinner." She held it up for Elizabeth to see. Elizabeth was not entirely deaf but she needed to see the lips of the person speaking to her to understand what was said. She smiled and said, "We are in funds, then, my love."

"Yes. I shall get our meal. I shall call you when I am ready." And Elizabeth turned back to the paper on the table.

Hannah passed into the corner of the room curtained off to make a little kitchen. Deftly she took her market purchases from their wrappings, rinsed, pared, chopped. It was a pity they had nowhere to put a block of ice to preserve things so that she did not have to buy in such small quantities,—like a French housewife, she supposed, and yet French housewives had a reputation for superlative food, so perhaps she should not repine.

She glanced through the gap in the curtain across the room at Elizabeth, once more absorbed in what she was writing. Happily, the decline of their fortunes had not outwardly affected Elizabeth's spirits. The true scholar's equanimity of soul, she supposed, though she knew the bitterness that underlay that cheerfulness. Sometimes it welled up in Elizabeth. There was one advantage in the eclipse of Elizabeth's reputation as a scholar. No longer were they subject to diatribes and censure from jealous colleagues and outraged male academics. How frightened they were of a woman with real pretensions to intellectual worth! Few people were willing, even now that there were colleges for women, to admit that there was such a thing as a female scholar, and an elderly female scholar was even more outlandish. An old man who had spent his life among books would gather honors as he grew older—deference, respect for his work, the mantle of wisdom that age alone was believed to confer. But a woman—a woman was only a figure of fun in such a context. And yet had not Elizabeth, with her book, changed the course of thought among those whose learned lives were spent in reconstructing the culture of the twelfth century? But she could not even command a post in one of the new women's colleges on the strength of her erudition. She was too suspect.

Her deafness, they would say. But deafness would be excused in her male counterpart.

She put the dinner on the table and went across the room to rouse Elizabeth from her scholarly reverie. When they were seated, Elizabeth said, "It is delicious, as always, dear love."

"I was too late at the market to find anything else. I did not expect to be held so long."

Elizabeth watched her lips. "Sadly, dear heart, I must admit that I do not remember where it was you were to go."

"To Mrs. Head. You remember, I made an exception in her case to my rule not to pay private calls on my clients."

"And who is Mrs. Head?"

"A wealthy woman—the wife of W. T. Head, the silver king, whom they call Colonel—a fictitious title, I am sure. She lives in a mansion on Sixteenth Street—a French chateau, perhaps, transplanted to Washington. She is not a happy woman."

"The Colonel. His affairs are often in the papers. Rather a notorious person."

"He is. But his wife is quite otherwise."

"She has undertaken the study of the occult?"

"She has joined the groups I sometimes speak to. She made a personal appeal to me. She needs reassurance. She is frightened."

"Frightened?"

"Frightened of what may be in the unseen. She accepts the idea that there are mysterious forces beyond her ken and she is fearful of what effect they may have on her future."

" 'Who, indeed, can see the gods, when they are in no mind to be seen?' Well, then, my love, she will have you to guard her from these fears—or these forces."

Hannah gave her a sharp look. "Are you laughing at me, Liz?"

Elizabeth's eyes twinkled. "Of course not. Haven't you guarded me all these past years from the consequences of my disbelief?"

"Pshaw!" But Hannah's annoyance evaporated. "Mrs. Head has a more practical and immediate worry. Like most married women, she is dependent upon her husband's whim. He is an ill man and not likely to live long. Yet he keeps her in the dark about what her situation will be when he dies. She fears that she will not be provided for."

Elizabeth looked perplexed. "I am no lawyer, dear love, but surely she will have her widow's portion regardless of what he does?"

Hannah thought for a moment. "I suppose that must be the case. Perhaps she is not aware of this fact. Or perhaps —"

Elizabeth waited for her to continue and when she did not, said, "Perhaps she wants more—though I should think that her portion would amount to a good deal of money."

"No, I don't think that is it. I don't think that Mrs. Head is a greedy woman. She does not understand much about money— what it really means to be as wealthy as her husband is. I think rather she sees his failure to act on her behalf as a slight to her- self—something that will not look well in the eyes of others—as if he took this means of saying that she was not as satisfactory a wife as he expected."

"Well, love, you are better able to judge than I. If that is the case, it is unkind of him. But from what I've heard, he is not a man to consider other people's feelings, even his wife's."

"That is so. Oh, Liz, I wonder whether the day will ever come when women, so many of them, won't have to hang in the balance on a man's whim!"

Elizabeth laughed. "Perhaps some time in the future, my love. But we should not look for it tomorrow. Just be thankful that you and I are free of the annoyance of a man. We may starve to death but not because of a man's whim."

"We are not in danger of that nor will we be as long as I am able to prevent it."

"Yes, yes, dear heart. I have every confidence in you. But let us go back to Mrs. Head."

"I spent most of the time with the husband."

"Ah. and what is he like?"

"I would describe him as an old devil."

"Really. That in general is his reputation, is it not?"

"Yes. I am sure he has earned it."

"How did it come about that you saw him?"

"Mrs. Head wanted me to. She said she thought that he was uneasy about himself—about the fact that he probably does not have long to live and he fears death."

"That is one fear the greatest of sinners cannot escape. What *does* lie on the other side of that bourne from which no traveler returns? Were you able to comfort him? What a curious enterprise for you, love—to comfort an elderly reprobate in whose torments many would rejoice." She stopped speaking when she saw that Hannah looked distressed. "What is it, love? Was he—unpleasant?"

"He alarmed me. He fell into a rage, because he at once suspected that his wife had sent me in to see him in order to discover something of his arrangements for her. I feared that he would have another stroke. His condition makes him even more suspicious and vengeful than he must always have been. And it is true that he fears the hereafter. He is a very cunning man but an ignorant and superstitious one also."

"So you will not be going to see him again?"

"Oh, yes, I will! He invited me back."

"And you intend to go?"

"Of course. It is an opportunity I cannot neglect."

"An opportunity?"

"Liz, I have a purpose in mind. Why should I not bring comfort to the old reprobate, if there is an advantage to us? I had thought that perhaps Mrs. Head would be a generous patroness. Now I see that the Colonel may be even more our friend, in spite of himself."

Elizabeth's eyes lingered on her. She murmured, "I am still after all these years amazed at the quickness of your perceptions, dear love."

Suddenly Hannah looked at the clock that stood on the mantel of what had once been a fireplace. She got up hastily and began to gather up the plates from the table.

"I had forgotten. I have an appointment for seven o'clock and it is already ten minutes to. I found a card under the door downstairs—a Mr. Wilmot, a stockbroker, wishes to consult me."

"Dear love! What company you keep! Members of Congress, rich men's wives, stockbrokers—surely your range of counsel is wide."

"Why shouldn't it be?"

"I do not say it shouldn't, sweetheart. But forgive me. The credulity of the human race seems to be a constant that does not change over the ages. It is not wonderful that the dweller in the twelfth century in Europe should believe in miracles. His faith taught him that his whole world, seen and unseen, was based on the miraculous. So why shouldn't he credit a tale that the Virgin Mary appeared to shepherd children in a deserted countryside? And why shouldn't he believe that the woman who lived alone in a hut in the forest could, if she had certain powers, summon up the Devil to bewitch him and make him lose his way, make his cow drop her calf beforetime, poison the water in his well? But surely in this day of scientific marvels, when we have the steam engine, the telephone, why, even electric trolleys on the streets of Washington—to say nothing of colleges for women—it is too strange that there are so many people—and in such exalted positions—who believe in the supernatural!"

Hannah smiled at her. "Perhaps the discoveries of science are only a corroboration of things that people have believed by intuition to be possible under the guise of magic."

"Ah, dear love, you have argued that point with me before. Well, perhaps. Sometimes you give me pause when I observe things you are able to perceive. Even Hamlet—'There are many things, Horatio, that are beyond the reach of your philosophy'. But I cannot believe that, if these extra-normal powers exist, they can be interested in predicting the outcome of political campaigns or the future course of stock prices in the market place."

"But, Liz, these may be only a part of the whole."

"In other words, love, you—I mean, you yourself—can deduce the particular from the general."

"There are currents in the Universe which govern our activities. I use what gifts I have to understand them. I listen carefully to what people tell me. The answer to their questions is often in what they say to me."

"Yes, love. I can well understand that. You have a most extraordinary way of seeing into people and a patience in dealing with them which to me is simply angelic. Yes, it is true, dear heart, that people tell you much more than you tell them."

"But there is, Liz, much in the universe that is not understood by most human beings and yet it is the sea in which they live. Is it silly of me to try to fathom what I can?"

"Of course not. I cannot be dogmatic on either side of this question." Elizabeth paused for a moment. Her eagle glance went to the clock. "But, my dear, you must hurry to your stockbroker. Put those dishes down. I will attend to them." Hurriedly Hannah placed the dishes in the small sink. "Leave them, Liz. I can deal with them afterwards."

"Go, go, my love. You need a few minutes before he arrives."

For a moment they stood together, with sudden tenderness putting their arms around each other and kissing, gently, unhurriedly, smiling into each other's eyes. In a moment like this their troubles seemed to recede and they were once more the two much younger women who had found each other in the most unlikely circumstances. It was a moment of balm.

CHAPTER THREE

The room downstairs was dark and mustily cool. The closed
and draped windows and the brick walls of the old house kept
out the fresh warmth of the April evening. With the confidence
of habit, Hannah found her way around the shadowy furniture
to the big gas lamp and lit it. It had a multicolored glass shade
that allowed only a diffused glow to lighten the gloom. She
looked around briefly, an automatic check she gave the room
whenever she entered it. The heavy black chairs, the ornate
false columns around the walls, the dull crimson velvet curtains, gave an air of brooding silence, a silence nevertheless
capable of being broken by unexpected sounds. That was the
effect she intended. She kept the room locked but ever in the
back of her mind was the possibility that curiosity might
sometime prompt someone—the lodging house keeper, perhaps—to try to enter. If someone did, she counted on the
sepulchral atmosphere to frighten him away.

She did not go in for any of the trappings that were the
stock-in-trade of the usual mediums and clairvoyants. She had
no secret devices hidden in the wall, no mechanisms for causing
objects to fly through the air, no hollow places in the furnishings or walls where assistants could be concealed. She scorned
such things, the props of charlatans—persons unworthy to call
themselves the elect of the powerful forces that governed the
universe beyond the reach of human senses. But if the general
effect of her rooms was to create the fear of hidden traps, she
did not mind. It was a safeguard.

She did not have such things because she knew what abilities
lay within herself. She had no need of duplicity. She knew how
to read people's minds from their unconscious movements, the
very words they spoke to her, the anxieties that so obviously
shone in their faces, through the outward manner in which

they sought to disguise their inner fears.

Her train of thought was interrupted by a soft chime. The doorbell, one she had had installed for this room. She opened the door into the vestibule warily. More than once the bell had been rung by some neighborhood urchin, who had run away at once. But she feared also that perhaps on some such occasion there might be someone bolder who might rush upon her.

Tonight, however, this was not the case. A man stood under the dim center light of the vestibule, a man dressed in a smart suit of clothes, who took off his fedora hat when he saw the door open slowly to reveal a narrow glimpse of a portly woman wrapped in an exotically colored shawl. His hesitation, his nervous concern at finding himself there, in this dirty street in this poor neighborhood, was instantly apparent to her. Without a word she stepped back and motioned to him to come in.

He thrust a card at her as he crossed the threshold. "I am Sturgis Wilmot," he said. "You were recommended to me by Mrs. Head."

She inclined her head and closed the door behind him. She still had not spoken, deliberately using silence as a means of reinforcing the effect the quiet, darkened room had on him. She saw him glance nervously behind him as he heard the soft thud of the door closing.

She walked majestically across the room, her feet noiseless on the thick carpet, to the table under the lamp. She sat down on the farther side and motioned to him to sit down facing her. The hooded lamp cast a bright spot of light on the table, which reflected up into their faces. He saw a rounded face, with smooth weathered skin, a firmly closed mouth, the straight upper lip slightly overlapping the curved lower, a pair of slightly bulging light eyes beneath dark eyebrows. Their expression struck him as being at the same time penetrating and unfocused.

She watched the uncertainty, the embarrassment in his face. He wore a moustache but no beard and she could see his lips tighten. She knew he was for the moment regretting his decision to come and see her.

He pulled himself together, to say in the voice he undoubtedly used in ordinary business meetings, "I have come to consult you about some financial matters that are giving me grave concern. Do you give advice on such things?"

His misgiving was plain in his voice. She said, "My advice is to you, to indicate to you the astral forces that should govern your decisions. The subject matter is of lesser importance. I will say, however, that you have serious uncertainties about your associates. You wonder if you have already gone too far in relying upon them."

He stared at her. She watched his reaction. Obviously he was not a man who was used to stepping out of the world he knew day by day, his office, the stock exchange, business dealings. She went on, "You have sought Mrs. Head's opinion of me. You have in mind a new venture. You sense a danger in it."

He was startled. "Yes, that is it. Can I trust these men? The investment required of me is a very large sum, for me."

"But to them not so considerable."

"Exactly. They are speculators. They are accustomed to the possibility of large losses, which they have the means to recoup. But I —"

He hesitated and she carried on his thought. "But you are a steady man. You are not a gambler. What you gain you wish to keep."

"Yes, yes. That's right."

"However, there is the promise of a very large gain, and for that you must speculate."

"Yes, of course. That is understood." He paused uneasily and then went on. "I could afford to lose what I would invest. It would be a great burden but I could stand it. What they want me for, really, is my reputation, my experience in floating new companies —"

Again he faltered. She continued smoothly, "You are uneasy about the methods you think they may use."

He nodded. "The loss of my reputation, my regular business, that would be very grievous."

So he is out of his depth, she thought. And he discussed this with Mrs. Head. Or at least told her he was troubled by business concerns. She took a long shot and said, "The transaction relates to a very dangerous commodity, one that has been of national concern for a number of years."

He answered without forethought. "Indeed! Indeed! Anyone dealing in it cannot escape public notice."

"In fact, you are about to speculate in silver."

"How can you know this?" He was aghast.

She shrugged and ceased to look at him. Instead she sat hunched over, as if in deep thought.

He leaned across the table towards her. "Tell me, what should I do?"

After a silence she answered, "There are two things you are chiefly concerned with: whether you should join with these other men whom you dislike and how long will Colonel Head live?"

"The Colonel —!"

She was observing him closely. "There is an aura of distrust, of fear that hovers about you when you think of the Colonel. You were thinking of him when you came into this room. It was because of him, really, that you have come to see me."

"I cannot deny that. This whole scheme depends on him— whether he is capable of thwarting it—whether he still has his wits about him, how long he will live. If he was out of the way, there would be no real obstacle to what we want to do. But if he lives and is able to forestall us— He has vanquished many men in his life. He has the cunning of the Devil—excuse me, but I am very alarmed."

Hannah leaned back in her chair so that her face was no longer in the glow of the lamp. "You must wait. I shall see if I can summon a messenger."

He glanced hurriedly around behind him, as if expecting someone to be standing there. But she paid no attention to him and sat wrapped in silence. The minutes passed without sound in the muted air of the room. His nervousness grew and his attention grew more and more concentrated on the half-seen bulk of the woman opposite him.

She said in a soft voice, "We of this world are surrounded by vital forces we know nothing of. In our ignorance we exclude them from our consciousness. Yet they flow about us, control our actions, our thoughts. Thus we suffer many sadnesses, many defeats."

She fell silent again, her eyes, hidden from her visitor by the lampglow between them, watched him fixedly. She saw him draw out a handkerchief and dab at his upper lip. Obviously his nerves, already on edge when he had arrived at her door, were quivering now from the effect of the room, of her manner. When she spoke again, he started as if she had touched him.

"I see the Colonel as very strong. His mind. His body. His will. His spirit goes forth from his body with vigor. He is not as hampered by bodily weakness as those around him believe. He is still an adversary with the power, the will, to conquer those who oppose him."

The man gave a long sigh and sat back in his chair. "Then you advise me —?"

"Do nothing precipitate. Don't be frightened into taking sudden actions. Resist the persuasions of these associates of yours. They are foolish men who are rushing into disaster. You will not suffer great losses if you are able to hold back and wait. There is much more for you to gain by waiting. Can you do that?"

"Yes. I can hold off by taking no action. I can temporize. What I fear is that by waiting I shall lose opportunities."

"There are none for you to lose at this time. If you will wait, you will outlast your associates. You will gain much more in the long run."

"Are you sure of that? Are you sure I can just let time go by and not make some positive effort? A businessman cannot afford to let opportunities go by."

"Wait. No success is ever achieved in defiance of the rhythm of the astral forces. You must learn patience. You must learn to resist the pressure of the ignorant and incredulous."

He sighed, as if in great relief. "You seem very certain," he said. "I am grateful to you. I came here almost mad with anxiety. I do not feel so unsettled now. Thank you. May I come and consult you again?"

"Certainly. I hold meetings here every week—a few friends who wish to learn about the forces that control their lives. If you should care to join us —"

He shook his head vigorously. "No, no. That is not for me. I shall depend on you." They had both sat forward again and could see each other in the light of the lamp. "I hope I can rely on your discretion—that you will say nothing of my visits to you. Professionally I wouldn't want it to be known that I have consulted you."

"As you wish. Of course you may have every confidence in me."

She stood up and he followed. There was satisfaction in his voice as he said, "I do believe that I may." He seemed anxious now to leave yet aware that there was something more he must do before he left and uncertain how to go about it. She raised her hand slowly and pointed to an ornate glass bowl that stood on the top of a small stand near the door.

"When we have a gathering here of earnest souls who seek enlightenment, I receive contributions of whatever each may be moved to give. But this is a private consultation and I charge a set fee of fifty dollars."

His eyes widened at the sum but he reached at once into his inner coat pocket to take out his wallet and extract the bills. He hesitated still and finally said, "You have relieved my mind of a great burden. I'm very glad I came to see you, though I must confess I had misgivings. You are everything that Mrs. Head said of you. Perhaps an occasion will arise when I can be of service to you."

She said nothing but bowed as he went out. Then she stood for a moment looking at the bills in her hand. Fifty dollars would go pretty far during the next few weeks. But how impatient she was to achieve a more stable income for Elizabeth and herself.

Slowly she climbed the stairs back to their room. The interview had tired her more than she would have thought. Or perhaps it was the accumulation of the day's efforts. It was this constant understrain of anxiety about their welfare that caused her fatigue, she knew. She smiled to herself. After all, she should practice for herself some of the advice she gave others. And when she thought of it in that light, she did have a sense that there would be an ultimate triumph for them. She could not believe otherwise. They had lived through such bad times— the bank panic of five years before had climaxed their troubles. It was only her inner goad that had sent her to the bank to draw out their few dollars before the bank closed its doors. And she had succeeded, simply because she had had the strength and determination to fight her way through a mob of angry men in the street. After that they had kept their bits of money in a dresser drawer until some of it had been lost to the lodging-house keeper's thieving servant. Elizabeth was no watchdog. Between her deafness and her scholar's absentmindedness, they could be robbed of everything before she would notice.

She reached the landing and rapped loudly on the door. She listened intently and heard the slight sound of Elizabeth's steps on the other side. Elizabeth opened it, exclaiming, "Ah, there you are, my love!"

The anxiety in her voice reached Hannah's ears. Something had caused Elizabeth to be on the watch for her return. This sort of anxiousness was another reason she wished the day to come when they could afford to move to more suitable quarters. She hated to see Elizabeth's blitheness vanishing. Of course, they were both growing older and she could not expect either of them to retain the self-assurance, the optimism that had seen them through hard times in the past—could not expect it under the difficult circumstances that beset them as unfamilied spinsters.

She answered Elizabeth's questioning look. "It was a profitable interview. I charged him fifty dollars."

Elizabeth's eyes grew wide. "Fifty dollars, my love!"

"He made no objection. I think he was very well satisfied. I have saved him from financial disaster. He will be aware of that before many days are past."

"Really, dear heart? You seem very certain."

"I am. He was sent to me by Mrs. Head. Of course, I am sure she had no idea of what he wanted to know. She is a woman who eschews any concern with business matters. But I was very soon able to fathom what was the cause of his panic."

"Panic?"

"Yes, it was nearly that. He finds himself in the hands of a group of men whose business methods he suspects. But the lure of large gains had led him into this situation. These men are waiting, like vultures, for Colonel Head's death. I assured Mr. Wilmot that the Colonel is not going to die very soon and that his faculties are so far unaffected. He has wisely decided to follow my advice and wait. The transaction, of course, is concerned with silver. The thought that the Colonel will lose control of his silver empire is a very tempting one to such greedy men."

Hannah with a weary gesture sat down in the chair by the table. Elizabeth studied her for a moment. She saw the traces of fatigue in Hannah's face—sturdy, tireless Hannah, whose store of strength, spiritual and physical had always seemed inexhaustible. But at last the worry and the ceaseless work to provide for them both was beginning to tell. Elizabeth was aware that during the last few months Hannah's spirits had been flagging. It was an uphill battle for two elderly women striving to maintain their independence in an inhospitable world. It had no place for any women except the ideal stereotype—the protected wife and mother. Spinsters and barren wives were outside the norm. And yet how many wives and mothers were truly protected, content to graze like cows in a safe meadow? Elizabeth thought of all the outrageous statements she had heard men make over the years since she had first set out to earn her living as a teacher. The true destiny of Woman, said Thomas Carlyle, was to wed a man she could love and esteem and to lead noiselessly under his protection the life prescribed in consequence. There were two words there of significance—noiselessly and prescribed. For women were not only to accept the sphere dictated for them by men but they must do so without complaint.

And the amazing subservience with which so many women endorsed this nonsense. Catherine Beecher, she remembered, forty years back, had declared that women should be teachers, not for their own advancement or wellbeing, but simply "to do good." What fruitless, ridiculous attitudes, thought Elizabeth, when teaching was almost the only resource for women like herself who needed to earn their own living and did not wish to be a factory hand or a domestic drudge. In the end she had been defeated by such attitudes, defeated by that sort of prejudice— and this damnable deafness that had overtaken her so insidiously. Defeated, so that she had had to relinquish to Hannah the full weight of their support instead of carrying her own share. In the last months she had tried not to let Hannah see her own struggle to stave off despair at the loss of her profession, of her ability to provide at least half their living. She did not regret—in good conscience she could not regret—her own actions in defence of principle that had led to her dismissal from the teaching post she had held for fifteen years. But the burden of years was taking its toll.

Hannah's voice interrupted her. "Liz, you're woolgathering."

"I was thinking of your remarkable gifts, love," Elizabeth lied defensively.

Hannah eyed her. Elizabeth went on, "How providential it was that you had met the Colonel before your stockbroker came to call. You were able to judge for yourself of his condition."

Hannah smiled. "Providential, Liz?"

Elizabeth laughed, "You caught me there! If it was not Providence, then something else must have helped."

"I have explained to you before—people tell much more about themselves than they realize. A great deal of prophecy is an astute reading of people and events."

Elizabeth quoted:

" 'There is a history in all men's lives,
Figuring the nature of times deceas'd,
The which observed, a man may prophecy,
With a near aim, of the main chance of things
As yet not come to life, which in their seeds
And weak beginnings lie intreasured.' "

Hannah raised her eyebrows.

"The Earl of Warwick, my love, to King Henry IV. Or so Shakespeare says. So you think that there are beginnings of something intreasured in today's events."

"I can't tell yet, Liz. But I know that we shall succeed in some way before too long."

"Dear heart, I hope you are right," said Elizabeth fervently.

The evening was still warm. The setting of the sun had brought no chill and the night beyond the open window was filled with sounds. It was not a neighborhood that was ever really quiet. But Elizabeth said, "You've had a long day, sweetheart. Shall we go to bed?"

They put out the lamp and undressed by the light of the

street lamp that shone into the window. The window shade was frayed and they mistrusted the degree of protection it could offer from the gaze of passersby on the sidewalk below. The bed creaked loudly as Hannah joined Elizabeth in it. The mattress was lumpy and the spring sagged, but at least it was clean, thought Hannah. Elizabeth had said, the first night they had slept in it, that it was a good thing that they enjoyed lying close to one another, were so used now to the comforting feel of the other's body that they would have drawn together even if the old bed had not caused them to roll one against the other. But we should have something better than this, Hannah fretted. Her sleepiness overwhelmed her as she became aware of Elizabeth's long-fingered hands stroking her body. At first her preoccupation wrapped her around so completely that she was only partly aware of the loving touch. Yes, she knew that something in the day's events had aroused a hope in her, a real hope. She could give no reason for this tantalizing feeling of something in the offing, some turn in the road that lay ahead.

Elizabeth persisted in her caresses. The welcome, familiar touch soothed her as she felt Elizabeth enjoying the smooth plumpness of her stomach, thigh, ample breasts and cheeks. Even at this age she had few wrinkles. Her skin, said Elizabeth, was satin to the touch, warm, slightly moist. Even the faint scent of sweat that the humid night brought forth was agreeable, said Elizabeth, kissing her neck. Her little goose girl. Hannah remembered that Elizabeth had called her that the very first night they had spent together in the cottage at the girls' seminary so many years ago. It was wonderful how at the very first moment of their acquaintance they had both recognized their bond.

Hannah suddenly stirred and rolled over on her back. She reached for Elizabeth, drawing her strongly into her arms, enveloping her bony, eager body with her own. Elizabeth laughed and yielded.

CHAPTER FOUR

Dear little goose girl. She was already asleep. It was rare that Hannah failed to fall asleep within minutes of coming to bed—unless they played together as they had this evening and then sleep overtook her promptly as they finished. But even asleep Hannah did not seem to go away from her but to be so wholly and so comfortingly hers.

Yet Hannah was a puzzle still in some ways. Her belief in something otherworldly. There was no doubt that she believed in an orderly scheme in the universe and that some humans, like herself, had the power to discern it—or at least glimpse it—and use it for their own benefit. It was hard to disbelieve Hannah altogether. There was a magnetism in her. Now she was old and ungainly, but as always through the years since her youth, people sought her out. She had the knack of drawing forth confidences. And at the same time no one had a greater contempt than Hannah for the trappings of occultism—the voices from the dead, the supposed ghostly presences in seances, the writings mysteriously appearing from invisible hands. But there had been occasions in the past when she had, skillfully and deliberately, made use of these things, when she deemed it necessary. She had told fortunes, predicted the future by the stars—without the slightest trace in her manner of what she really thought.

Hannah had told her about her childhood in some small mountain settlement in western Maryland—a place of a few clapboard houses with a grist mill to serve the surrounding farms. The house her family had lived in had been a ramshackle place, overflowing with too many people, quarrelsome, shouting, often drunk, capricious in their treatment of the children. She had learned very early how to dodge out of the way to avoid being switched by some stumbling, irate adult.

Various members of her family had through the generations

claimed second sight. In her early teens she had hit on the device of pretending trances in which she could foretell the future. She discovered in claiming psychic powers that she had found a potent weapon not only to protect herself but also to cast fear into those who would otherwise torment her. Later she had gone to Baltimore to work as a servant. But she had used her quickness of mind to learn to read and write and cipher. In this she aided herself, when it seemed feasible, by the use of her psychic gifts, sometimes in ways that roused her own contempt.

Hannah and she had first met in the autumn of 1865. Could it really be thirty years ago? The nation was just beginning to settle down to peace after the Civil War. She herself was teaching at the girls' seminary in the lush countryside of Pennsylvania. Her post was, as such things went, a well paid one for a woman. At the time the seminary found itself sought by an unusual number of new students, daughters of men who had made money in the war or its aftermath and as evidence of this new wealth wished to send their daughters to a well-established young ladies' school.

At the moment she had been alone in the cottage in which she served also as housemother. She remembered the golden early October days, savoring her few days of freedom before the new scholars arrived. For to her, in spite of the comparative luxury of her situation, the school seemed a prison from which she could not escape. How difficult it was to convey to anyone else this feeling. For almost twenty years, since her father's death, she had earned her living as a teacher in girls' schools. Glad that she had this means of livelihood yet enraged at the waste of energy and the confinement of mental vigor it entailed. For she could not teach girls as they should be taught—to open their minds, stimulate their intellectual curiosity, coax them to try the wings of their fancy, as boys were taught. Girls must not be given tasks that would overtax their minds, must not be disciplined to excel in mathematics, philosophy, science. If they were not already sufficiently docile, they must be forced to become so. For otherwise—so said the trustees of their schools and the preceptors of female education generally—society would suffer from their rebellion. And most of the girls she taught were the true products of their parents' prejudices—inattentive, incurious where learning was concerned, thinking only of the life they had been trained from babyhood to wish for, as submissive wives and mothers, complacent in the restricted sphere assigned to them by fathers and husbands.

Where in such a narrow world was there stimulus for such a woman as herself, who refused the domination of men over her body and mind? If it were not for the periods of the year when she could absent herself from the classroom, go to some library where she could immerse herself in the books that opened the doors of mediaeval literature to her, she would long since have despaired. But these excursions of hers she kept prudently hidden, disguised, aware that such a pursuit for a woman would not be favorably seen by those who hired her to teach. A man had no such handicap. It was assumed that he would use his free time as he saw fit. But she must remain within a woman's sphere, unambitious to go beyond it. A man's sphere was what he chose to make it, with the width of the physical and mental world open to him.

A woman's sphere. Most of the girls she taught accepted that concept, accepted the notion that their brains were not the equal of their brothers', that it was unwomanly—that terrible word!—for them to aspire to anything beyond a domestic world. If occasionally she was confronted with a girl who was by nature rebellious, who questioned the subservience in which she was bred, Elizabeth recognized a great danger. A teacher who did not conform in her own role as a docile instructress of docile pupils courted disaster. Not only might she be dismissed, but she would also find it difficult to get another post.

And then, to emphasize the true character of the education meted out to girls, there was this constant distraction of domestic duties. To gratify these silly men, the trustees of the school and the fathers of the girls, the girls must spend a large part of their time in practicing domestic arts. The women who ran the school—like those who ran all schools for girls—used this as a means of reassuring the parents. Whatever little learning they acquired would thus not turn them from their appointed destiny as wives and mothers, which, everyone said, was divinely ordained.

How she had raged sometimes, Elizabeth remembered, at this foolish waste of her own time—those precious few moments she might otherwise have spent on her own work used instead in supervising girls in household duties. She was no seamstress. She knew very little of the art of cooking—a result of having been motherless from an early age. The seminary required its teachers to live each in a cottage with a group of girls. There were only a few servants. The girls did most of their own housework. The fact had a chastening effect on any female who might be tempted to place reading and intellectual pursuits above the making of beds. Occasionally, through the centuries, some few women had escaped these strictures. She remembered having heard that Wordsworth's sister Dorothy had had the scandalous habit of reading Shakespeare before lunch, with the housework undone.

When Hannah arrived Elizabeth herself had just returned from a summer spent in Washington at the Library of Congress, long, blissful days passed among the heaps of books and papers that crowded the narrow space alloted to it in the Capitol Building. The first news she had had on getting back was that she must be prepared to welcome a new teacher who would share the cottage with her, a young woman whose care was to be especially the younger girls. She saw in this announcement the fact that the Principal of the seminary had recognized her failings on the domestic side and had acted to supply the lack. She had often thought that the Principal had a secret sympathy for her and did what she could to shield her from criticism. But who would this new teacher be—what sort of woman would she have to share her daily life and probably even her bed at night? The school would be very crowded this year.

Elizabeth remembered very well their first meeting. The cottage was still empty. The girls had not begun to arrive and she sat in luxurious ease in the sittingroom, books and papers spread on the table in an unusual freedom from interruption. She did not hear the bell or a knock, if there had been either. She had looked up to see Hannah in her bonnet and shawl, standing in the open door.

She exclaimed, "Oh, are you the new teacher?" and Hannah answered, "For the little ones."

Elizabeth got up from her chair and they stood for a moment looking at each other. Elizabeth noticed Hannah's tanned skin. Her face and hands were brown, like those of a farm woman. Surely a woman who cared little for a sunbonnet. There was, in fact, a gypsyish air about her, but in the place of the darting, acquisitive glance of a gypsy there was a calm self-assurance about Hannah. Not the usual sort of woman who sought and found a teaching post in this sort of girls' school.

But she held back her questions. "Ah, then, we are to work together. Let me show you our living quarters."

The one-story cottage housed twelve girls, in four large, airy rooms. The seminary prided itself on following the precepts of such mentors as Catherine Beecher in providing a healthful, cheerful environment for its pupils. A fifth room, narrow, with one window, was squeezed in next to the kitchen and the still-room. It was crowded, Elizabeth's writing table and a bureau and a clothespress taking up nearly all the space not occupied by the bed. She had cherished this room as a haven from the restless adolescent girls she had to oversee. Its smallness had made it a reasonable thing for her to have it to herself. But now, with the new teacher —

Hannah had cast one swift glance around it without comment. No doubt, thought Elizabeth, she was used to even more crowded quarters. A bed shared with another teacher or with a pupil was commonplace in many girls' schools and in the boarding arrangements for young teachers hired for their public schools by the people of many new townships in the western part of the country.

"Perhaps," said Elizabeth, as Hannah hung her shawl and bonnet in the clothespress, "you would like to join me in a cup of tea?"

Hannah nodded and said, "I'll fetch my carpet bag. It is on your porch."

Elizabeth left her and went to the kitchen to prepare a tray with teacups and a teapot and several bread and butter sandwiches—a part of her duties was to instruct the girls how to preside over tea parties, and she had the paraphernalia at hand, though she did not often trouble to use it for herself alone. Probably, she thought, Hannah was weary and hungry from travelling. She carried the tray into the sittingroom and waited for Hannah to appear.

Hannah came into the room and sat down in the chair opposite her. Elizabeth gazed at her covertly. Her hair was simply dressed in two smooth wings over her ears. It was a soft bright brown—like a thrush's wing, thought Elizabeth. Not my age but nearly.

She said aloud, "Most of our girls have not arrived yet. You and I shall be alone together for a few days."

She offered the statement as an invitation to Hannah to speak for herself. Hannah seemed to recognize this and replied, "Then, we shall have a chance to become acquainted."

Elizabeth nodded. She herself did not suffer from shyness. A sense of her own capabilities gave her self-assurance. But she recognized shyness in others, especially in girls and women, and in fact expected it, feigned or real, a reflection of the habit of self-deprecation in which they were trained. In Hannah she sensed reserve but was uncertain whether shyness was part of it.

"I am Elizabeth Beaufort. Minerva Elizabeth. I am known as Elizabeth. Of course, I should have introduced myself before this."

Hannah smiled a disarming smile. "Yes, I know. The Principal told me. My name is Hannah—Hannah Morgan. I've never taught in a school like this before. I am afraid you will have to instruct me as well as the girls for a few days."

"You will learn our way of doing things very quickly. The schoolrooms are in the main house—where you saw the Principal. There is a chapel there, too, and rooms for visitors. Parents sometimes come to see how their daughters are taught. Here, in this cottage, we—you and I—are responsible for instructing them in how to discharge the duties that will devolve upon them in the future, as wives and mothers. Girls, you know, must be bred to be modest, agreeable and above all submissive. I am afraid that any education they get beyond that is superficial. Parents and husbands have been frightened by physicians who say that a girl's health will suffer if she is required to study too closely. So we make sure they learn to cook, sew, keep a house. In this way the Principal can reassure their parents that there is nothing to fear in sending their daughters here for—for a social polish."

Elizabeth stopped suddenly and looked at Hannah, aware that she had been carried perhaps too far by her own feelings. But there was a smile still on Hannah's face and a lively sympathy in her eyes.

"Where have you taught before?"

"Oh, nowhere like this, as I have said before." Hannah glanced out of the window at the broad sweep of the grassy hillside that led up to the handsome brick house perched there overlooking the cottage and the farm buildings that surrounded it. It had once been the country estate of the man who founded the school as a memorial to his only daughter and it retained enough of its original elegance to serve as an attraction for well-to-do parents seeking a socially polished education for their own daughters. The outskirts of Philadelphia were not far away.

Hannah went on, "Just little schools—in Baltimore and the South. But I have not always been a teacher. I have earned my living in other ways also."

"So how did you come to get a post here?"

"By a recommendation from Mrs. Lipscomb, the widow of Major Lipscomb, late of the Union Army. He was, I think, once a trustee of this school."

"Yes." Elizabeth recognized the name. "We heard that he died of wounds he received in the seige of Petersburg."

"He lingered for some time," said Hannah. "He was in the military hospital run by Captain Sally Tompkins of the Confederate Army in Richmond, Virginia."

Surprised, Elizabeth exclaimed, "Indeed? A woman an officer in the Confederate Army?"

"Yes, the only one. She refused all pay for what she did, though she cared for many wounded and lost only a few. Major Lipscomb was fortunate. I was able to give him some assistance at the end, when he realized he would not recover. I wrote a letter at his dictation, to his wife. When General Lee surrendered at Appomattox, I took the letter and his personal belongings to her in Washington. She was grateful and asked if she could help me. I told her that I needed a means of livelihood and that I had been a teacher. She said she knew that the seminary needed new teachers and that she would give me a recommendation. So I came."

Either an intrepid young woman or a desperate one, thought Elizabeth. "Wasn't it rather a chance—to come all this way simply on a recommendation?"

"It seemed a good enough chance."

"But what would you have done if the Principal had not accepted you?"

Hannah looked directly at her. Her eyes were disconcertingly clear. "I knew I would have a haven here."

A haven? Elizabeth was at a loss both at her choice of words and at the unobtrusive but definite air of assurance with which she spoke. Finally she asked, "Were you a sympathizer with the Southern cause?"

"I do not believe in war for any cause."

"Ah, then you are a Quaker?"

"I am not the adherent of any church."

"Oh, dear! As definite as that. Does the Principal know your views? A great deal is made here of a suitably pious atmosphere."

"She did not ask me any questions about my religious beliefs."

"She must have assumed that you hold the same tenets as Mrs. Lipscomb, who is, I think, a Presbyterian."

"Is this important?"

"Yes. Religious observances are emphasized here. You will be required to attend chapel."

"I shall make no question about it." Hannah paused to look at her for a moment. "What are your views?"

"I am nominally an Episcopalian." Elizabeth hesitated. It was extraordinary, she thought, how this unassuming young woman drew her out of herself. She had been about to say that she was in fact an agnostic, that she had no religious faith, that she thought most Christian sects used Biblical doctrine to subjugate women. But she stopped herself. This young woman was a stranger. She did not know how safe it would be to make her a confidante.

She was startled when Hannah said, "You mistrust religious groups. You are out of sympathy with religious people."

Elizabeth temporized. "Like yourself, I do not subscribe to any church. However, I am required, as everyone here is, to attend services in the chapel and engage in evening prayers. When put to it, I prefer the forms of the Book of Common Prayer. Unlike the more fervent preachers we have here, I do not believe myself to be under God's curse."

That was the first time Hannah laughed. She gave easy answers to Elizabeth's questions about her childhood, about her life in Baltimore as a young woman. When it came to her activities during the War she was less specific. Obviously she had worked in military hospitals. She seemed also to have been in Washington part of the time. She was not, she insisted, attached to either side in the struggle. Humanitarian principles governed what she did. Whatever else she engaged in she passed by—spying for the Southern cause, perhaps, Elizabeth wondered.

"You were not an abolitionist, then, before the war?"

"I was not a member of any organized group. I do not accept the idea that any human being should be in the power of another. I have always acted on my own."

"You have never married?"

There was a quick flash of what looked like scorn in her eyes. "I would never be any man's servant."

In spite of herself, Elizabeth cried, "Ah, there we have something in common!"

Hannah smiled again. "Of course."

"It is assumed that if we don't marry it is for want of opportunity. In my case, because I have frightened men away with my learning. I would be useless as a wife, I've been told, because I have no patience with domestic duties. And I am not submissive. What a dreadful word—submissive. To submit, to submit one's body, one's mind, one's spirit, to the limitations imposed by another. I am told I feel this way because I have never felt passion—never felt the kind of love that would carry me beyond my self. Yet it is disgraceful for a woman to succumb to bodily desire. She must only endure another's. How disgusting!"

Hannah was still smiling, as if she was applauding what Elizabeth said. Elizabeth said, "Forgive me. I do not have many opportunities to speak to a sympathetic ear." And Hannah said, "I find what you say of the greatest interest."

They went on talking, Elizabeth alternately drawing back and impulsively expressing her feelings. Hannah sat listening attentively, self-possessed, adding a comment when it was needed.

Finally it was five o'clock and Elizabeth realized that they must go to the main house for supper with the Principal and the other teachers who had already arrived. Together, in their bonnets and shawls, they walked up the grassy slope in the long rays of the setting sun, whose warmth no longer dissipated the crisp coolness of the autumn air. They spent the evening in the big drawingroom of the seminary, under the gaze of the painted images of the founder and benefactors of the school. Elizabeth, while talking to one or another of the several teachers already arrived, watched Hannah. Hannah, shabbily dressed in comparison with the prim elegance of the other women and plainly unlike them in social manners, nevertheless was self-possessed. She must be aware of the scrutiny she was being subjected to, thought Elizabeth. For if Elizabeth herself had been surprised at her appearance, the other women were even more nonplussed at this new addition to the staff. She obviously did not wear stays and there was no hoop under her skirts. They stared more than they spoke, yet Hannah seemed untroubled. It is as if, thought Elizabeth, she is secure in some knowledge they lack. There was no rusticity in her manner of speech. She simply was not the same as the rigidly conventional women who surrounded her.

After supper and the evening's sociability, she and Hannah went back to their cottage, the brightness of the full moon lighting their way. They would be alone, said Elizabeth, because the old woman who served as a general helper, one of the few servants at the seminary, who had slept in the cottage with her the last few nights, would now return to her regular quarters in the main house. She had used one of the beds in one of the girls' rooms. Perhaps Hannah would like to sleep there till the arrival of the pupils forced them to share her small bedroom.

Hannah, following her into the cottage and waiting while she sought in the dark for matches to light the oil lamp, said, "If you would prefer that, Miss Beaufort. It means another light, doesn't it? Do you have candles?"

"Yes." Then suddenly Elizabeth came to a decision. "We must, in any case, get settled for the winter. Let us share our room tonight."

With the same equanimity Hannah agreed.

In the narrow little room, Elizabeth prepared for bed circumspectly. She noticed that Hannah was not as self-conscious as herself. She took off her outer garments and stood bare to the waist to wash in the big china basin for which she had brought hot water from the kitchen, first for Elizabeth and then for herself. Elizabeth's eyes dwelt on her breasts, plump, generous, smooth-skinned with brown-tinted nipples. There was nothing in Hannah's manner of the prudery so many women displayed, as if fearful of seeing their own or another woman's body. In Hannah there was an economy of motion in the way in which she bathed and changed into the voluminous nightgown. When she joined Elizabeth in the bed, Elizabeth turned out the lamp.

In the dark, lying carefully on her side of the bed, she thought back to what the Principal had said when she had first arrived back. There would be a new teacher, she had said, but obviously she had not known that it would be Hannah, for Hannah had said the Principal had known nothing of her before she came that afternoon. Of course she had realized that the Principal had been at her wits' end to find qualified teachers at short notice. That was as much as she had known, for she had always maintained a certain aloofness from discussing the administrative details of running the school. It was a prudent attitude that saved her from annoyance. If she knew nothing about the practical problems, she would not be drawn into the little wars that from time to time erupted among the teachers. But there was something quite strange about this present situation. She felt a certain dismay, there in the quiet dark, Hannah obviously already asleep beside her, at the remembrance of the freedom with which she had spoken to Hannah. She was uneasy about having to deal with Hannah again in the morning—rather like, she supposed, a drunkard must feel the day after when the half-remembrance of yesterday's extravagance assailed him. Eventually she also slept.

A sound at the door awakened her. It was just daylight. Hannah stood there, still in her nightgown, holding a tray on which was a pot of tea and two cups. She brought it over to Elizabeth's side of the bed and set it on the nightstand.

"Why, Hannah! What a delightful surprise! How did you know that I like tea first thing in the morning?"

Hannah smiled at her, the same easy smile of the evening before. She did not answer but sat down on the edge of the bed to pour out the tea and take a cup for herself.

"You have bewitched me," said Elizabeth.

CHAPTER FIVE

It was the beginning of a momentous week. The fine autumn weather held. In its cheerful brightness they spent the sunlight hours together, Elizabeth ostensibly introducing Hannah to the mode of life at the school. But in reality, she knew increasingly, they were establishing a sort of friendship she had never experienced before. They seemed to begin with an intimacy she had not before granted to anyone. She found herself unable to hold back from voicing to Hannah her most inward thoughts,— opinions, feelings, beliefs she had never explored with any other person. She was baffled by this loose-tonguedness. Hannah did not appear to make any effort to draw forth these confessions.

Of course, the biggest inconvenience she foresaw was Hannah's intrusion on the few hours she tried to save for her work. At night, for example, when she found it hard to sleep, she had been able to have a light to read by. Now —

On their second night together, wakeful, she listened in the dark for Hannah's breathing. It was regular and quiet. Hannah must be sound asleep already. She decided to try an experiment and reached carefully into the drawer of the nightstand for a candle to put in the candlestick. She lit it and in its wavering light looked over at Hannah. Hannah slept serenely on her back, one hand outside the cover on her chest. Elizabeth reached down to the floor where several books were stacked and pushed her pillow into a better prop for her head.

When she woke in the morning Hannah was already in the kitchen getting their tea. "I hope," she said, "I did not disturb you with my candle last night."

"Oh, no." Hannah stood with the tray, waiting for Elizabeth to clear the books from the nightstand. "I'm never disturbed by things that are not harmful. If I rouse, I go back to sleep, unless there is something that means danger."

"You must have experienced many unpleasant moments during the War. Do they trouble you now?"

"Not often. Sometimes I have a nightmare. Then I may disturb *you.*"

That afternoon, as they sat on the porch of the cottage, Hannah swiftly and accurately sewing a new dress for herself, she broke a peaceful silence to ask: "What is it that you are working at? You have so many books."

Elizabeth, confronted by such a direct question, sat and thought. "For years I have been working on a book I wish to try to publish."

"What does it concern?"

Again Elizabeth took thought. How to convey what filled her mind so much of the time, to someone who perhaps had never heard of the subject? "I have always been fascinated by the singers and poets of the Middle Ages. There is not a great deal known about them. Their lives and their work—we have only fragments that have come down through the accidents of the centuries to go upon in reconstructing them."

"It must be difficult to look for such writings when you are so far away from places where they may be found."

"It is indeed. I save every penny, I use every moment that I can escape from teaching to seek what I want. I am considered eccentric, you know, because I do not spend my holidays as do the other women. In the first place, I have no family, no parents, no brothers and sisters. I am a lone woman and that, perhaps as you know, is to be at a grave disadvantage in our society." She stopped and looked at Hannah.

Hannah, without looking up, said, "That is my situation. I do have blood relatives living, but I have long since lost touch with them."

Reassured, Elizabeth went on, "My work is my life, really. But that is not accepted by those with whom I live surrounded. It is not self-sacrificial work nor is it done in any spirit except that to obey my most powerful inner urge." She paused again but Hannah said nothing. "The focus of my work is Marie de France. Who she was is almost lost in the mists of time. She lived in the twelfth century and is supposed to have gone to England to the court of Henry II and Eleanor of Aquitaine and there found patrons. She was a poet and her Lays are some of the most beautiful of early writings. They also portray a profound change in the social outlook of her time. In them love is seen in a new way, not the reflection of violence, as in the chansons de geste and not as the posturings of courtly love. She speaks with a modern voice, of the individual —"

Stopping herself in full flight, Elizabeth stared at Hannah, who had put down her sewing and was looking at her attentively. Elizabeth gave an embarrassed little laugh. "It is all so foreign to this life of mine—this circumscribed, narrow sphere of a teacher of ignorant and heedless girls. There is a fascination for me in the life of the twelfth century which I perceive in what I have studied. Such sweet singers they were, some of these wandering poets, men and women, free, untrammeled. My vision of them is quite different from the view held by most of the scholars in this field, whose minds, I think, are too rigid, too governed by their own preconceptions. My view is based on their own words—what has been salvaged through the ages. Marie de France, for instance, tells the story of Tristan and Iseult and there she says of their love—it is as the hazel tree and the honeysuckle, twined together—if the two be pulled apart they both die—'Fair friend, it is the same with us, There will be no you without me, nor me without you.' Do you see what is there—the ideal of a love between two individuals, not two stylized characters? A love unconcerned with extraneous things, subject to social rules. Such a freedom of spirit —"

Again Elizabeth stopped short, but Hannah still sat listening to her. "Legends—you see, part of what I am trying to do is to discover how much there is in these ancient legends that refer to actual persons. I do not think they can merely be assumed to be figures of the imagination. These wandering singers—they were players and singers, sometimes with a little learning in Latin, and sometimes they were women. Marie de France's patron was said to be William Longsword, one of the sons of Henry II and Eleanor of Aquitaine. She was his jongleuse or glee maiden. She was greatly appreciated and was called the Sappho of her age. Of course, not all of the jongleuses or glee maidens were refined and learned, like Marie de France. Some of them were wenches who traveled about the country alone or as companions of gleemen or minstrels. They played the lute or sang while the men juggled or tumbled to entertain people at a fair, for the sake of a few pence."

Hannah was smiling at her, her eyes twinkling. "You would have liked to have been a gleemaiden, wouldn't you?"

Elizabeth blushed. "The sense of freedom one gets—For a woman it is such a prize, always beyond reach. You are either respectable or free. You cannot be both. Respectability was so little regarded then. Not as it is with us. They had a freedom we can scarcely grasp—a true freedom of spirit—we in our corsets, our hypocracies, our fearfulness, of what others will think, or what will bring us to hellfire hereafter." She paused for a while. "But it was a dreadful age in many ways. The horrors of wars and pestilence —"

Hannah interrupted. "We've had a taste of that."

Surprised, Elizabeth gazed at her. "Oh, of course! You must be more aware of that than I."

They were both silent for a while. Then abruptly, Elizabeth asked, "Why did you come here? Yes, I know that you have said you needed a livelihood and Mrs. Lipscomb offered you her recommendation. But was that all?"

Hannah answered calmly, "I came here because of you."

"Because of me? How could that be? You knew nothing of me until you arrived here."

"That is not altogether true. I felt I must come here from the moment Mrs. Lipscomb spoke of the seminary. And before that, I felt a compulsion, beyond the need to make good on my promise to Major Lipscomb to take his letter to his wife. I could have sent that by other means. No, I knew then that there was a reason for me to go to Mrs. Lipscomb and when she mentioned the seminary, it was quite clear to me that I must come here. You are right. I am destitute and do need to earn my living. But I could have done it in other ways. I could have obtained employment with the Federal government in Washington. But there was no doubt in my mind that I should come here. The moment I laid eyes on you I understood."

"You understood what?"

"That it was you I was sent here to find."

Elizabeth stared at her, baffled. "I cannot understand you."

Hannah nodded in sympathy for her bewilderment. "Yes, it is difficult to explain. Before I came here I could not have said your name nor have described you. But when I saw you writing at your desk, I knew at once that you were the one I was destined some time in my life to meet. I knew then that the strong pull I felt while I was journeying here was to you, that there was no other reason for me to come."

Elizabeth was speechless. Hannah said comfortingly, "I know that I take you by surprise. But I think it will be apparent to you before long—apparent that we were destined to meet."

Elizabeth said cautiously, "Do you—are you often visited by these premonitions? Do you believe them to be supernatural?"

Hannah was thoughtful. "I've always known that there is more to the world than what I could see and hear and touch. When I was a child I thought this feeling might be connected with the gift of second sight which various members of my family claimed to have. But when I grew older I changed my opinion, especially when I had the chance to educate myself and read about the theories that have been held about the occult. I began to doubt the idea of the transference of images by nonhuman means—at least in the ways claimed by mediums and clairvoyants. I have come to believe that there is an ancient wisdom that surrounds us which we have lost through ignorance. I think it may be retrieved—by those who have the gift of receptiveness—those who can wait and reach for what may lie beyond the barrier of the human senses."

She spoke with such a modest certainty that Elizabeth's stiffness melted in spite of herself. "My dear girl, I am sorry that I cannot accept such an idea. My thought, I'm afraid is bounded by the rational. I don't care to dethrone the mind for the purpose of believing in the miraculous. I never could feel the force of the biblical admonition to become childlike in order to invite revelation of the divine." She stopped, aware that she had spoken with more vigor than she had intended.

But Hannah seemed unperturbed. She did not respond and after a silence they began to speak of other things. But Hannah's confident explanation of how she had been led to come to the seminary lingered in the back of Elizabeth's mind. Early in her life she had turned away from a religious focus in her thinking. Quite often she wondered what in fact her own viewpoint was. Her father had been a deist. There was a divine will that governed the world, but he rejected the idea of the supernatural, of divine revelation as the Christians believed. Perforce, because she had had to teach in schools under the aegis of one or another religious sect, she had learned a good deal of the details of their tenets. Hannah's belief in the foreshadowing of events did not appear to be the predestination that the Presbyterians embraced. Was she, therefore, an adherent of a cult based upon the stars and the planets? Elizabeth, alone at the moment and preoccupied with her thoughts, shook her head. The idea of the future, of future events affecting people, the world, the universe, being already set forth, lying ahead and merely awaiting the passage of time to arrive as the present— instead of being a fluid element that would crystallize into events as the result of physical laws—this she found very difficult to grasp. What were the governing principles of the universe —cosmic accidents, the influence of human ideas and actions? She sighed and decided to lay the matter aside as for the present at least insoluble.

But though she could put the riddle of the universe out of her mind, she found it impossible to turn her thoughts from Hannah. Not that Hannah intruded. When she sat in the sitting-room working, Hannah found quiet, unobtrusive things to do that nevertheless enabled her to stay close by. There was a soothing quality to Hannah's presence. How sweet this wordless companionship was! And how quickly the days were passing when they could enjoy it thus. Elizabeth put down her book and turned to talk instead.

Hannah was not reticent about her own background. When she was in her early teens, she said, her father had succumbed to the Western fever and had loaded his family onto a wagon to join the train of others headed for the frontier. She had made up her mind that she would not go, that this was her opportunity. She went to Baltimore and worked as a servant in a doctor's family—till she had enough book learning to become a teacher in a dame school. Her working career after that had been varied. At one time she worked for a woman who practiced palmistry, clairvoyance and card reading. She had soon grasped the essentials of this trade. In the course of the years since she had used this knowledge to earn a living in hard times.

Elizabeth asked, "How old are you, Hannah?"

"Thirty four. You are forty."

"How do you know?"

Hannah smiled. Elizabeth gazed at her and said, "You must know, then, how terribly fraudulent most of this trade in occultism is."

"Oh, yes." And Hannah related several episodes in which she had taken part in which she had helped fake the mysterious rappings and ghostly appearances.

"Oh, Hannah, Hannah!" But at Hannah's bright smile she could not help laughing. "All right, then. I shall call you Morgan le Fay. She was, you know, King Arthur's sister and a very powerful witch."

"And you?" asked Hannah. "You are from New York."

"Yes," said Elizabeth and found herself talking without reserve of her own life. She had never known her mother, she said. Her father had been a professor at Columbia College, a renowned classicist in his day, and she had grown up in a scholarly atmosphere, a child among learned men. It was only after she was grown that she realized what an odd childhood it was. "I learned all about the ancient world—Greece and Rome. It seemed a living world to me then, more so than the actual one of New York City. I still find myself bringing to bear on current events the criteria of ancient history. My father made no question of educating me as if I had been his son. He thought my mind good and therefore to be cultivated."

"That is why he named you Minerva as well as Elizabeth."

Elizabeth paused in surprise for a moment. "Yes. Of course. I have not thought of that before. But I was always very interested in the goddess as she appears in the *Odyssey*. You remember, it is Minerva who succors Ulysses when all the other gods treat him with despite."

Hannah shook her head to indicate that she was not acquainted with the story but Elizabeth went on, "But my education was invaluable to me when I came to earn my living. The young men who came to my father to be tutored in Greek and Latin and Hebrew were rather frightened of me. I was really quite grateful for this, because I found them very boring, and otherwise I should have had to entertain them. Oh, I know, the wives of my father's friends thought this very dreadful. I should never get a husband, they said, and they tried their best to make my father understand what an awful thing this was. Poor man. He fended them off for my sake. He had no interest in assuring me a husband. I am sure he thought I would make my own way, which in fact I have done since he died twenty years ago. Both of us took it for granted that I would be a teacher. He knew I would need a means of livelihood and he had no property to bequeath me. It was too bad, he lamented, that there were no schools for girls that were the equal of the colleges and universities for young men. The nearest thing to such a school was Mary Lyon's Mount Holyoke College. I did not go there, for there were no teachers who knew as much as I did in my field. Are you an advocate of womens' rights, Hannah?"

Hannah looked up sharply from her sewing. "I have always been."

"Well, then you know that it has always been a subject that has aroused heated debate and violent attacks from the hidebound. I attended the first Woman's Rights Convention, in Seneca Falls in New York in 1848. Do you know, that is almost fifty years ago! And so little has been accomplished since. Oh, yes, the War has intervened and the leaders of the women's movement agreed that they should set aside their concerns in order to aid in freeing the slaves. And now we must still stand aside in case we hinder the granting of voting rights to black men. I object to this. All citizens should have the right to vote for those who represent us in legislative bodies and the executive. Why is it always assumed that it is the role of a woman to step back for the benefit of someone else? It is a false idea, Hannah, very false. Until the position of women in our society is corrected, there will be no progress for anyone."

Hannah was gazing at her. What patrician features she had, she thought, and now so flushed with the indignation that rose so easily in her. Ah, Elizabeth, how happy I am that I have found you! Aloud she said, "I am quite sure you are right. But I expect you have suffered more from these injustices than I."

"Perhaps, because of the way in which I have earned my

living. I have told you of my upbringing. When I first went out
as a teacher I was greatly disillusioned. I had the odd notion
that my merit—the quality of my education, my dedication to
the ideals of teaching—would mean everything. I very soon
found out that that was not the case. My first shock came when
I had to deal with the women who run the sort of schools I
must teach in. They were not supporters of this new concept of
female freedom. They were too circumspect, really too frightened—of the men who provided the money to found and run the
schools and pay the teachers—to espouse the cause of woman's
rights. The men must be humored and reassured that educating
females would not destroy the absolute authority that they
claim as husbands and fathers. I was dismayed especially when
these women appeared to agree with their boards of trustees
that women were not capable of sustained mental effort, that
burdening them with a thorough education would destroy their
health and sanity. It was then that I discovered that I should,
for my own sake, hide the work that has always filled the
greater part of my life, the study of the literature of the Middle
Ages. I learned to be devious—which was something I had
always despised before. Only on the rare occasions when I had
the money and the opportunity to go back to New York and visit
some of my father's old friends could I talk about my work and
find stimulus from other scholars. Even there I had to be careful. Many scholarly men—most of them—gave no credence to
the idea that a woman had anything to offer in intellectual matters. It has been a very frustrating experience for me. Whenever
I have journeyed somewhere to hear Mrs. Stanton speak on
woman's rights I have been careful to make no mention of the
fact, much less discuss what I heard her say. She has always attracted me because she has a broader grasp than most women —"

"Elizabeth Cady Stanton?"

"Yes. She is considered a radical, you know, because she
questions the idea that a woman cannot be trusted with intellectual, political, religious—and sexual—freedom." Elizabeth
paused and glanced at Hannah.

"That will be the last freedom a woman will ever be granted."

Hannah spoke so positively that Elizabeth stared at her in

surprise. "But, Hannah, women have not always been so hampered in their personal lives. It is the terrible necessity to be respectable. Respectability is such a fraud. Its worship makes for such dreadful hypocrisy. Why is it that a woman can only be a sheltered, mindless creature suitable only for producing and raising children or else a creature of the streets?"

"Why, because that is most convenient for the men, don't you see?"

"Well, yes, of course, I can see that. But nevertheless I find it repugnant. Any intelligent, sincerely upright person, man or woman, must find it repugnant. And these ridiculous clothes we must wear —" Elizabeth stopped and looked again at Hannah. "Forgive me for mentioning it, but I have noticed that you do not wear stays. I have never had the courage to wear the costume Amelia Bloomer has devised but I am told by some women who have that the freedom it affords is simply marvelous—one need not keep one hand ready to manage one's skirts, for example."

"Stays and hoopskirts are quite impractical when you're looking after wounded soldiers."

"Of course. I see. But the Principal made no comment on this to you when she interviewed you?"

"Oh, no. She was anxious to hire me—partly because she needs new teachers desperately—at least temporarily—and because she was anxious to oblige Mrs. Lipscomb."

"And if she raises the point later —?"

Hannah smiled back at her. "I always allow the future to take care of itself."

"Hm. However, I must warn you that conformity is something insisted upon here." She paused for a moment and then added, "I have always had a trump card. It is hard to find a woman as qualified as I am to teach as many subjects. A man teacher would require a much higher salary—perhaps twice what I am paid."

Hannah nodded.

∿ ∿ ∿ ∿ ∿

It was the evening of their last day alone. The thought haunted

Elizabeth with the sense of an imminent and irreparable loss. From time to time she cast a glance towards Hannah. Hannah seemed to be her usual composed self. Occasionally she would suddenly raise her eyes and meet Elizabeth's directly. Elizabeth would look away in embarrassment.

It was as if she suspected Hannah of looking beyond her eyes into her mind. And what would she find there? Not the orderly and disciplined thoughts of a middle-aged school teacher. She longed to reach out her hand and touch Hannah, as if by doing so she could hold her back from the inevitable separation they would experience when the students arrived and the cottage would be filled and this great freedom of interchange between them would be lost. The very intimacy of the way they lived— spending all day together, sharing the same bed at night—would emphasize the distance from each other that they would have to practice. Did Hannah feel this? she wondered. Hannah gave no sign.

As usual they had eaten supper with the other teachers and the Principal. Now they were back at the cottage, whiling away the short time before they went to bed. Elizabeth, seated by the lamp with a book before her was silent. Hannah, sewing, said nothing, as if waiting for Elizabeth, as usual, to talk. This intimacy of women together, thought Elizabeth. It was understood to be the one prerogative women had, to commune together without the presence of men—but subject always to the instant dissolution of that intimacy if a man intruded. An intimacy, yes, but one without physical closeness beyond fleeting kisses, brief hugs, a denial that under their cumbersome garments there were bodies sensitive to the touch of loving hands, capable of being awakened to passion. What nonsense to maintain that women felt no pleasure in bodily contact, that their bodies were meant to feel only the pains of childbirth. In physical terms, between men and women there could be only the meeting of tyrant and slave. Between women, without the presence of true lust, there could be only sentimental sham. It has not always been thus. Her reading in the classics, in the literature of the Middle Ages, of the Renaissance, had taught her that.

In her adolescence the physical stirring of approaching womanhood aroused her interest in human relationships. When she first began to equate what she read with what she knew of life around her, she became aware that close friendships between women were possible and not subject to the strictures that affected any but the most distant acquaintanceship with men. Surrounded chiefly by people much older than herself, she groped for an understanding of the rebelliousness she felt and the role she was expected to play as a maturing young woman. The possible union of two women, she was told, was a rare and valuable form of friendship, but it was a matter of the communion of souls. Bodies had nothing to do with it. And yet her own body left her in no doubt that there was such a thing as desire. She drew back from the idea of a man in this context. She enjoyed the company of the men who surrounded her father—learned, kindly, willing to treat her as the possessor of a mind. But it was women who attracted her physically, who stirred her emotions.

Instinct warned her not to allude to this knowledge, even to other women. Women could be much more open and candid with each other than they could be with men. But when the subject of men arose—or the question of what men would think of what they said—women ran to ground. It was after all a man's opinion that counted with them. In her innermost being she longed for a companion, a woman, another girl, to whom all these buried feelings could be expressed. In time she came to accept the idea that this was a forbidden thing that would never come to pass.

Later, when she was already a teacher, she was fascinated by the courage Mrs. Stanton displayed in her writings and speaking on woman's rights, on the subject of the inequality of the laws that governed marriage and divorce. Mrs. Stanton had dared to say, "Our religion, laws, customs are all founded on the belief that woman was made for man." Every day of her life, teaching nubile girls brought up in that pattern, her soul rebelled. She would never surrender herself to a man.

Then she made acquaintance, on a visit to a feminist meeting in Philadelphia, with several of the women doctors striving against great odds to establish the Women's Medical College there as a respect-worthy school to train women in the practice of medicine. Among these women she found congenial company—women not afraid to discusss the realities of women's physical lives, the true character of a woman's sexual nature. The idea came clearly to her then: it would only be with a woman that she would ever explore the demands her own body made. And even in this company she instinctively buried this knowledge. It was too dangerous to seek to find another woman who had longings like hers.

And then of course there were the girls in the schools in which she taught. It was a commonplace problem, the excessive affection of one adolescent girl for another or for a teacher. From her self-knowledge, it was the result she knew of the bodily stirrings that they were forced to suppress. She herself had been the target of such feverish adulation more than once. The girls themselves did not understand why she kept them kindly but firmly at a distance. It was in their society an acceptable thing, this sometimes passionate affection between females, something indulgently looked upon as a foible of the weaker sex, to be erased by the arrival on the scene of a suitable man. She, with the knowledge of the dangerous depths that might lie hidden beneath this superficial fondness, drew back into the protection of a cool indifference.

But how little these girls, even sometimes these young women, understood or recognized the physical basis for this outpouring of emotion, love and jealousy, how horrified they would be to have it defined as sexual in origin, a lust sometimes as strong as that contemptuously assigned to the male. Women and girls, it was assumed, were of a finer nature, destined, it was true, to be the bedfellows of men and the producers of children—that most grossly physical of human processes—but nevertheless knowing love only as an idealized emotion, in no way tainted by sexual desire.

What rubbish, she thought, aware of the vigor, the swelling of unacknowledged concupiscence, in these burgeoning bodies. How ridiculous it was for those in charge to recognize only the danger of male seduction—whenever a male teacher taught the girls there must be a chaperone present to satisfy the proprieties. What of women like herself, as tempted, as delighted as any man at the sight of fresh young bosoms, lissom young bodies? She had always turned resolutely away from these thoughts. Yes, through the years she had learned discipline.

∿ ∿ ∿ ∿ ∿

Hannah had not spoken but Elizabeth, suddenly aware of the prolonged silence between them, looked up at her and exclaimed, "I am very sorry, Hannah, to have become so abstracted."

Hannah shook her head. "You were deep in thought—about the gleemaidens?" Her quick smile ravished Elizabeth.

"Oh, no! Not really. Something much closer to home."

Hannah looked her question.

"We shall not have such opportunities for chat after tonight. I have enjoyed our few days together, Hannah."

"So have I. But why do you think that this ends?"

"Why, we shall have very little time free from interruption after this."

"Well, that's so. But we do have our own room."

The matter-of-fact way in which she spoke took nothing away from the impact of what she said. Elizabeth stared at her for a moment and then Hannah went on asking about the duties they would face the following day.

A while later, in their bedroom, getting ready for bed, Elizabeth found herself standing in the middle of the floor, facing Hannah. There seemed to be something of the utmost importance that she should say in order to arrest the inexorable flight of time that would bring this idyll to an end, yet she was tongue-tied. Hannah stood waiting, respectfully silent. When the minutes had passed, Hannah smiled and turned away to undress.

In the dark Elizabeth lay on her back, her feelings in a turmoil that gradually subsided, as Hannah sank at once into sleep. She felt a great desire to touch Hannah, to stroke her, to move closer to the warmth of her body. For a few moments she lay motionless, hovering over Hannah and then with a supreme effort she rolled away to her side of the bed.

Still she could not sleep for thinking of the day to come.

Tomorrow would be the end of this tranquil communion,
tranquil yet alive with the undercurrent of attraction between
them. Tomorrow they would be surrounded by a crowd of
girls eager to establish their own places in this new world.
Her life with Hannah alone had flowed sweetly through the
sunlit days. Without saying much about it, Hannah had taken
over the few household tasks necessary. Elizabeth noticed the
deftness of her movements, the swiftness and sureness with
which she did anything with her hands. In the afternoons they
had often sat in the kitchen, Hannah at the big deal table paring
apples for a pie, Elizabeth in the rocking chair beside the
window, her book forgotten in her lap. The autumn sun stream-
ing in at the window warmed the big tortoise shell cat asleep
in another chair. The thought had crossed Elizabeth's mind,
a more disarmingly domestic scene could not have been
imagined by the seminary's board of trustees.

But that would be all gone now.

She was startled to hear Hannah groan. Sometimes, Hannah
had said she suffered from nightmares. Elizabeth was not to be
alarmed at this. A touch would awaken her and dissipate the
dream. Now Elizabeth wondered whether she should wake her.
But Hannah settled back quiet again.

She wondered what disturbed her rest. Perhaps some memory
of the ghastly sights she must have encountered during the
months she had served as an army nurse—for that was indeed
what Hannah had been for a while. The last battles of the Civil
War had been fought not far away, in Virginia, and the dead
were often left lying unburied on the battlefield for months.
What a stupid carnage. It was men who sought wars. As if
fighting would ever solve a rational argument. All this war had
achieved had been bitterness and frustration, even for the
former slaves—and wealth for the war profiteers.

How strange, this tale of Hannah's about the feeling that led
her to the seminary and their meeting. Could one really believe
in this claim of otherworldly direction, bringing her here to
seek someone she knew nothing of? Hannah was neither stupid
nor ignorant, nor hysterical. There was a remarkable quality
about her—yes, in that modest garb there was a woman with a
sense of command. It was difficult to deny what Hannah

asserted, simply because of the manner in which she spoke.

Hannah stirred, turned over on her back and lay muttering in her sleep. Elizabeth raised herself on her elbow, listening. There was a moment of absolute quiet. Even Hannah's breathing was soundless. Then Hannah said, "I have been dreaming. Did I disturb you?"

"No. I was not asleep. Hannah —" Involuntarily she put her hand on Hannah's breast, felt its resilient softness. Hannah did not move. Elizabeth leaned over her, eager for something she could not formulate, aware that at this moment she was sweeping aside the prudent withdrawal she had practiced for many years.

"Hannah —" She could get no further than the name.

But Hannah did not hang back. Her strong arms encircled Elizabeth and pulled her down on top of her. She felt Hannah's capable hands reach inside her nightgown, travelling thrillingly all over her body. She felt Hannah's lips on her skin, heard the inviting chuckle in Hannah's throat. A thousand fantasies suddently became reality. She gasped and sank helpless onto Hannah's warm, abundant body. Time had no meaning nor place. She knew only the fulfillment of Hannah's touch. In the end they sank comfortably into each other's arms. Eventually Elizabeth slept, aware only that she had moved from ecstasy to the land of bliss.

She woke abruptly, at first bewildered, not sure whether she was waking from a dream of joy. The sky out of the window was barely light. Half-guilty with the remembrance of the night, she rose carefully, anxious not to rouse Hannah, and went out into the kitchen and poked the embers in the stove into a flame sufficient to boil a kettle of water. She had not finished preparing the tea before Hannah appeared in the doorway.

"Let me take the tray," Hannah said. "It is cold this morning. Let us have it in bed."

Elizabeth glanced at her uncertainly and quickly looked away, relinquishing the tray. Obediently she followed Hannah and got back in bed. Hannah put the tray on the nightstand and got in under the covers beside, lying down on her back.

Looking up at her, Hannah said, "Minerva was Athena to the Greeks, wasn't she? I sometimes tell stories about mythology to the little ones." She paused and smiled up at Elizabeth. "Pallas Athena, in panoply. That is right."

Elizabeth blushed.

∿ ∿ ∿ ∿ ∿

All that was so long ago, and yet, in this lumpy bed in this dreadful lodging, the perfume of that long ago moment returned like a charming ghost to wipe out the vexations of the present. Indomitable Hannah. She felt sure they would not long linger here. But how to understand Hannah's intent?

She leaned over Hannah to feel the regular rise and fall of her breast, to reassure herself of Hannah's tranquil nearness. She would not wake her, though the yearning to share this recollection of their own past was great. It was childish to disturb the rest Hannah so much needed simply to gratify herself.

II

CHAPTER SIX

Daisy came down the great staircase of the Colonel's house with quick, soft steps, buttoning her glove. At the bottom she stopped to listen. The big doors of the drawingroom were open and she wondered if Aunt Edie was there. No sound came to tell her, but then sounds did not travel in these enormous, thickly carpeted spaces. Was she there alone, leafing through the latest issue of the *Ladies Home Journal*, upon which she depended for fashion news, consoling stories and spiritual advice? I should be more punctual, thought Daisy, and not keep her waiting. But how I hate these rounds of calls. Thank goodness, Easter will be here in a week or so and the season will be over. The summer is coming and we won't have to be having these interminable ladies' luncheons. I don't mind the dinners so much when there is dancing. If only Aunt Edie did not make such a point of my accompanying her on these calls. I can't say she forces me to, but the darling gets so hurt if I don't. And of course she thinks this is all part of what we should do to get me a rich husband.

Daisy paused to look at herself in the great floor to ceiling mirror. She had grown used to big looking glasses—rather like those in the palace at Versailles, she thought. They were everywhere throughout the house—part of Uncle William's mania for the ostentatious display of his wealth. She pitied some of the less sophisticated of her aunt's visitors on first encountering these great sheets of reflecting glass. She remembered her own dismay when she had first come to live with her aunt, how startled she was to see herself so small a figure in the surrounding vastness captured in the mirror.

Now she turned one way and then another to judge her appearance. She saw a slim, not so tall girl with a lovely complexion. There was a general air of elegance about the fine silk walking dress with its elaborately embroidered cuffs and collar and the wide-brimmed hat with the French ornaments around the crown. Yes, she knew she made a very pretty picture. The trouble was that these expensive clothes, this slightly aloof manner which she carefully cultivated, gave a false impression. People thought, because she lived with Aunt Edie and Aunt Edie provided her with everything that a young woman could need or want, that she was an heiress, when in fact she hadn't a penny. This, when she complained of it, did not trouble Aunt Edie, who said complacently that the misconception would surely lead to marriage with a suitable man, by which she meant a young man of family and wealth.

But it hasn't happened yet, thought Daisy, with satisfaction, and I am twenty-two years old—an old maid.

She crossed the wide hall and stood for a moment in the drawingroom doorway. Aunt Edie was not alone then, for she heard the murmur of women's voices. For a moment she was perplexed and then wary. Surely not. But, yes, it was that strange looking old woman who had first come to see her aunt a week or so ago and who now seemed to be at the house every day. What was it she called herself? Madame Aurora. Nothing more or less than a fortune teller. Aunt Edie was altogether too susceptible to such shady characters. Her natural credulity made her an easy victim and people like that knew it as soon as they saw her.

The voices drew nearer and Daisy stepped quickly back into a corner behind the newel post—one of the few spots, she had discovered, where one would not be reflected in the great mirror. Her aunt came out of the drawingroom, an elegant little woman dressed for the calls she was about to make. The woman with her was short and broad, in a voluminous skirt and a brightly colored shawl.

Aunt Edie was saying, "I am so grateful to you, Madame Aurora. I must go out now to make calls. But the Colonel, I know, will be very glad to see you."

Madame Aurora bowed slightly. Daisy watched them in the lookingglass, Madame Aurora walking slowly to the staircase, her aunt fluttering in her wake.

Her aunt said, "I won't go up with you. I am expecting my niece down at any moment."

Daisy found herself looking straight into Madame Aurora's light, strange eyes. Madame Aurora said, "I believe she is waiting for you here."

Daisy, blushing, stepped out from behind the newel post.

∿ ∿ ∿ ∿ ∿

Daisy, sitting next to her aunt in the carriage, said, "Who is that funny old woman who comes to see you almost every day?"

She saw, out of the corner of her eyes, that her aunt was offended. "Daisy, she is not a funny old woman. She is Madame Aurora, who is noted now in Washington for her psychic powers."

"You mean, she is another fortune teller."

"I mean nothing of the sort. She spurns such tricks. She is a person of great gifts. She has really taken Washington by storm."

"With your patronage, I'm sure."

Her aunt pursed her mouth. "Daisy, you must not be so cynical. I have had little to do with the success she has made. I am simply very fortunate that she consents to come to see William."

Daisy turned to stare at her. "To see Uncle William!"

"She doesn't come to see me. Though I think she would if I needed her. She is a kind woman. I see her at her gatherings. She has quite large groups of people who meet to hear her."

"Seances?"

"No. She refuses to hold seances. She is a teacher—a teacher of spiritual things. It is very inspiring to hear her."

"But, good heavens, Aunt Edie, why is Uncle William interested in her?"

"Honey, he is an old man. Everybody begins to think about the hereafter when they get old. It is only natural. I think he is quite unhappy. I believe he broods on the past. Madame Aurora has cheered him up. He was getting quite gloomy."

Daisy was silent for a moment, listening absently to the clip-clop of the horses. They were getting close to their first call. "Don't you think it is rather dangerous to let someone like that get too friendly with Uncle William?"

"Dangerous? Why?"

"Well, sometimes somebody like that gets to have too much influence, especially since Uncle William sees practically nobody else now that he is an invalid."

Again her aunt looked offended. "Honey, Madame Aurora is not a mercenary woman. Her mind is on higher things. She is being very considerate of me to come and talk to William. Well, here we are at Mrs. Conway's. My, I shall be glad when the season is over. It is getting so warm."

∿ ∿ ∿ ∿ ∿

She won't listen to me, thought Daisy, following her aunt up Mrs. Conway's steps. She was very fond of Aunt Edie. But from the time she was a little girl she had been aware of Aunt Edie's foibles. She was kind, affectionate, with a strong sense of family feeling. But she was also stubborn and clung to her own opinions, which she almost never put into words, so that it was difficult to reach an understanding with her. Like a good many other people, she had often wondered why Aunt Edie married the Colonel, how this unlikely match came about. She had been too young to understand the circumstances when Aunt Edie had astounded everyone by becoming Mrs. Head—a pretty, modest little woman from the vicinity of Easton on the Chesapeake Bay, a true lady but unused to sophisticated society, who for some unaccountable reason had remained single into her thirties. Capturing this fearful creature—for capture was how it was seen among her friends and relatives—this fearful creature who was many times a millionaire, with a shady past—this had been a nine days' wonder.

But she had moved to Washington to inhabit the Colonel's monstrous house, built by him to outshine the great houses of wealthy senators by which it was surrounded. Aunt Edie loved entertaining lavishly. She was very soon known as one of the more successful of Washington's hostesses. There was grace and charm and lively conversation at Mrs. Head's dinner parties, excellent food and sometimes music. She blossomed in the atmosphere of respectful attention that she received from everyone. It obviously occurred to no one to bracket her with the Colonel when critical things were said about him. The Colonel himself treated her with affection. Daisy had often seen him watching his wife surrounded by the mighty and the wealthy, with a sardonically approving light in his eyes. Putting it bluntly to herself, she thought he was savoring the excellence of his bargain in acquiring such a woman as his prize, a prize whose value everyone must acknowledge and which no one would have supposed he could have achieved.

Five years ago Aunt Edie had sent back to the Eastern Shore for Daisy, the child of her dead brother, whose mother had recently died. There was one overriding idea in her mind, which she made plain to Daisy at once. Daisy was to marry well and soon.

$\sim \sim \sim \sim \sim$

The afternoon was spent by the time Aunt Edie told the coachman to take them home.

She leaned back in her corner of the carriage and said, "Tomorrow will be our last dinner for this season." She said it with an air of fatigue and Daisy was aware that she welcomed the fact. In the morning she would go, as she did more often than not, to the Center Market, with the black manservant in tow, to pick out the crab and the terrapin and the game, the new peas and asparagus. Perhaps, she said, there might still be oysters. She wanted some Mme. de Wattville roses. She preferred the delicacy of their fragrant, blush-marked white petals as table decorations to the more spectacular visions achieved by some of her friends—forests of evergreens down the center of the table, dotted with carnations or other similar creations.

Her aunt went on, "I've had such trouble with the seating arrangement for the dinner."

Daisy, used to her nervous worry about the details of a dinner party, said soothingly, "You always worry, Aunt Edie, and there is never any reason to."

"Oh, but this time I have a real problem—an extra guest at the last moment, and a young unmarried woman at that."

"Why did you have to invite her?"

"I could not refuse. Mrs. Thurber asked me to—she is the

wife of a senator, you know, and her brother is an important man in California. This girl is his niece. She has just come to Washington. Her parents are close friends of the governor of that state. One must be careful of these connections, Daisy. Mrs. Thurber is anxious to introduce her to Washington society."

"Well, in that case, did you find a place for her?"

"Of course. But for a while I really did not know how to go about it."

"Oh, Aunt Edie, you're never at a loss!"

"You may think so, honey, but I've never had a situation just like this one. She is an unusual girl."

Daisy's curiosity rose. "Unusual?"

"Yes. She has been to college and now she has come to Washington to take a position in the government."

Daisy recognized in the tone of her aunt's voice her dislike of bookish women. Aunt Edie disapproved of women who sought what she considered to be a man's education. No woman, she contended, could really achieve intellectually what a man did and if she tried, she would only lose what was far more important, the status of a womanly woman whose sphere in life was bounded by her home and family. When her aunt had become the wealthy Mrs. Head, Daisy knew that she was perfectly willing to send her to a good finishing school. She saw that as an avenue to a circle of suitable friends and thence to an advantageous marriage. But she would never consent to send her to college, even to one which was entirely for women.

"What sort of position?"

"I really don't know. It is something to do with the Library of Congress. It sounds most unsuitable, to me, for a young woman."

∿ ∿ ∿ ∿ ∿

A good deal of the time Daisy was bored to tears by the dinners her aunt gave. She tried to cover her boredom with a disguise of amiability, listening as patiently as possible to the chattering ladies and the self-important men. But Mrs. Head cast her social net wide and often there was someone of greater interest—a world traveler newly arrived from China, an artist returned from a sojourn in Paris to paint portraits of his wealthier fellow Americans, and in the last few months Army and Navy men talking about the Spanish in Cuba.

Her aunt's comment about the extra guest for this evening titillated her interest. She kept a watchful eye on the guests as they arrived. Her aunt had not mentioned her name but by looking at the place cards on the dining table she determined that the newcomer must be the Eleanor Purcell who was to sit between the third secretary of the British Embassy and old Mr. Alsop, retired from the Department of the Treasury.

Eleanor Purcell proved to be a tall young woman with decidedly red hair, not goodlooking but with bright inquisitive eyes behind spectacles, self-possessed, dressed in an excellent gown that was nevertheless not in the very height of fashion. There was to be no dancing this evening, so that it was easier, after dinner, for Daisy to maneuver in the drawingroom, eluding the young men who always gathered around her. She succeeded in getting the newcomer alone for a few minutes' conversation, behind one of the white marble Grecian nymphs, draped in flowing robes and holding baskets of marble fruit that filled the corners of the room. The young woman was standing by herself, looking around eagerly as if taking in a new, enthralling scene. When Daisy spoke, she turned to look straight into her eyes with friendly interest.

"Miss Purcell," said Daisy, "I'm Mrs. Head's niece."

"Oh, yes! Of course, I remember. We were introduced earlier. My name is Nell."

"And I'm Daisy. You're from California?"

"Yes. My father is an astronomer. He and my mother teach at the University of Berkeley."

"You're a newcomer in Washington."

"Yes, but it is not my first visit here. I went to college here in the East, at Bryn Mawr and after that to the Library School at Columbia."

"The Library School?" Daisy's wonderment was obvious in her eyes.

Nell laughed. "Yes! I am a librarian. I've come to Washington because I have been promised a post on the staff of the Library of Congress when it has moved into its new building. I am sure you have heard all about that magnificent new building. The newspapers are full of it. They have begun to move the books already from the old quarters in the Capitol. I tell you, it is quite an achievement to have obtained one of the new staff positions. There are many, many more applicants than positions and of course there is a lot of political patronage. But I do have thorough training."

Bewildered, Daisy asked, "But what do you do?"

Nell, looking into her puzzled eyes, laughed again. "Oh, I know! You think a librarian is either an old man with a beard or a mousy little woman sitting behind a desk afraid to speak above a whisper. Well, let me tell you, things have changed a lot. I am a cataloguer. I examine books and describe them and identify the author and the publisher so that they can be listed and readers can find what they want. This is really one of the great events of this century, moving what amounts to our national library to a fine new building and cataloguing its contents so that we can know for the first time what they are. To me, this is most exciting."

Daisy listened, bemused by Nell's enthusiasm about a subject entirely new to her. She had never before encountered a young woman who spoke with such vivacity about something so impersonal as a lifework among books. Fleetingly she thought how dismayed Aunt Edie would be at such total disregard for the important things in the social world. For this young woman with so many obvious disadvantages—red hair, wearing spectacles, having no trace of regular beauty and none of the usual social graces—was entirely self-confident, apparently untroubled by the fact that she was an oddity. Nell seemed oblivious to the idea that a young woman's sparkle and vivacity was exclusively for the benefit of eligible men, not to be wasted on another girl.

Their chat was brief, for Daisy was very soon called away to join in other conversations. She was amazed when at the end of the evening, the guests gone, her aunt thanked her for being so kind to the newcomer.

"Why, I enjoyed talking to her."

"You're always so kind, honey. You made the poor girl feel right welcome, I'm sure."

∿ ∿ ∿ ∿ ∿

In fact, she found she could not bear the thought that this bird of strange plumage should go out of her life as abruptly as she had entered it. The season of formal entertaining was over but her aunt held small evening parties at which visiting musicians performed. Daisy, counting on the power of familiarity to make Nell's idiosyncracies less noticeable to her aunt, was able to invite her several times. She was helped in this by the fact that, in her aunt's eyes, Nell had impeccable antecedents—well-to-do parents who were people of considerable importance in their own part of the world and who were well-connected in Washington political circles. Perhaps, Aunt Edie remarked, her forthright manner was merely the natural exuberance of Californians.

Nell, eager to show appreciation for being so singled out, said effusively, "Oh, Mrs. Head, it is such a treat to come. I don't play any musical instrument. I don't think I have the talent. But I love music. It is wonderful to be able to hear so much of it."

Mrs. Head smiled, gratified. Nell had lingered this time until after the other guests and the singer and her accompanist had left.

Mrs. Head said, "Daisy plays the piano very well, for a girl. But I don't really approve of a professional musical career for a woman. It takes her too much into public. Though I don't deny that Madame Morini has a very fine voice."

Nell rushed in. "But if a woman has a great talent, she must feel the same need to use it as a man would!"

Daisy, recognizing the slight tightening of her aunt's lips, went quickly to the piano and began to play ragtime. She played with spirit and Nell, astonished, tried hard to look grave as she saw Mrs. Head's annoyance and realized that Daisy was engaged in a diversionary tactic.

"I don't know where Daisy picks up these vulgar tunes," said

Mrs. Head, with distaste. "She tells me some of them are even written by women."

She turned away as if to close out the sound of the piano and said Goodbye with an appearance of unconcern.

∿ ∿ ∿ ∿ ∿

One day Nell tentatively suggested that perhaps Daisy would like to come and visit her. She was, she explained, living in a boardinghouse, one frequented by congressmen and other prominent people who, either because they could not afford their own houses or were too transient in Washington, required a suitable lodging. Mrs. Haines' boardinghouse, said Nell, was expensive but very well appointed. She was the only unattached young woman living there.

"I am," she said further, "nearly always home on Sunday afternoons. At least, I always can be if I know you may come."

So, in the somnolent calm of one Sunday afternoon Daisy, greatly daring, set forth on foot down Sixteenth Street. When she reached Pennsylvania Avenue at the trolley stop near the White House, she had a long wait, for the Sunday service was leisurely. She felt very conspicuous, standing there in her white lace-trimmed dress and big hat, aware of the covert glances of the frumpish middle-aged woman and the two straw-hatted men who waited with her. At last the trolley came and she rode up the Avenue and around Capitol Hill.

Nell's boardinghouse was right in the shadow of the massive new granite building of the Library of Congress. She had heard discussion of this boardinghouse among her aunt's friends. The proprietor, Mrs. Haines, had always had only the most genteel clientele and it was a matter for comment when she for the first time had accepted as a boarder an unattached young lady, the graduate of one of the new women's colleges, earning her own living as a member of the staff of the newly expanded Library of Congress. Mrs. Haines did it, of course, because the young woman had been vouched for by the wife of one of the justices of the Supreme Court.

When Daisy arrived and Nell had been summoned downstairs

by the smart black maid whose eyes were bright with curiosity, they sat through the warmth of the early June afternoon in Mrs. Haines' parlor, happily deserted on that occasion by everyone else.

~ ~ ~ ~ ~

The second time Daisy went to visit Nell there were others in Mrs. Haines' parlor and Nell suggested that they go up to her room. It was a large front room with a view of the Capitol dome across the trees. The idea of a young woman of her own age living alone in the house of a stranger, no matter how respectable and well-appointed it might be, aroused awe in Daisy. Nell, watching her, took a certain pleasure in emphasizing her own independence.

"Rather nice, isn't it? You know, when I first said I was coming to Washington, some of my mother's friends were alarmed. They thought I should stay with relatives. That I did not want to do. I am not afraid. I can take care of myself and I haven't any use for this old-fashioned idea that a woman must always be protected. Protected against what? Some man who may take advantage of her? Well, I'm not putting up with anything like that."

"Aren't your parents worried?"

"Oh, no. They expect me to be independent. In fact, they have taught me to be, as if I was a boy. After all, this is almost the twentieth century. Women don't have to live in perpetual seclusion from the dangers of the world."

Daisy said nothing.

Nell was saying, "Don't you get bored sometimes, Daisy, not having anything to do all day?"

Surprised, Daisy exclaimed, "But I have plenty to do!"

"I mean, something to do that means a lot to you."

Daisy thought for a while and then said, "I don't know just what you mean."

"Well, I know you live with your aunt and you don't have to earn a living. But there are so many things a woman can do these days. Why, you know my mother is an astronomer, like my father. That is, she trained to be one and when she married she kept right on as his assistant. They both teach. She never has idle moments."

"Oh, you mean a career."

"Yes. Have you thought of it?"

"Well —," Daisy was silent for a moment. "I haven't got your kind of education —"

"Would you want it? Would you like to go to college?"

"Aunt Edie would never hear of it."

Nell said delicately, "You would have to have her consent?"

Daisy smiled. "I haven't a cent to my name. Aunt Edie pays all my expenses, buys all my clothes, provides all my luxuries."

"So naturally you must please her."

"It's more than that. I would never hurt her if I could help it. My father died when I was little and Aunt Edie invited my mother to bring me and come and live with her. She wasn't Mrs. Head then. She had a house she had inherited and some income from a farm. My mother was glad to have a home. We went on living there when Aunt Edie married. Then when my mother died, she sent for me to come and live with her here. She is the kindest person in the world and she has a very strong sense of family feeling. But she does not approve of modern young women with college educations."

"Like me!"

"Yes. She likes you now, because she has become used to you and you don't seem alarming. But she distrusts your independence."

They were both silent for a while and then Daisy said hesitantly, as if she was shy of speaking of something close to her, "There is one thing I do which I like doing."

Nell was alert. "What is that?"

"I write a social column for an Eastern Shore newspaper—all about the goings on in Washington. Aunt Edie thinks I do it just for fun. But I get paid for it."

"Bully for you! Then you do know what it means to be independent."

Daisy looked at her ironically. "I wouldn't say it means independence. It is only a pittance."

"But it's the idea!"

"I've never told anybody else. Just the editor of the paper knows about it and he has promised not to let on."

They went on talking until it was almost five o'clock and neither of them had noticed the passage of time. The long clear June evening had not warned them. Daisy hurried to put on her hat and gloves. When she was ready, they stood for a moment facing each other, caught in a joint emotion that neither was able to explain or articulate. In the end they turned away and Daisy ran down the stairs with Nell following close behind, wishing her goodbye.

CHAPTER SEVEN

They were in Daisy's room, enormous, with velvet-draped windows. It was after dinner—a family gathering, and Daisy knew that her aunt's attention would be completely absorbed in the conversation of her relatives from the Eastern Shore.

Nell, glancing over her shoulder, felt intimidated by the two long lookingglasses, which increased the impression of the size of the room, one on each wall. How, she wondered, could Daisy put up with this intrusion, for that was what it was. The big mirrors shattered any sense of intimacy. Nell was startled by the sudden glimpses of herself and Daisy when, absorbed in their talk, she least expected to see them. This absurd splendor—obviously the whole house spoke of this inappropriate grandeur, the Colonel's intent to call attention to his immense wealth. This room was indeed an incongruous setting for Daisy's fresh young grace.

"How do you stand it, Daisy?"

Daisy, looking to see what she meant, said, "Oh, the mirrors. I've learned not to look at them, except when I'm getting derssed for dinner or to go out. They're blank walls otherwise."

"You've got more fortitude than I do, then."

"Let's sit over here," said Daisy, indicating a love seat with its back to the mirrors.

She sat down and Nell dropped down on the seat next to her. It was the first time they were physically so close to each other. For a while neither of them found anything to say.

Finally, Nell asked. "Do you stay here all summer?"

"We do this year, because of Uncle William. He can't travel. Sometimes we've been abroad, to Europe. But we usually go down to the Shore, several times, for long visits. Uncle William used to like to fish, so he didn't mind going there. But now, since he had his stroke, he doesn't want to go anywhere and Aunt Edie won't leave him."

"Not even for a short holiday?"

"I don't think he would like it. She feels she should stay with him. It's part of her bargain."

After a moment Nell said, "She did make a bargain, then—whatever it was he wanted from her in return for the status of a wealthy matron. Oh, don't get offended, Daisy, but that is it, I'm sure. So many women make that sort of bargain—only there is not always so much money involved."

Daisy was on the defensive. "Well, what else could she do? She had very little to live on and she had given up hope of marrying the sort of man she had been brought up to expect as a husband. It must have been a breathtaking offer—to be the wife of the richest man in the country—that's what some people say he is—and live in luxury for the rest of her life."

Nell looked at her closely. "Would you have done it?"

Daisy did not answer her look. "I don't think so, but then, how can you say what you would have done in somebody else's place?"

"You don't like him, do you—the Colonel?"

Daisy was slow to answer. "I shouldn't say anything about him, since I'm living off his bounty. He didn't marry to have children. He obviously didn't want any, but he never objected when Aunt Edie brought me here to live with her. As far as I know, he has never begrudged her the money she spends on me."

"So you have to be grateful." There was a touch of scorn in Nell's voice. "Your aunt did make a good bargain."

"There was no one among her friends who didn't believe she was marvellously fortunate."

"But, Daisy, don't you see, that sort of viewpoint is so wrong! Women shouldn't sell themselves for social position, for luxurious living—in fact, just for a meal ticket —"

"What are you talking about?" Daisy stared at her angrily. "Women are supposed to marry as well as they can. What else can they do? What kind of life does a woman have unless she has a husband and children? She's just an old maid, a fifth wheel —"

Nell's face flamed. "Is that the way you feel about it—for yourself? Women should be able to do anything they want to—just like men. Do you think I'd settle for that sort of servitude?"

Daisy's anger drained away. "It's not supposed to be servitude. It's supposed to be the highest calling, for women. Oh, you're different. You've got something you want to do and you have the chance to do it."

"Because I chose to! Daisy, you can't mean that you look foward to that sort of life?"

The moment the words were said, they both were transfixed, as if something hidden had suddenly come to the surface. They stared at each other.

Daisy said slowly, "I don't want to get married. I don't like the idea. I want to be myself, to listen to my own inside thoughts. But that is what Aunt Edie wants me to do. She is set on it. She does not want me left with nothing."

"Well, she can prevent that by leaving you something, can't she?"

"If she has it to leave."

"Well, why wouldn't she?"

Daisy shrugged. "She seems to be quite uncertain whether the Colonel will leave her anything when he dies."

"What a strange idea! She'd be his widow."

"I don't know. I just know she worries about it."

"Well, in any case, if you're left on your own, you can learn to take care of yourself. Other girls do now and I think they are a lot better off. Times have changed. Women can get educations now—I mean, real educations so that they can earn their living at something worthwhile. We're not as ignorant as we used to be. Why, a generation ago, most girls didn't know anything about what marrying a man meant—that you had to go to bed with him and have children whether you wanted to or not, whether it damaged your health or not —"

Daisy cut in impatiently. "What makes you think a lot of girls aren't that ignorant now?"

Nell's eyes were anxious. "You're not, are you?"

Daisy smiled. "Oh, I guess I don't know as much about it as you do, but I'm not a ninny."

"I'm glad of that. You know, women have been kept in subjection by ignorance. Why do you suppose men don't want us educated? Because we'd see through them and rebel against all the silly prohibitions they lay down on us. Why do you suppose they say we shouldn't ride bicycles or we'll damage our female organs? Because they don't want us to be free to go where we like. But things are changing and it is because women have been able to get educations. They've banded together and worked for women's rights. That's made a big difference already, but there is still a lot to be done."

"Are you a suffragist?"

"Of course. I want to do everything I can to make things change. I find it intolerable to live in a society that tells me to my face that I'm not a complete person, that I'm a creature incomplete by nature, born unequal to any man, no matter how stupid he is and how intelligent I am. I won't put up with being told that I can only reach fulfillment as a woman by becoming some man's property, to have children to be brought up to perpetuate this kind of world. I can't understand why any woman is willing to continue to be a chattel when she is offered the chance to be her own person."

"Well, please don't say all this to Aunt Edie."

Nell was brought up short, speechless.

Daisy went on, "It's bad enough that you live in a boardinghouse by yourself and earn your living doing a man's job." Daisy paused to put her arm around Nell's shoulders. "I couldn't bear to have her say she doesn't like my being friends with you."

Nell grew stiff. "Would you cut me off to please her?"

"No." Daisy's voice was soft. "But I don't want to create a situation that can be avoided."

Nell sat silent, her feelings seething just under the surface. She found herself caught in a strange cross-current of emotions. She remembered the first evening she had seen Daisy. She had been excited, under the spell of this new venture in her life, for the first time independent financially of her parents, meeting new people every day who saw her as a modern young woman, on her own, perhaps as an iconoclast. This role suited her. It compensated for the shortcomings in herself of which she was very much aware. She had grown up knowing she was not pretty, not with the sort of prettiness people admired in girls. She knew she lacked the sort of pliability that girls were supposed to have. From her childhood she had learned to make her cleverness, her quickness of mind take the place of these things she lacked, to give her the outward appearance of self-confidence, and later, social aplomb. She felt awkward with boys and then young men and used her book learning to make a shield betwen herself and them.

But sometimes her nerve failed.

So, on that evening she had been grateful to Daisy for the gentle amiability with which she had welcomed her. At first that was all she had thought of it. But she realized, after the evening was over, that something about Daisy had made a lasting impression on her. She remembered wishing that there was some way in which she could make Daisy a friend and she was overjoyed when Daisy contrived to invite her to her aunt's musicales. Daisy's visit to her boardinghouse had sealed the fact that they were indeed to be friends.

Now sitting next to Daisy, she felt a great urge to do, to say something that would draw them still closer together. But what? Since her earliest childhood she had read compulsively—history books, novels, biographies, diaries, everything that came her way. She was aware of a sort of hunger for something beyond the printed page, a hunger for physical fulfillment. While she was growing up this longing took the form of wishing that she could be a boy and do what boys did in the stories she read—go to sea, be a warrior, explore the wild places of the earth, discover treasure. When she got older and read novels that were concerned with the relationship between men and women she felt a sort of frustration, because she could not enter into the emotions and desires depicted in the women, even after she learned what the sexual act was and how it was euphemized in literature. She found she really disliked the idea of being kissed by a man, of being overwhelmed by his embrace. Curiously, she found more interest in the pursuit by men of women. Or, rather, she found more pleasure in imagining a man's desire for a woman, more pleasure in imagining the softness and compliance of a woman in her arms.

Later, when her reading became more sophisticated and she came upon forbidden books, she realized that there were aspects of sexual desire and its satisfaction that were never alluded to in the world in which she lived. In studying the classics and poetry, she came upon Sappho and learned that, after all, there were women who like herself preferred to think of erotic desire in a feminine context. But all this was between the covers of books. She had come to realize that there were ardent friendships between women and girls. She had a few such in her teens—at least, passionate devotion directed to a teacher or older girl but never really acknowledged. She quickly learned that such things were not to be brought out into the open. Single women—spinsters and widows—might maintain households together but the nature of these relationships were clearly defined as simply the poor second best that women without men could achieve as a normal way of life, practical arrangements in which the erotic had no part.

Or if it did, then they must either hide the fact or be the subject of ostracism. For that reason she had been wary whenever she found herself approaching or being approached by another woman in moments of mounting emotion. It had not been too hard for her to exercise this sort of self-discipline, for she did not find herself too greatly attracted.

Until she met Daisy. And then at once Daisy held her in the palm of her hand. She despaired that anything could ever come of it. There were too many obstacles to the development of the sort of communion she longed for with Daisy, not least Daisy's own attitude. She could not guess how Daisy might feel about such a thing. She wondered, in fact, if Daisy had ever considered the existence of such a thing. A woman could not just invite another woman to go to bed with her—at least, not the kind of women she and Daisy were. But even if nothing ever came of it, she knew it would always be Daisy who would be the standard of comparison with every other woman in her imagination. Daisy was the embodiment of the ideal. Whenever she was with Daisy she felt an almost overwhelming desire to touch her, to kiss her, to try to arouse a response to her own desire. She was held back by the devastation that would occur if, should she reach out, Daisy recoiled in horror. With Daisy she teetered on the brink of an abyss.

Now the touch of Daisy's hand on the back of her neck turned her to stone. Daisy, aware of her tension, said, "Nell, I have never felt for anyone what I feel for you. I don't know whether it is right or not."

"Right?" Nell was breathless with the effort to speak. "What do you mean? What could be wrong with being friends with me?"

"Friends? Of course, we're friends. You're the closest friend I ever had. But that's not what I mean. People talk about being in love. I've never been in love. But I think I must be in love with you. I don't think I could ever feel this way about a man."

Daisy was looking at her with a perfectly open face, slightly puzzled and anxious. Nell took a deep breath. Nell sat gazing back at her, motionless. She said softly, "This is impossible. It can't be true. Daisy, Daisy —" She was not able to say more.

Daisy put her arms around Nell's neck and leaned her head on her shoulder. "I do love you, Nell. I want to feel you—not just look at you, talk to you. I've never felt this way about anyone. I didn't know this sort of feeling existed." She tightened her embrace.

Nell said into her hair, "Daisy dear, I can't believe it is true—that I am here with you and that you have told me this. Daisy —"

She stopped as Daisy raised her head and slowly ran her fingers along the line of her jaw. "It seems perfectly natural for me to feel this way about you. I'm sure I could never feel it for anyone else. It is not just a vague yearning. I want to—make love to you, to have you love me. I know now what people mean when they say that. It is something I must have—with you. Do you feel what I do?"

Nell caught her tightly to her. Daisy responded by grasping her hand and thrusting it under her skirt to the cleft between her legs. "Feel me there, Nell, there—there —"

∿ ∿ ∿ ∿ ∿

In the following weeks Daisy found it was not as easy as she had thought, to journey up on Sunday afternoons to Nell's room on Capitol Hill. She had long since grown tired of the young men who found that time convenient for calling, to invite her out to play tennis or to cycle in Rock Creek or simply to sit and chat. It annoyed her that her time was seen to be of so little consequence that the visit of any casual young man should immediately preempt it. So she had fallen into the habit of seeing Hugh Carson on Sunday afternoons. Aunt Edie approved of him—a sober, ambitious young man whose parents she knew, who was making rapid strides in his profession. Daisy found him easy to deal with. His seriousness was less annoying than the banter of the livelier young men and he was almost straitlaced in his view of how young women should behave, so she had no problem in curbing his amorous advances. But she realized now that her acceptance of his regular visits, an acceptance based on inertia, out of boredom, had given both him and her aunt the firm impression that she looked upon him as the man she preferred. So confident was her aunt that this was the case and so much did she approve Hugh that she ceased to be present as chaperone when he came to visit.

It was her own fault, thought Daisy, because she had followed the line of least resistance and had allowed all these assumptions to be made that now entrapped her. Fortunately, Hugh was in the habit of coming fairly late in the afternoon. He was a conscientious man who spent much of his time keeping abreast of his duties. She contrived to be away from the house before he arrived. If this happened too often, of course, he was likely to complain to her aunt that he never saw her and then she would have explanations to make. But the importance of being with Nell overrode these hazards.

∿ ∿ ∿ ∿ ∿

Nell waited impatiently for Daisy to come. All day she had tried to occupy herself with reading and letter writing—her parents counted on getting long, sprightly accounts of the day's events in her new job—to help the hours pass. She had the habit of waking early, even on Sundays. Daisy had told her that she, too, was an early bird. She knew that on Sundays Daisy went to eight o'clock communion at the Church of the Ascension on Massachusetts Avenue close to the Sixteenth Street house. Daisy had told her that she and her aunt were Episcopalians but that Mrs. Head preferred to go to the later service at St. John's at Lafayette Square, where she encountered many people she knew. But Daisy did not like that.

That was a curious facet of Daisy, a part of the essential downrightedness of her nature. Daisy had a decided streak of religious feeling which she seemed to preserve and shelter not only from the jibes of those who ridiculed devout faith in what they termed this enlightened age, but also from those who would confine it to a narrow set of prejudices. Sometimes Daisy brooded and at such times it was difficult to reach her, difficult to establish that easy flow of communication between them. At such times Daisy seemed rather far away, in a realm in which she could not follow her.

At last she heard the doorbell and the sound of the maid going to answer it. Then eagerly she listened for Daisy's voice. In a moment she opened the door to welcome her into the room and close it upon them.

Daisy took off her big hat—"that monstrous thing!" Nell exclaimed. They moved together in embrace. "Now I can kiss you."

Then Daisy said, "Don't you see what a wonderful baffle it is when Hugh or someone else wants to kiss me?"

"Hugh or someone else!" There was disgust in Nell's voice. She was taller than Daisy by several inches and she looked down with indignation in her long-nosed, wide-mouthed face.

"Well, I do have to fend them off, honey."

"Yes, I suppose you do." Nell looked down into her long-lashed deep blue eyes. She added sulkily, "You've been a long time getting here."

Daisy bit her lip in annoyance. "You've no idea the dodges I have to use to come here and spend the afternoon with you. One of these days Aunt Edie is going to get suspicious and ask me where I am going. Then what shall I say?"

"You could say that you have something more interesting to do than entertaining Hugh or some other young man."

"You know that is silly." Daisy's gaze was ironic. "Am I supposed to tell her that I have no intention of marrying Hugh or any other young man and that the reason is that I am in love with you? You know we are in a very strange situation."

A chill reached Nell as it always did when Daisy said something to bring the truth of their situation out into the light. "Of course. I know. We are beyond the pale."

They dropped the matter there. Apart, the time for each of them seemed filled with the awareness of the other, of the briefness of the time they could spend together. When they were together the heat of their feeling crowded out every other consideration. The practical aspects of their situation seemed to vanish and they lived, for a short while, in a strange state of remoteness from their normal surroundings and circumstances. They were no longer Daisy and Nell as their separate worlds knew them. They were Daisy and Nell as they saw and felt each other.

Their awareness of this caused them both misgivings. Were they, Daisy asked, unlike any women who ever were? Nell said that was impossible. There must be others, though no one ever spoke of them, or if they did, it was in veiled terms, as something abnormal. We can't be abnormal, because we are two whole women, physically. Daisy said, we're just ourselves. Does it matter if there is nobody else like us? Nell asked, you're not bothered by your religious beliefs? Sometimes I wonder if that makes you broody. And Daisy replied, what you are to me cannot be evil. What we do cannot be wicked. I shall answer for it. I do not accept everything that people tell me about my religion.

This dialogue, half-spoken, half communicated without words, flowed between them whenever they were together. This time Daisy said, "I love you Nell. It is so very simple when I am here with you."

"I try not to think of anything but you when you're here—not about other people, not what they would think of us."

"Well, then, show me you love me now," said Daisy, putting her arms around Nell's neck. She sighed as Nell began to undo the buttons down the back of her dress. In a few minutes they lay on Nell's bed, naked, luxuriating in the feel of each other. Their nakedness in itself was an affirmation of the rising strength of what they felt for each other. Naked together they were, without even clothing to come between them. For Nell there was defiance in this fact, defiance of what the world might think of them. In the uncertainty of their situation, in the misgivings that assailed them about this carrying out of their desire for each other, this coming together served as a balm, a reassurance. After a while the peacefulness of a happy consumation held them quiet.

∿ ∿ ∿ ∿ ∿

Then they began their private game of imagining what people would say if they announced their engagement and set a date for the wedding. This originally was Daisy's invention, humorously mimicking the marriage announcements of the girls in her circle of relatives and friends. But Nell had given it embellishments and eccentric twists. They embroidered on it until Daisy, suddenly aware of the passing of the afternoon, sat up.

Nell, looking up at Daisy's beautiful, high-riding satin-skinned breasts, said lazily, "Midnight is about to strike and the coach will become a pumpkin. Or are we the pumpkins?" She raised herself on her elbow and looked at the small clock on the mantel. "It's only four o'clock. You were here early—though at the time it seemed to me you took an age to get here."

Daisy yawned and stretched. "I must get back there and see if Hugh is waiting for me. I don't want him complaining to Aunt Edie."

"Will he?"

"He might. But I'm not sure that she will be there. She may be attending one of Madame Aurora's gatherings."

"Madame Aurora?"

"Yes. You know, Aunt Edie isn't being any more honest with me than I am with her about what we do on Sunday afternoons. She talks about going to visit Cousin Ardis, who is laid up with rheumatism just now. But I don't think that is where she goes at all. She goes to hear Madame Aurora."

"Who in the world is she?"

"You must be the only person in Washington who hasn't heard of her. Here, help me button this dress, Nell. Madame Aurora is a clairvoyant—I suppose that's what you could call her—who is all the rage right now. She holds gatherings on

Sunday afternoons at various people's houses and I know that Aunt Edie just can't stay away. You know, Nell, she is very easy prey for anyone who claims to have psychic powers. She is always visiting clairvoyants and fortune tellers and palmists. She always has."

"Is she worried about something?"

"Uncle William, of course. She hopes Madame Aurora will be able to influence him about what he will do to provide for her when he dies."

"Is he superstitious like that too?"

"I think he is. I think he knows he is going to die soon and he's afraid of what's lying in wait for him on the other side."

"Well, from what I've heard of him, he probably has good cause to be afraid."

"Don't be facetious, Nell. I think he really is terrified."

For a moment they were silent as Nell helped her fasten her shoes. Then Nell said, "You know, my parents are agnostics. They don't believe in anything not of this world but they are willing to give other people a hearing, just out of fairness. I know you are devout, Daisy, but I can't say I really believe in anything. Are you afraid of the supernatural?"

Daisy answered slowly, "I was afraid of ghosts when I was a child, because I was surrounded by people who were. You know, my relatives are country people. They've all lived in old houses with legends about ghosts and hauntings. Aunt Edie is true to her inheritance. One of the reasons she wanted my mother and me to come to live with her was that she was afraid to live in her old house by herself. But as for me—when I grew up I realized that all that did not fit in with what I believed about God. I couldn't believe that God and his angels would go around playing tricks on me and I couldn't believe in the Devil as Mephistopheles. Oh, I think there are demons, but they are the kind you create for yourself."

"Then you're not likely to become a devotée of Madame Aurora."

"No. But I am worried about the hold she seems to have on Aunt Edie. You know, she comes to the house almost every day and she is in with Uncle William for hours. Of course, I'm sure Aunt Edie is happy about that because it keeps him occupied.

He's not so hard to live with. But don't you see, Nell, I'm sure she is getting a very firm hold on him and I mistrust that sort of thing."

"But from what you say, she is your aunt's friend."

Daisy gave her a long look. "What can you tell about that sort of person—whose friend she is?"

III

CHAPTER EIGHT

"Ah, dear Madame Aurora! It is so kind of you to come and cheer my poor invalid."

Mrs. Head came toward her, holding out her hands.

Hannah calmly ignored the gesture. "I believe my visits are beneficial to him. Since he is not able to come to my gatherings, I must come to him. He seems to wish to become an earnest student of the occult."

Mrs. Head, daunted by her steadfast gaze, turned away with a flutter of her hands. "He is waiting for you. He becomes very impatient when he is expecting you."

Hannah did not reply but followed her up the stairs to the door of the Colonel's room, which she opened and called to him that Madame Aurora had come. The Colonel's male attendant as usual rose and went out without a word.

The Colonel sat hunched in his wheelchair, a rug over his knees in spite of the warmth of the day. He growled, "Well, what do you have to tell me today? Silver's down. What's your theory?"

He was watching her with sharp, challenging eyes as she crossed the room and sat down in a chair drawn close to him.

She said, "That you have had some people manipulating sales on the exchange."

He grinned, his false teeth showing unnaturally white and prominent. "You don't pull any punches, do you? What makes you think I can do that?"

"You have told me so. Besides, you are the owner of the largest stocks of silver in the country and you also own silver mines here and in foreign countries."

He looked at her cannily. "What are you doing? Trying to pump me for information you can sell to the newspapers?"

"I don't deal with the newspapers."

"Then you've got some clients who'd like some inside tips."

Hannah fastidiously arranged her voluminous skirts. "I have no need for that. My psychical perceptions can give me any information I may need."

He stared at her half-belligerantly. "You know, I wonder about you. You have told me some things I wouldn't expect you to know. How do you do it?"

"I have explained to you before," she said patiently. "I have the power to learn from elemental forces not perceived by my eyes and ears. It is a power, a primitive power, that has been lost to most people through the predominance of the material things in our lives. It is my object to teach those who wish to learn to retrieve this power by loosening their grip on the material world, to reach out to the immaterial."

He chewed the end of his moustache for a few moments. "I've spent a lifetime building up a very material fortune. Have you ever seen silver in the ore? It is black. It was thrown away by the first ignorant bastards who came across it while looking for gold. Have you seen it in the lump? It fits in your hand, something solid to hang onto. I know what silver is like. I've grubbed for it in the dirt—not like those rascals that deal in the market in Chicago. They wouldn't know an ounce of silver or any other commodity they deal in, if you handed it to them. Talk about the immaterial! Silver is immaterial to them."

"But obviously not to you. It has a character, an essential nature, does it not? It is not simply a lump of matter."

He looked at her with deep suspicion in his eyes. "I don't know what you are talking about. Silver is material to me. I keep a lump of it by just to feel it." He reached a shaky hand out to the half-open drawer of the table beside him and drew out a greyish, dull lump which he cradled in his palm. "Yes, that's what I said. I've spent a lifetime building up a very material fortune and I don't know what makes you think I want to dematerialize it."

"Because your earthly life is drawing to a close and you are uncertain what lies ahead."

His eyes blazed. "Don't threaten me! I'm not about to die yet! This stroke wasn't anything. I'll get over that. I'll show all these crepe-hangers, all these vultures, how they're miscalculating."

But the fear underlying his bravado was clear to her. "For the moment you may be right. But we must all at some time pass over the bridge into the astral sphere. How much better to be prepared for this great change."

His belligerance drained away and they sat in silence for a while. All at once he said, "How'd you like to help me win a gamble?"

Hannah looked at him warily. "I am not a gambler on the stock exchange."

"But I am. There's a little game I want to play. There ain't nobody around here I can trust for this sort of thing. But maybe you — Suppose I put up the money and you use your psychic powers to make a play on the stock market. You sound as if you have a pretty good idea of what goes on in the stock market—for somebody who hasn't much use for the material world."

He was enjoying his jibe but she saw the brightness in his eyes as he weighed his idea. She said carefully, "I will act only when and if I feel the moment is right. I must have a free hand, with no interference."

He grinned broadly as if he had won a point. "All right. If you're successful, you get half the profits. If you lose—well, we'll know what your astral guides—that's what you call 'em, ain't it?—are worth then."

She sat for a moment stunned and unwilling to let him see how she felt. He must have often in his life enjoyed this sense of power in offering a prize to some penniless gambler. But she knew he had no idea of what he was offering her—no idea of what it meant for her in opportunity for financial freedom, nor what that freedom would mean to herself and Elizabeth. Here at last there was perhaps within her grasp the means of taking them out of their slough of despond. She made no effort to confront his gloating but kept her eyes cast down.

∿ ∿ ∿ ∿ ∿

She spent another hour with him while he talked at random about his past, about men and events that meant nothing to her. She knew that this was what he wanted her there for—an audience who could make some response to his talk, who had some understanding of what he was talking about. He obviously did not expect anything of the sort from his wife and she judged that he had outlived most of his chosen associates and had quarrelled with the rest.

When she got up to leave, he said, "Next time you come I'll have some cash here for you."

She did not depend on his promise. He might well forget this conversation with her and on the other hand he might remember but change his mind about entrusting her with money to lay out for him in speculation.

But the next visit she paid him, after they had sparred for a while in the usual way, he began to scrabble with his good hand in the half-open drawer of the table next which he sat and finally brought out a large roll of bills.

He thrust it towards her. "You remember what I said. See what you can do with that."

He held the money out to her in a shaky hand. She took it as he added, "Count it and make out a receipt for how much it is, two copies, one for you and one for me." He pointed to a pad of paper on the table.

She counted it. Five thousand dollars in large bills. He was watching her with hawklike eyes. "Nice little stake, ain't it? There's many a time I'd have given my right hand for a sweet little roll like that."

She sat very still. She had never held anything like such a sum of money in her hands before. She strove mightily to maintain an air of unconcern while she placed the roll in the satchel she carried. Apparently she did not betray her own trepidation because finally he relaxed and leaned back in his chair.

She spent the rest of the visit listening as attentively as she could to the Colonel's rambling account of how, in days gone by, he had bested Commodore Vanderbilt, Jim Fisk, Jay Gould and other renowned speculators in financial deals. She noticed that his eyes strayed continually to her satchel, as if drawn irresistibly by the thought of the money he had seen her place there. This was her cue to act is if it was for the moment of no further concern to her. When she got up to leave, he said that he would be looking for an accounting of her success or failure soon. She brushed his remark aside.

"I shall have to await the propitious moment," she said. "I must consult my astral guides."

He grinned and said, "They'd better know their business."

She walked out of the room, careful to maintain her usual air of confidence. With Mrs. Head, who came to chat with her for a few minutes, she was easier. Any abstraction in her manner would be interpreted by Mrs. Head as a preoccupation with higher things.

On the trolley ride home she sat bemused. She decided, conscious of the money in her satchel, not to visit the market and instead walked from the trolley stop straight to the lodging-house. When she got there she did not go up to their room. Elizabeth, she thought, might well be still at the Library. Instead she let herself into her consulting room and sat down in its musty coolness to consider what she should do.

For a long time she sat still without clear thought about the present situation. Her mind went back thirty years. Yes, thirty years. She remembered the first time she had seen Elizabeth, seated at the table in the cottage of the seminary with books and papers spread out around her—a cameo-like profile, a woman completely separate from her surroundings, as alien to her setting as it was possible to be. Yet she had recognized Elizabeth, recognized her as the object of her search. And such a jewel. Elizabeth had not believed her when she had said that she had come there in search of her. It did not trouble her that Elizabeth remained skeptical of these strangest impulses that impelled her actions. It was not Elizabeth's nature to ridicule her. She knew Elizabeth to be sometimes bemused by her views, to wonder sometimes how much reliance to put upon her impulses.

Perhaps it was because Elizabeth had her own imagery, her own world of the spirit, the recreation of the twelfth century in the songs of its poets. She had been entranced, in those early days especially, when Elizabeth spoke of this inner world of hers, of the word-splendors she sketched, of the vividness of the scenes and characters she called forth in imagination.

It was her book she spoke of, the study of the strolling singers of Aquitaine and England which she had been working on for many years, ever since she had embarked on the life of a scholar. She had early realized that she interpreted the life and poetry of these ancient singers in a way quite different from that of the few scholars who had up till then dealt with the subject.

"My dear love," Elizabeth said, "the chief point of my book is that I disagree with those who have gone before me. The poetry of the troubadours, of the strolling singers in the twelfth century is love poetry, of course. They personify love, they see it as a natural force powerful enough to cause a sensible person to lose his wits and thus suffer misery and grief—if he does not save himself in time by abandoning his beloved and this is a shameful thing to do. Thus love is outside other considerations. It cannot be limited by the tenets that govern marriage, marital fidelity, the social status of the lovers. Marie de France had her own particular concept, as one can see from reading her poetry thoughtfully. She saw love as a thing in itself, which sets it own terms. If it is hampered by the laws that surround marriage, religion, it would die. Love, she says, is not worthy if it is not equal, if lovers are not in their own eyes equals, if they do not place the beloved above all exterior considerations. The reason for this, she says, is that loyalty is a necessary part of love—fidelity to the beloved—is undermined if one partner believes himself superior, with the right to require the other to love him. True lovers give themselves to each other completely. A true lover finds his happiness not in himself but in the happiness of the beloved."

Hannah remembered how Elizabeth had looked up at her from her books as she said this and smiled that sweetest of smiles. She had stopped at this point in her explanation for a few moments and then added, "Don't you see, love, how contrary this is to our contemporary notions of love? We don't really understand it at all. We don't really value it. We do not praise lovers in our society. We think only of marriage partners. We teach girls that they cannot be equal partners in any relationship with a man. They must be obedient to their husbands and the loyalty that is demanded of them is one-sided and not required of the man."

Hannah remembered that she had interrupted here. "But you say nothing of women, love between women."

Elizabeth's eyes had lighted. "Ah, that is another matter altogether!"

Elizabeth had worked five more years on her book. Together they had gone in every holiday to some city where she could find the books and papers she needed to consult. Then it was ready for publication. She had saved over the years the money needed for this. Cannily she used as author only her initials—M. E. Beaufort. To Hannah she explained:

"I want my book to be received with attention and be given serious consideration. With simply my initials it will be assumed that I am a man. Only a few of my father's old friends will know otherwise. Nobody would suppose that a woman would write a learned work and certainly not one on such a subject. There has really been very little research done on these early poets and much of it is erroneous. M. E. Beaufort may be given a hearing. Minerva Elizabeth Beaufort would be laughed at."

At first the book was not noticed among American scholars. But then it caught the eye of a learned professor in an English university and at once a controversy arose about the thesis it presented. Articles appeared in learned journals. The first question raised was, who was M. E. Beaufort? Who was the unknown who dared to put forward such innovative theories about the identity of Marie de France and the significance of her poetry—who dared to claim for her at least second place to Chretien de Troyes?

Hannah rembered that at this stage of things, Elizabeth had been elated, jubilant over the arguments and counter-arguments aroused by her theories. It was obvious that she was being granted not only the attention of many scholars but respectful attention, that the value of her work was recognized.

Elizabeth supposed that it was one of her father's old colleagues who eventually revealed her identity. He acted, she knew, from the kindest of motives, impelled by the thought that she should not go unrecognized. But the result was not what he had anticipated. First there was a great clamor at the idea that a woman could have the learning and the intellectual power sufficient to conceive and write the book. This was bad enough and gave rise to some scathing comments by ruffled professors who could not accept the fact.

But, then, after the debate had raged for a while, a new outcry arose, this time about the immodesty of the theories put forth, that the author should so lose her sense of womanly reserve that she would write on such an outrageous subject as profane love untrammeled by the strictures of religion and society. Perhaps it was true that in the twelfth century women might be depicted as lovers who abided by the dictates of love alone, but no modest modern woman, in a community subject to the rigorous demands of a Protestant ethic, would even contemplate the discussion of such a thing. Elizabeth, reading this diatribe, realized that here she had the revenge of a man who could find no other means of attacking her.

It was thus that Elizabeth's book proved to be their undoing. It took a while for the uproar among the scholars to reach down to teachers and parents of the girls in the seminary. Even when she had first heard of the interest aroused by Elizabeth's book, the Principal was restrained in her appreciation. It was gratifying that one of the seminary's teachers should have demonstrated such an unusual degree of learning as to call forth the praise and blame of renowned scholars, but in the background of her mind was the fear that for a woman recognized excellence in intellectual work might not be viewed with wholehearted approval in a teacher in a girls' school. Her misgivings were well-founded. One of the trustees, a man of conservative views and the pastor of a large church, heard of the charge of immodesty. He knew nothing of the twelfth century in France but a brief glance at the book showed him that not only was the poetry immoral, but the author set forth ideas about carnal love that were nothing short of licentious.

His views were not entirely shared by all of the trustees but he was too influential a man to be gainsaid. So a year or so after the publication of Elizabeth's book she was dismissed from the teaching staff of the seminary. The Principal, mindful of her fifteen years as teacher and knowing that she could never find anyone who could really replace her, was plainly distressed in informing her that her contract would not be renewed in the coming year, nor would the seminary be able to recommend her to another comparable institution.

The Principal was not prepared for Hannah's resignation. She protested, saying there was certainly no need for Miss Morgan to go simply because Miss Beaufort would no longer be with them. Hannah, with barely restrained scorn, said she could not think of remaining in the face of such unjust treatment of a valuable teacher. The Principal was clearly offended. Hannah herself had never been treated with any great regard by the other teachers. Her value to the seminary had been the skill and discipline she used in teaching the younger girls the domestic arts to the satisfaction of their parents. To be spoken to by Hannah in this way was an affront the Principal would not forget.

The tag end of that year, then—the Principal could not replace Elizabeth with teachers for so many subjects at such short notice—was a curious interlude for them. The other teachers had not failed to see that their close companionship extended beyond the period of the year they spent teaching. It was known that they passed their holidays together, that they seemed never to separate. It was true that neither of them had families to go to. They seemed to pass their free time in a vagabond way. But Hannah had a trump card which she used to deflect or at least blunt criticism. Her reputation as a clairvoyant very soon spread and she was often visited, in secret, by various women in moments of anxiety. Her advice was too eagerly sought to allow for any real attack upon them.

Hannah sighed, seated in the darkening room, remembering the years that followed. Elizabeth had been defiant, angry and humiliated. She had refused to seek another teaching post right away. Instead she sought less restricting work, travelling to lecture on the New York Lyceum circuit and to the newly established Chautauqua Institute in New York State, sometimes being a visiting teacher at one of the new colleges for women. But she was unwilling to subject herself again to the regime of social and religious coercion that any regular post meant for a woman teacher.

"Hannah, my love," she had said, "we're free, don't you see. Let's not sell that freedom for money unless we have to."

For a while they did very well, for Elizabeth commanded a good salary, for a woman, wherever she taught, and she soon had an excellent reputation as a tutor of difficult subjects. The book seemed, however, to dog their steps. With the years it became a standard work, found in every library, used in many schools, often without royalties to Elizabeth. But a faint aura of the scandalous clung to her reputation, too vague to put one's finger on but enough to make her suspect that sometimes she missed out on a lucrative post because of it. No one really remembered what all the fuss had been about. All that remained was a notion that Elizabeth was a woman who would prove difficult to defend if she was hired to teach girls. It's as if, said Elizabeth, they think I advocate free love, like Victoria Woodhull.

This was nevertheless, Hannah remembered, probably their most contented period. They were free, as Elizabeth said. They could live very much as they liked—aside from such problems as the difficulty of finding landlords who would rent to two single women or of obtaining payment for their work of at least two thirds of that paid to men. Hannah herself engaged in many different types of work. Work for the Federal Government was the best paid, though often under wretched working conditions, whenever they were for a time in Washington. But their life was peripatetic. They were both members now of the National Woman Suffrage Association—Elizabeth had been from the beginning—and they attended every annual meeting. But there, too, there was a shadow over them. They were by no means the only single women present but they came without the usual appurtenances—family attachments, church affiliations, a visible anxiety to deny that what they sought in working for woman's rights was the restructuring of society despite the opposition of men. Even in that group of active, aggressive women they did not fit. By no means all of their fellow members had Mrs. Stanton's candid and fearless attitude towards the subject of sex and women's subservience in their relationships with men.

During the 1880s it became apparent that Elizabeth was growing deaf. At first she joked about it. After all, she said, Harriet Martineau had become deaf at the age of fifteen and had never hesitated to take her ear trumpet into any gathering and even across the Atlantic to observe the habits of the Americans. But inexorably her deafness cut into Elizabeth's professional engagements. Gradually their income shrank, in spite of

Hannah's efforts. They were both aging. Elizabeth was close to seventy and the natural enthusiasm that had carried her through all the problems and hardships of the previous decades began to flag. The bank panic of 1893 had brought them to their lowest ebb.

During all these fluctuating fortunes Elizabeth had worked on her second book, intended to carry further the ideas she had propounded in the first and to be an answer in some measure to her critics. Their journeyings were curtailed. The effort to find the material she needed was greater. But in the last few months Elizabeth had talked more and more of its completion. She did not say this as if she expected it to be published since she knew they had no money nor did she expect that what reputation she had left would be sufficient to interest a learned press. She knew herself to be largely forgotten as a living scholar. The satisfaction she would receive on finishing the book would be simply that from the achievement of the goal she had set for herself. Hannah had watched her as she sat sometimes, lost in musing, her hand resting on a pile of manuscript. At such moments, Hannah's resentment of their poverty seized her anew.

But now perhaps —

A sound from outside the room broke into her thoughts. Elizabeth must be arriving home. She picked up her satchel and went out into the vestibule to follow her up the stairs.

CHAPTER NINE

"Ah, love, you're already home!" Elizabeth exclaimed as Hannah touched her on the arm. "I'm afraid I lost track of the time."

They were in front of their door and Hannah unlocked it and they went in. As she did so, Hannah automatically glanced about to see if anything had been disturbed. Everything was as she had left it earlier that day. Elizabeth's books and papers were spread out on the one table they used for meals and for her study.

She listened with half an ear while Elizabeth cleared away her work and stacked the books and papers on the floor. Elizabeth was usually talkative when she returned this way from the Library and found Hannah home, full of anecdotes of the people she had observed and encountered. And usually Hannah enjoyed her recountings, happy in the sense of the communion they thus renewed after a few hours' separation. But this evening she could think only of the money in the satchel.

What was she to do with it? In the preceding weeks she had listened while the Colonel talked about money, how it was to be made in speculation, how it was to be manipulated. Her quick, retentive mind had picked up a great deal of information about the stock market, the buying of futures in commodities, about the maneuvers of large corporations. But it was information that she had merely stored away, having no special use for it except as another fund of material from which to draw in dealing with her clients. It was obvious that she could invest this money in some profitable way. That is what the Colonel expected.

In the meanwhile, how was she to safeguard it? There was nowhere safe in the house and she shrank from the idea of carrying it about with her. She had no illusions about her accountability for it in the Colonel's eyes. It was odd that he had given it to her in cash. He could have given her a draft on his bank. Perhaps this was an aspect of the essential primitiveness of his outlook. He had spent much of his life where wealth was carried about in specie and bullion. Even paper money in such places was disregarded.

But on the other hand perhaps the reason was that he did not want it traced, that he wished the transaction to be truly between himself and her. It gave her a strange feeling of outlawry, as if what she held in her satchel was the proceeds of a theft. And yet that was silly. Perhaps the money was stolen but if so, it was stolen through channels of financial manipulation, through the maneuvers of very wealthy men contending with each other for the power that very large sums of money conferred.

She brought her mind away from that subject back to the question of what she was to do with the money. When he had made his suggestion, her heart had leapt up at the thought that a way was opening in which she could increase the store of cash she was slowly gathering as a safeguard for Elizabeth and herself. Since that first moment of jubilation she had felt stunned by the problem that confronted her. She found it difficult to contemplate the steps she must take to make good her undertaking. She had never been in a stockbroker's office —

But, ah, there was her solution! Sturgis Wilmot was the answer to her need. Elizabeth broke into her musing.

"Hannah, love, what is the matter? You are standing there as if you are in trouble."

Hannah made a vague gesture with her hand. "No, no. There is something I must think out, something I must seek guidance in."

Elizabeth gave her a long look but said nothing more.

Hannah's thought immediately closed over her again. She knew how to reach Sturgis Wilmot. She could not go to his office. It was understood between them that no one was to know of his reliance on the advice she gave him. He came to see her every so often, early in the evening, probably on his way home from his office. But she could not wait. She must contrive to find a telephone directory and a telephone. In the meantime she would keep the money in the satchel and say nothing of it to Elizabeth. The idea that she had it, that she had made such a bargain with the Colonel, might alarm Elizabeth. She did not want to have to explain to Elizabeth that she was about to embark on a career of speculation in the stock market.

In dealing with Wilmot in the preceding weeks, she had been careful never to pass on to him the bits of financial news that the Colonel let drop. But she had used the information she obtained to give him general advice, to warn him of possible coups that might be hatching among various of the large speculators. Various bits of information she gathered might sometimes fit into a mosaic whose pattern was thus clear to her. So that on occasions she had saved him from a loss by a word of warning. Or pointed out an action that resulted in his gain. He had come to have the greatest admiration for her psychic powers.

And now she needed him. Tomorrow morning she would contrive to bring him to her door.

∿ ∿ ∿ ∿ ∿

That first episode unfolded with an ease that took her breath away. Wilmot was a little surprised at the size of the sum she entrusted to him for speculation. She stipulated that he must tell her what he would choose in which to invest, why and the details of any background maneuvers he knew about that might affect the deal. She had, after some debate with herself, decided to stake the whole sum at a throw. The inner voice that so often seemed to speak to her assured her that this was the moment for a bold stroke. Wilmot demurred at the idea. If she insisted on speculating, she should do it in small amounts. He was quite certain she could not afford a serious loss. The sum she presented to him, he privately thought, considering the humble place in which she maintained her consulting room, must surely represent her life savings. But she swept away his objections. She had indications, she said, from her spiritual guides that this was the path to follow.

The venture succeeded. Wilmot had watched the transaction

with as much anxiety as he would have any of the much larger ones he carried out for himself. But things went as if by magic. When Wilmot placed in her hands a sum almost double what she had given him, she felt an exultation she was careful not to show. She bewildered him by demanding the money in cash. He protested against the danger of carrying such enormous sums around in money. If it was stolen, it was gone, untraceable. But she insisted and he brought it to her in bills.

She saw the Colonel the next day. With a demure air she placed the money on the table beside him and watched with amusement while he counted it out.

"By jingo! You've done it!" he exclaimed, and made her count out the bills another time. When she had done so, he told her to count out half of the sum. Half of that, he said, was her share of the profit.

"All right now," he said, pushing the other half towards her, "take that and see what you can do with that. But you have to tell me how you did this."

He listened with gleaming eyes as she recounted what Wilmot had told her. Occasionally he exclaimed, as if he were watching a horse race, she thought. The only other times she had seen such animation in his face was when he had flown into a rage. This liveliness came from pure enjoyment.

∿ ∿ ∿ ∿ ∿

She found, as the weeks went on, that she had not only a taste for financial speculation but also a natural talent for understanding the workings of the money market. Her ventures were not always as successful as the first one, but she never lost the stake she put up. She also learned to make her own choices, to direct Wilmot what to do, rather than rely entirely upon his judgment. Sometimes he protested that what she chose to do was foolishly dangerous but she did not allow him to deflect her from her course. He became more and more convinced that she had extraordinary means of foreseeing events.

One day she astonished Elizabeth by saying she would go with her to the Library of Congress.

"There is a newspaper room there, isn't there, Liz? I should like to read some of the financial news."

"Why, of course, love. Are you going to emulate Hettie Green?"

"She deals only in real estate," Hannah retorted.

But she wondered how much Elizabeth's sharp eyes had noted of what she was doing.

∿ ∿ ∿ ∿ ∿

It was a two-way battle of wits with her—the financial market on the one hand and the Colonel on the other.

On one of her visits he suddenly said to her, "I'd like to know how you do it."

Wary as she always was dealing with him, she nevertheless kept her usual expression of grave thoughtfulness and waited for him to say something further.

"You've doubled your stake five times since you began and you've taken regular plunges. I wouldn't have expected to do that well myself. There are not many experienced brokers who would try what you've tried. You've got to have more help than you can get from them."

This told her that she was winning in this battle of wits but she also knew that there was an unpredictable element in him. She did not know how much belief he placed in the supernatural powers which she hinted were at her beck and call. Undoubtedly his staking her to play the stock market was a game which he had devised for his own amusement, to see how far she could go without disaster. She had exceeded his expectations. But sometimes she felt acutely insecure, as if the ground she stood on could be pulled out from under her by him at will. She knew he watched for signs of this insecurity, pleased if he found any, amused, a cheerful loser, if she disguised it.

Most of the time, after they had begun to play this game, he was in a cheerful mood. Mrs. Head, welcoming her at the door, spoke of this fact, showed a touching gratitude for the change her visits had wrought. But the gloomy fear that she knew to underlie his other moods was always there. As the novelty of the game began to wear off, he became less cheerful, less absorbed in the details of transactions that she described to him.

If she came with a disappointing report, he did not react as he had at the beginning, chiding her, making insulting remarks about her unseen preceptors. Now he seemed to take it all on a matter-of-fact basis, as if he were preoccupied with something more personal. She wondered if this decline in alertness meant that his health was deteriorating. She did not mention this to Mrs. Head.

One day, after she had given him the money she had brought, he pushed it all back to her, saying, "Take it all with you. I don't want it."

She picked up the bills and put them methodically into her satchel. It was a very large sum and she was uneasy at this development, but she said nothing and waited.

He began to talk, in a mumbling, rambling way, about his own life, harking back to the years of his youth, when he had set out from a small, rural township in New England to seek his fortune in the wilderness that in the 1830s lay beyond the Mississippi River. He had arrived in California well before gold was discovered at Sutter's Mill. He had later gone to Colorado to mine silver, like many others of his kind ignoring the Civil War. In the 1870s he had gone to South America, to Peru and Bolivia. It was in those days that his fortune had burgeoned. Hannah had heard bits and scraps of this biography but he had never narrated it in this way, as if he were recapitulating his life to himself, in search of reassurance.

Thus she learned about his son. He had married a woman in California, he said, and had left her there with a two year old boy when he had gone to Colorado.

"I married her in a weak moment. Probably I was in my cups and she was too, for that matter. She had a boy. I don't doubt he was mine, in spite of the kind of life she lived. She went her way and I went mine. I never saw her again."

He broke off his narrative at this point and fixed his eyes on her with gloomy intensity. He demanded, "What's going to happen to me, if I meet somebody on the other side who's waiting for revenge?"

Hannah returned his stare with composure. His abrupt question interested her. She had known from the start that he was afraid to die. The man who had lived a life full of physical danger, wild speculation, unrestrained violence, was now facing his own end and some elemental fear that had been with him as a child and which he had ignored through his adult life was coming to the surface to torment him. Those buried memories of his Calvinist childhood which he had fled in young man-hood were more alive to him now than the realities of his day to day existence, here in this great house that he had erected as a monument to his own glory. That was the reason for this ac-count of his life that he had retold himself and her.

She said in a measured tone, "You mistake the nature of the sphere into which you will pass when you leave this earth. Earthly passions, including revenge, will have no place there."

He was disappointed. "That's no kind of an answer."

"Then you prefer to believe in fire and brimstone, the cauldron of hell and eternal punishment?"

He turned his eyes away.

She continued, "You have wronged someone—or more probably a number of people—in the course of your life. You fear retribution now because the sense of your own mortality is borne in on you."

"Wronged somebody? It was give and take, I tell you. Dog eat dog. Eat or be eaten. There's nobody you can trust. Take that sniveling coward, my son." He brooded for a while and she waited silently.

A strange grimace appeared on his face. If it was a smile, it was one full of vindictiveness. "He decided to come and look for me in Bolivia. He had heard that I had struck it rich there. So I had but it was no place for cowards. I didn't want him around. I don't allow anybody to ride my coat tails. I told him to go back to California. That was 1880 and things were getting pretty civilized out there in the mining camps. He said his mother was dead and he thought he'd have a better chance with me."

"Did he go back?"

"He did not. He decided he'd do better for himself by help-ing my enemies, since it didn't look as if I was going to do much for him. But he stuck around me long enough to learn quite a bit about my affairs and he used his knowledge to trade off with them." His old man's eyes gleamed with hatred and malice.

"He didn't profit by it. Nobody had ever profited at my expense and lived to enjoy the proceeds."

"What did you do?"

"I didn't do anything. He hung himself with his own rope. There was a lot of violence in those days in the mining fields in those countries. We were all playing for high stakes. He was shot in an ambush—got in the way of a bullet intended for somebody else."

He still had his eyes on her. Hannah kept her face impassive. Nevertheless, he was sure that he had disturbed her. "Surprise you, does it?"

"No. I have always been aware of an aura of violence about you. But you do not regret your son's death? It has left you without an heir for your vast holdings."

He laughed without sound. "I don't give a damn about that. Whoever comes after me has to scratch for himself." His mood changed and he said morosely, "What I'm interested in is what happens to me. I've always known how to handle this world. I've fought my way through it, no holds barred, but —"

In the long silence Hannah said softly, "Now you have no idea what may lie beyond the curtain of your death."

"Do you?" He glared at her.

She eyed him. "You half believe that I do. And perhaps I have a better idea of it than you do." She paused. "There are many people who think there is nothing."

He drew his breath in as if he felt a draught of cold air. "Sometimes I'd be glad to think that when they plant me, that'd be it. But on the other hand —"

He seemed at a loss to continue. Hannah said, "You certainly cannot take your wealth with you, nor the power it gives you among mortals."

He made an impatient gesture with his good hand. "That's understood. I've never been afraid of losing a fortune. I've lost several, but I've always made another, bigger one. That's what riles me—that I won't have another chance."

"Then what you fear is extinction."

He did not answer for a moment and then he said, "You've put your finger on it. Where am I going? I can't just—be nothing."

"You've never hesitated to ride roughshod over others. You've never concerned yourself about other men's ambitions, except as they provided you with adversaries to conquer. Other men's deaths were not important. But now your own —''

She saw he was no longer looking at her. She sat still for a while before she got up to leave, thinking that perhaps he was ready to doze off as he sometimes did. But the moment she moved he was alert. He seized her hand. She was surprised at the strength of his grip.

"You'll be here tomorrow?"

She temporized. "I have many engagements. Besides, it will be several days before I have anything to report to you about this." She indicated her satchel with the money in it.

There was a gleam of malice in his eyes. "You know why I have been playing this game with you, don't you? Nobody knows what I am doing this way. You're just a woman fooling around with something she doesn't know anything about. If I told my brokers what I wanted them to do, everybody would be on the watch, reading all kinds of meanings into every move I made. This way we can try out all sorts of tricks."

Hannah took a deep breath. "I do not engage in anything that is not proper."

"Proper!" He laughed again silently. "What's proper got to do with it when you're dealing with money? Money ain't respectable. It don't have any morals."

"But *you* know whether something is right or wrong."

He made a scornful noise in his throat. "I don't give a goddamn for what's right or wrong. They're equal to me. It's what I want that's important."

"Yet you are afraid of an accounting when you die."

Again he seized her hand. She waited till his grip relaxed and he sank back in his chair. Then she left him.

∿ ∿ ∿ ∿ ∿

When she came out of the Colonel's room she found Mrs. Head nervously walking about the hall.

She cried, when she saw her, "Oh, Madame Aurora! Can you spare me a few moments?"

Alert to the distress in her voice, Hannah said, "Of course," and followed her down the stairs to the drawingroom, to the two chairs where they had sat when she first came to the house. A tea service was arranged on the table and Mrs. Head offered her a cup. As they sipped, she said,

"Yesterday my husband's physician warned me that his condition is worsening—that he may have another stroke at any time and perhaps a fatal one. Have you noticed anything in his manner?"

"Sometimes he dozes off while we are talking. But his mind remains perfectly clear."

"Yes. He requires more sleep now." She was silent for a while. Hannah noticed the nervous movements of her hands.

"You are upset, dear lady. Perhaps if you confided in me —"

"That is what I wish to do. I do depend upon you to understand me and not to think me unfeeling." She fumbled for words. "I have said to you before this that I am deeply concerned about my husband's arrangements for me in case of his death. I feel it is important that he should make some while he is still able."

"You think he has not acted?"

"I have spoken, in the last few days, to Hugh—Mr. Carson, his legal adviser. Hugh tells me that he has still not been able to persuade him to make his will."

"That is indeed very bad, in the light of his vast financial concerns."

"You have said nothing to him about this?"

"I do not think that I can. If he were to initiate the subject, of course, I should certainly encourage him to do so." Hannah saw the disappointment in Mrs. Head's face. "Don't you see, dear friend, if I raise this question, he will at once believe that you have prompted me to do so and that will work against your interests. He has a deep suspicion of everyone."

"Indeed I am very much aware of that. A few days ago I tried to speak to him about this. He got very angry—I was frightened. He has never been angry with me, though he is famous for his rages. I realize that I must never mention the matter again to him."

After a pause Hannah said calmly, "But you do realize, don't you, Mrs. Head, that as his widow the law allows you a certain share in his estate? This cannot be denied you. Mr. Carson must have spoken of this."

Mrs. Head's distress did not seem to be dispelled by this reassurance. "Yes," she said, "I believe Hugh tried to explain to me some such thing—using a great many legal terms I cannot understand. But, don't you see, dear Madame Aurora, how unpleasant it would be for me to have to claim such a share? It would be apparent to everyone that William took no thought of me —"

"However," Hannah interrupted, "that may be the very reason he feels no compulsion to make a specific provision for you. If he cannot face the thought of making a will—there are many people who are superstitious on that score—he may justify himself by reminding himself that you will have your widow's portion—which in your case will be a very large amount of property."

But Mrs. Head was unwilling to be comforted by this reasoning. She sat in dejection for a while and Hannah waited for her to speak. Presently she began timidly, "I have hoped that you could perhaps use your great gifts to foresee something of what lies ahead for me. You must see what a terrible state of suspense I am in. I have always been seen as a woman whom fortune has favored with a wealthy and attentive husband. If William fails to provide for me in a fitting way—Oh, dear Madame Aurora, I cannot face the humiliation." Noticing the stern expression that appeared on Hannah's face, she rushed on, "I know—you have made it plain—that you do not act as a medium—you do not hold seances. You have told me that you doubt the genuineness of these things —"

Hannah was frowning. "They are very suspect. You must know that there have been recently a number of scientific investigations into the matter—some people who have claimed to be mediums and the purported psychic phenomena they have described have been shown up as fraudulent. Many earnest people have been duped for mercenary reasons."

Mrs. Head was stubborn. She must, thought Hannah, be very upset to stick to her guns like this. Mrs. Head's usual approach to any discussion was oblique. If she met with resistance, she would back off to try another tack. But now she insisted. "But some of these things are genuine. I know right here in Washington some eminent men—scientists and savants—who have made their own investigations and who believe that some psychic phenomena are genuine. You yourself have taught me that there are great forces just beyond our comprehension which perhaps we may be able to understand as we become enlightened —"

Hannah said blandly, "Certainly this is true, but nevertheless there are despicable people with no powers of mind or spirit who try to mislead others for their own gain. I assure you that we do not reach through our cosmic envelope to these forces by means of mediums and seances. These great forces are unaffected by our feeble petitions—as if we seek miracles. I warn you against becoming entrapped by charlatans."

Mrs. Head gasped. "Oh, dear Madame Aurora! I have no intention of seeking anyone's help but yours!"

"I must tell you that, if you do, I shall no longer be able to give you counsel."

"Oh, no, no! Please do not believe that I could ever do such a thing!"

Hannah could not resist her pleading eyes. "You wish me to read the future, to foretell by psychic means what will befall you when the Colonel dies. Such things do not come about at will. There must be thought, meditation first. Perhaps through deep contemplation I may be able to reach beyond the physical prison in which we live and, as you conceive, reach into the future."

Mrs. Head reached for her hands and clasped them vehemently. "Oh, dear Madame Aurora!"

IV

CHAPTER TEN

Nell stood in one of the alcoves off the main reading room of the Library of Congress comparing the information on the cards she held in her hand with items in the reference books shelved there. There were not many readers at the desks that surrounded the distribution desk in the center of the huge rotunda. She glanced up at the gallery around the base of the dome where a few visitors looked down at the scene below. Ever since the Library's new building had been opened on the first of November, crowds of sightseers had flowed through it. Nell, gazing upward, thought, it really is a glorious sight, this golden quilt as a newspaper reporter had dubbed it, the gilded and painted splendor of the ceiling.

When she brought her eyes back to the cards in her hand she became aware that someone was standing at her elbow. She immediately recognized the strange, gaunt woman with white hair drawn back from her face, dressed in a shabby skirt and jacket. She had often seen her in the reading room, and once she had glimpsed her striding along the street near the Library, her skirts swinging around her legs. In her curiosity about her she had asked the attendants of the service desk if they knew who she was. All they could tell her was that the books she withdrew were always concerned with the literature of twelfth century Europe.

The woman was smiling at Nell now but said nothing. Her blue eyes were sharp and clear behind her eyeglasses. Her white, large-knuckled hands held several cards covered with a fine handwriting.

Nell said, getting over her first bemusement, "Is there something I can do for you?"

She noticed that the woman's eyes had dropped, as if she was watching her face. Her smile bloomed and Nell thought, What a charming person!

The woman said, "I am trying to find this book. I consulted it once when the Library was still in its old quarters."

Nell took the card she held out and read the title written there. "I cannot tell you offhand. You know, many of our books are still stored. We are cataloguing a great deal of material. Where are you sitting? I will see what I can find and let you know."

The woman seemed to hesitate, with a slight frown. But then Nell's meaning became clear to her and she pointed to a nearby seat. "Number 38," she said.

"Well, fine. I'll come and find you as soon as I can verify this."

The charming smile bloomed again, and the woman turned to go back to her seat. Nell, interrupting her work to go in search of the volume she had asked for, wondered, What an odd person. Of course, as a librarian, one never knew what odd characters one might encounter, pursuing some strange, obsessive idea. Yet this woman did not seem a mere crank. Certainly she would not be seeking ancestors back in the twelfth century. Or be trying to prove the modern identity of the twelve tribes of Israel.

Half an hour later Nell returned to the reading room to desk 38. The woman sat absorbed in a book she was reading. Nell said softly, "Madam, may I give you the result of my search?" But the woman did not move. Instead she smiled at something she was reading and snatched up her pencil to write on a pad of paper before her. Again Nell spoke to her without getting a response and finally touched her on the shoulder.

The woman started and looked up into her face, half-alarmed.

"Oh, do excuse me!" said Nell. "I did not mean to startle you. I just want to tell you what I have discovered about the book you want."

The woman's face relaxed into a smile. "Oh, yes! How kind of you!"

Nell spread several slips of paper on the desk before her and began to explain what they meant. But almost at once the woman put her hand on Nell's arm and shook her head. Suddenly Nell realized, Why she is deaf! She wanted to say, I'm so sorry, but caught herself and began her explanation again more slowly, noticing that the woman had turned herself so that she could follow her lips. After several attempts she succeeded in making herself understood.

The woman thanked her and Nell returned to her interrupted task. But she could not keep her mind on the subject. The woman intrigued her. There were not so many women who regularly used the Library and a woman who seemed to be a serious scholar was unusual. Every so often she looked over to where the woman sat, once more bent over her reading.

Presently Nell saw that the woman looked up at the big clock over the entrance to the reading room, with its life-size figure of Father Time. Then she began to tidy the papers and books on her desk. She is going to lunch, thought Nell, watching her gather up her purse and a small parcel that obviously contained a sandwich. Obeying a sudden impulse, she intercepted the woman as she walked down the aisle between the desks.

"I see that you are going to lunch. Would you like to join me? It is too cold to eat outdoors, but there is a room where we can go to eat our sandwiches."

The woman observed her closely but said nothing until she had explained her invitation again. Then she smiled. "What a pleasant idea! It is much pleasanter to eat in company."

They walked into the center of the reading room. Nell felt a hand on her arm. The woman said, "I noticed, a little while ago, that you were looking up at the ceiling. It is beautiful. I never tire of looking at it. But don't you find something lacking?"

Her clear eyes sparked with mischief as Nell gazed into them. She looked up at the ceiling, puzzling, and back at the woman at her side.

"Really, not the ceiling itself. It is complete and beautiful. But there, the bronze figures on the visitors gallery. I see Moses and Isaac Newton, Beethoven and Francis Bacon, Shakespeare. But where are the women—Queen Esther and Sappho and Aspasia and Eleanor of Aquitaine?"

Nell gazed at her in surprise and then enlightenment. "Why, of course! I never thought of it!"

Delighted at her response, the woman went on, "We forget, don't we, that there have been remarkable women through the ages, women worthy of being memorialized in such a place as this."

Walking through the door under the great clock they emerged into the marble expanse of the exhibition hall, where they could speak more freely.

Nell said, "You know, that thought never came to me and I call myself a feminist."

The woman, watching her lips, replied, "There is one exception. Up on the second floor, at the head of the staircase, is a mosaic of the goddess Minerva. But then one could hardly have a place dedicated to wisdom that did not have a representation of the goddess of wisdom, could one?" Nell saw the mischievousness in her eyes. She went on, "We have not been taught to think of women that way. We have always been given the picture of women as handmaidens, the patient comforters of men—good women, that is, conforming women. Otherwise, female figures represent only abstractions. For instance, up at the base of that dome we have just been looking at there are eight figures, all in the guise of women. They represent, I believe, Philosophy, Science, Poetry, Art, History, Commerce and Religion. Again, the idea that women are the inspirers and nurturers of men. Men are certainly not willing to accept real women as philosophers, scientists, priests."

"We are changing all that," said Nell confidently.

They reached the room where they could sit among other members of the staff and eat their sandwiches. Nell chose a bench in a corner. As they sat down, the woman put a hand on her arm. She said, "My dear, you must realize that I am quite deaf. I cannot understand what you say unless I can see your lips."

"I'm so sorry," said Nell, shifting her position on the bench to face her. "Would a hearing aid help you?"

The woman gave a little laugh. "I refuse to use an ear trumpet. I do not have the self-confidence that Harriet Martineau displayed, presenting her trumpet to anyone she wished to catechize. I am afraid I am not as firm-willed as she."

"But there are devices, I believe, now that are not so daunting."

"They cost money, my dear."

Nell was embarrassed. Of course, she hasn't much money. She noticed the white shirtwaist the woman wore under her jacket. It was snowy-white but she detected the tiny stitches where it had been darned—a work of art in themselves.

The woman was speaking to her. "May I know your name? It would be nice to know that perhaps I could call on you for assistance sometimes."

"I am Eleanor Purcell. But I am not assigned to the reading room. I am a cataloguer. I just happened to be checking something when you spoke to me."

"I see. Eleanor—a queenly name, I have always thought."

Nell blushed with pleasure, though not sure why the comment by this woman should provoke such a sense of compliment. "I see by your request slips that your name is M. E. Beaufort."

"Yes, that is my name."

"But the M. E.?"

The woman looked at her for a moment, as if weighing her reply. "Minerva Elizabeth," she said finally, her eyes still closely on Nell's face. She smiled when she saw the surprise there.

Nell said impulsively, "It can't be!"

Elizabeth, reading her lips, said quickly, "Oh, but it is."

"I beg your pardon! I didn't mean—but are you really Minerva Elizabeth Beaufort, the author of *The Strolling Singers of Mediaeval Europe?*"

"Yes. I am surprised that someone as young as you are should know my book."

"I read in in college. It opened up the middle ages for me! There is no other book like it! Oh, Miss Beaufort, I am overwhelmed. It seemed so wonderful, to have a book like that, of the finest scholarship and yet so alive, written by a woman."

Elizabeth looked at her curiously. "How did you discover that M. E. Beaufort was a woman?"

"The librarian at our college told me. She said there had been a great furor about the book when it was first published. Some people said it could not have been written by a woman. How ridiculous! But you were acknowledged in the end."

"There is no one now who attempts to deny that I wrote the book." Elizabeth's words and tone were noncommittal.

"It must have been very distressing to you at the time."

Elizabeth nodded.

"You are working on another book now?"

"Yes."

"Is it on the same subject?"

"Yes. It carries my thesis a step further."

"Your thesis?"

"The nature of love." Elizabeth smiled at her.

"Oh, yes. That was the real fascination in it for me." Nell paused for a moment, half-embarrassed. "I shall be so happy if you give me the opportunity to help you."

"Certainly, certainly," said Elizabeth.

∿ ∿ ∿ ∿ ∿

"It is the boundless enthusiasm of youth, love. Someone that young cannot understand everything I said in my book."

The early evening was closing in and Hannah had arrived home laden with parcels of food for their dinner. As she sorted out her purchases, Elizabeth described her encounter with Nell.

Hannah, aware from the moment she had entered their room that Elizabeth was upset, did not reply.

" 'But they have had to acknowledge you as the author,' she said, as if the whole matter was easily solved. She is such a nice girl, but how can she know what that business cost me—us, in fact? She cannot, of course. The world has certainly changed in the last thirty years for young women like her."

Hannah, listening to the fretting note in Elizabeth's voice, said calmly, "It *is* over, Liz. No one can dispute about the book now."

"I thought it was a complete dead letter now—until this afternoon. I thought nobody would concern themselves with that old quarrel any longer, that the book would be consulted in a library and referred to in a footnote, like any other scholarly work. But, no. She says she heard the story of the controversy from the librarian at her college. I had hoped that if I could bring out my new book some time, it would be considered on its merits, not hampered by the past."

What should be, thought Hannah, is that the first book should be reprinted, brought out in a new edition so that the world can see what a brilliant thing it is. But she did not say this aloud. There was no use adding to Elizabeth's sense of frustration. Perhaps soon she would be able to say to Elizabeth, now, dear heart we have the money —

Aloud she said soothingly, "You have proof, from this girl, that there are people who value it." She looked critically at Elizabeth and thought, Such a pity that you should be wearing that blouse that I've had to mend so often. You so seldom meet anyone of consequence these days, it doesn't seem to matter that your clothes are getting so shabby. Perhaps presently you can have new ones, which you need. But first we must get out of this miserable lodging. It was a wonder you did not contract typhoid fever this summer. Washington was full of it.

Elizabeth had gone on talking. "It was by chance that she was able to find a copy of the book. I wonder if it would be better received now if it were republished?"

Hannah said cautiously, "It might well be. After all, Mrs. Stanton has just published her book, *The Woman's Bible.* It certainly is not more controversial than that."

∿ ∿ ∿ ∿ ∿

"But, Daisy, don't you see? She is marvellous—the complete scholar a woman who lives in her work, work that is entirely intellectual- -the sort of excellence that a man would be proud to claim. And yet she has such a sense of life. It is in her book and in the way she talks."

They were walking together along the curving paths through the green grassplots edged with syringa bushes that surrounded the Italian Renaissance splendor of the Library's grey bulk. The December day was mild, with the capricious warmth of a Washington winter, and Daisy had come to join Nell in her half-hour lunch period and they spent it thus, munching sandwiches as they talked.

Daisy glanced at her sideways. "She seems to have made quite an impression on you."

"It's more than that, Daisy. I've been able to talk to her several times now. She is very deaf but if I am careful to face her when I speak, she can read my lips. Do you realize—she is seventy-five—that in 1848 she attended the first women's rights convention in Seneca Falls in New York when she was my age? She has worked for woman's rights ever since. She knows all the women who have been working in the feminist movement since before the Civil War—Mrs. Stanton, Miss Susan Anthony —"

"Well, of course, if she's that old, she would know them."

Nell's ear caught the sulky tone in Daisy's voice. "Daisy, I wish you were more interested in woman's rights. Women will never make any real progress in changing things until girls like you take part in the organized efforts to gain equality for women."

Sulkier still, Daisy said, "I'm just not suited to it, Nell. I can't get all worked up over these abstract problems the way you do. I don't see that all these conventions and speeches make any difference."

"But, Daisy, they do! If you talked to Miss Beaufort you'd see how big a difference there has been in the last fifty years! But you know, a good many of these women who've worked at this for so long are getting pretty old. Mrs. Stanton is eighty-three and Miss Anthony is older than Miss Beaufort. We've got to do our share now."

"You, Nell, not me. You'll have to do my share."

"But, why, Daisy? It means as much to you as to me."

Daisy shrugged. "I should think it would be obvious. Can you imagine Aunt Edie putting up with my joining the Woman's Suffrage Association and going around carrying placards in public? I couldn't make speeches, anyway."

"There are a lot of other things to be done besides making speeches. Anyway, I wish you could meet Miss Beaufort. She's a fascinating woman. She can talk about the Middle Ages as if they happened in her lifetime."

"I'm sure you found that enthralling."

Nell laughed. "It does sound a little stuffy, doesn't it? But that's not what I mean. I mean, I'm fascinated by the idea of a woman who has been able to spend a lifetime being a scholar—she hasn't married, she hasn't had to drown her talents in a household of children. She's a rare creature."

"I'm sure other people would call her just an old maid who had to find something to support herself with."

"Daisy! You don't believe that! A man can spend a lifetime being a scholar and everybody thinks he is doing something worthy. He's looked up to. He's believed to have made a contribution to human progress. If a woman does the same thing, then she is just wasting her time and trying to be something that it is imposible for her to be. All the same, Daisy, even male scholars admit there has never been a book written about the twelfth century that equals hers."

"Then she is very well known?"

"No, not really. When she first published the book nobody would believe that a woman had written it. They had accused her of borrowing some man's research and claiming it as her own. Do you know what she told me? When she was working on it she used to come whenever she could to Washington to look for source materials in the old Library, when it was in the Capitol building. She could get a seat in one of the alcoves, among all the piles of books and periodicals that couldn't be housed any other way—there was no room to shelve them. But at first, she says—this must have been forty years ago—it wasn't thought to be a proper place for a woman. It was too public, they said. Isn't it amazing, Daisy, this idea that females should always be hidden from view? As if we all belong in harems or in purdah. And of course women could not speak in public. They couldn't even place their own bets at a gambling place or a horse race. A man had to do it for them. Things have improved a little."

"I wouldn't go to a gambling place. And somebody always places our stakes for me and Aunt Edie when we go to the Preakness."

Nell eyed her. "Well, you might as well live in India, then."

"But about Miss Beaufort. You say she is well-known among people like you."

"Yes. But it doesn't seem to have done her much good financially. She looks as if she doesn't have much to live on."

"Is she a teacher?"

"She used to be a teacher—back in the days when girls went to seminaries, not colleges. I suppose she doesn't teach now because she is deaf."

"Does she have a family?"

"I don't think so. She lives with a friend. She says she would like me to come and visit her so that we could talk but she says they're too poor, that they live in a place she wouldn't want to invite me to."

"What does her friend do?"

"I don't know. She doesn't say. I have an idea that the friend earns a living somehow for both of them. She says they've lived together for more than thirty years."

They had stopped at one of the curved stone benches that every so often broke the low granite wall that encircled the Library grounds. The pale December sun warmed this corner and Daisy spread the scarf she had been wearing so that they could sit down.

Nell said, "Do you suppose they're like us?"

"What do you mean?"

"That they love each other the way we do?"

"Of course not. They're elderly ladies. Lots of elderly ladies live together when they're spinsters and don't have any relatives."

"They were not always elderly. Miss Beaufort says they have lived together for thirty years."

But Daisy was unconvinced. "There is nobody just like us."

"I wonder. Daisy, there have been women in the past who loved other women. I've read about them. People don't admit it, but it is true. I've told you about them."

"Yes, I know you have. I don't think anyone ever has loved anyone the way I love you. I don't think even you love me that way. You're always thinking of too many other things."

"Daisy, that's not true. It is only because we're always so much on view."

Nell looked up at the grey wall of the Library building,

studded with the great windows looking down on them. She gestured towards them. "Just imagine all those people in the North Curtain watching two girls sitting on a bench to eat lunch. They probably think we're talking about the men we know and the prospects of marriage."

"And how improper for us to be sitting here in such a public place—right on the street, in fact."

Nell looked a little surprised. "Really? What could happen to us here in broad daylight?"

"We might be accosted by strange men, who think we're inviting their attention by sitting here."

"Pshaw! What nonsense."

"And young ladies do not say 'pshaw'."

Nell looked at her in indignation and then laughed. "Oh, Daisy, what a world you live in!"

"Quite different from yours. You see why Aunt Edie doesn't want me to go to college and get fast manners."

"Well, before you get further corrupted, you'd better leave me. Besides, my lunch hour is up."

They walked together to the corner, where Daisy would wait for the electric trolley. Reluctantly Nell left her there and walked swiftly up the curving driveway of the Library to the great flight of granite steps that led to the wide terrace in front of the big doors. She lingered for a moment to wave to Daisy over the heads of Neptune and his nymphs and horses in the fountain below.

Someone said behind her, "Ah, Miss Purcell! Did you enjoy your sandwich?"

She turned and saw the head of her division standing behind her, his felt hat in his hand. Before she could speak, he added, glancing in the direction of Daisy, "Your friend is a very pretty young lady."

"Oh, yes!" said Nell, feeling stupid, and rushed on to cover her awkwardness. "It was such a fine day—and in the middle of December!—that it seemed a pity to stay indoors."

"Yes, indeed. And you modern young ladies like the fresh air don't you?"

He walked into the building with her, his attention now obviously wandering to some preoccupation of his own. But he has noticed, she thought, and he has noticed us before.

CHAPTER ELEVEN

"But a house, love!" Elizabeth gazed at Hannah in astonishment. "I know you have been prospering in this new career of yours as—as —"

"Psychic advisor."

"Ah, yes. You've mentioned that we would shortly be able to move to better quarters. But a house!"

"Yes, a house. We can afford it. I've found one, a small house, almost across the street from the back of the Library. It will be like having your own scholar's retreat."

Elizabeth's eyes sparkled. "Have you signed the lease?"

"Not yet. I want you to come and see it first. It is a great find. The agent has lent me the key."

It was a small, square, two-story brick house set back from the street behind a patch of garden in which a few rose bushes grew. For the first few moments, walking about the square empty rooms, Elizabeth was speechless. Then she said, "Oh, Hannah! What a wonderful reprieve! We've not had a house like this before!"

"No, we haven't, Liz."

Spontaneously, without a second thought except to look quickly about them to see if they were really alone—a habit of years—they moved towards each other and embraced.

Still with her arms around Hannah, Elizabeth asked, "The agent made no question about renting to us, a couple of lone women with no visible means of support, no man to speak for us?"

Hannah's eyes were twinkling as they looked into Elizabeth's. "I told the Colonel I needed new quarters for my group of seekers after the truth of the cosmos. He's very indulgent these days. He said he would be my sponsor. The agent made no demur at all when he heard that."

Elizabeth went across to the recessed window and dusting the window-seat with her handkerchief, sat down gingerly on it. "This is lovely, sweetheart."

"Do you really like the house, Liz? I must tell the agent today whether we are taking it."

"Love, it is like a dream come true! Our own parlor! A room for a study. A little garden." She gazed out of the window at the narrow space beside the house enclosed by a high board fence. "It wants cleaning and perhaps we could paint the kitchen walls and hang new wallpaper —"

"I have arranged for all that, to be done before we move in. We shall have a clean place in which to live."

Elizabeth looked at her and laughed at her determined face. "My little conqueror! You sweep everything before you." She looked around again with satisfaction. "We must have a house-warming. Oh, not your aspirants to immortality!"

"Then who?" Hannah's question was absentminded as she measured the room by eye for a carpet.

"We do still have some friends. Some of our old colleagues. And there is that nice girl at the Library, who is always so helpful when I have difficulty finding what I want."

"Isn't she rather young? Everyone else will be our age."

Elizabeth laughed softly in her throat. "Dear love, of course! She is most flattering. She considers me the premier scholar of the century on mediaeval literature. She is always at my elbow when I raise my head from my book. Besides, she is a suffragist, a real firebrand when it comes to discussing the rights of woman. It is refreshing to meet so young a woman who is so eager to carry on the battle. I had begun to think that the movement for the equality of women would die with our generation." She paused to glance again at Hannah. "Dear love, don't tell me you are in some astral place from which the affairs of this world are seen as ephemera."

Hannah shot her a quick glance. "I was selecting furniture for this room."

Elizabeth laughed and Hannah grinned. It was wonderful to see Elizabeth so happy, looking forward to their new life with optimism.

In the next few days, whenever they were together, they

chose furniture, decided on curtains, the design of wallpapers, the colors of rugs. On one occasion, Elizabeth interrupted their calculations to say, "Dear love, don't you think we are rather old to be building our nest?" Hannah, surprised, looked up to see the mischief in her eyes. "It is never too late, Liz. It is only overdue."

"And what is to support all this splendor, sweetheart? What is the source of our wealth? Surely not simply your fees."

Hannah said blandly, "I've been quite successful in investing in the stock market."

"Ah, your broker. He has given you advice. But where did you get the money to invest?"

"From the Colonel."

"From the Colonel?"

"Yes. He has asked me to place the money for him in shares on the stock exchange, ostensibly as my own. He enjoys this sort of gambling, he enjoys deceiving people in such matters. He is afraid of people who will take advantage of him because he is a man with a great deal of money. He has earned that fear, of course. There are many people who would feel that duping him would only be a matter of justice."

"And what is your reward for doing this, love?"

"My share is half of the profits I may make in these transactions. I have been fortunate—or perhaps I should say that I have had good guidance. I have listened to my inner voice."

Elizabeth contemplated her for a moment. "Then this prosperity is not temporary?"

"Not if I can prevent it," said Hannah fervently. "I have had no losses so far. I have always at least broken even. He gives me a sum in bills—he always deals in cash—and when I report the result to him, he hands me back a quantity above the sum that is my share. I have been using some of the money for our living expenses but most of it has gone into our bank account. We have a little nest egg there now. If only there is not another bank panic. But this time I think I shall be prepared."

"But still you are uneasy."

"Yes. Our nest egg grows so slowly, especially when I feel we must use some of it—for the rent of this house, for example. If only I was more certain, I would risk some if it in speculation for us. But I hang back from that."

"I see. But I feel that you are also uneasy about these transactions because of the Colonel himself."

"Oh, Liz, you always see through me! Yes, I am uneasy, because of the way he handles these transactions. I can understand that he wishes to use me as a shield for himself in dabbling in the market. This is about the only entertainment he has these days. But I wish I knew why it is he insists on using cash—as if he wants to leave no trace of what he is doing. I have thought about this. I cannot see how it could get me into any difficulties— at least while he is alive. But he is not in good health."

"And you fear what may come up when he dies. You would, then, perhaps, love, have to account to someone else. Who would that be? Mrs. Head?"

"That is part of the problem. If I only knew the answer, I could tell Mrs. Head what she so much wants to know."

"And what is that, love?"

"The Colonel refuses to tell anyone what he is going to do with his wealth. His lawyer does not know. His wife does not know. You see, Liz, he is afraid of dying and he has a superstitious fear that by making his will he will bring his end sooner."

"That's not an uncommon fear."

"Mrs. Head is almost beside herself with anxiety about what her own situation will be when he dies—it is obvious that he cannot last much longer. She begs me to use my influence to persuade him to make a will. I must tread very carefully. He is a devious vindictive person. There are undoubtedly many things in his life he wishes to hide. Perhaps he has forgotten some of them and is fearful that he may unconsciously expose himself. His illness has taken a toll on him. What he is most concerned with now is himself, what will happen to him when he dies."

"Do you mean to say that an old sinner like that fears retribution? He has not acted—if one believes the tales about him— in the past as if he believed in punishment for wrongdoing. If you don't believe in Hell and you've vanquished all your enemies on earth, I shouldn't think that what will happen to you in after life would be a pressing concern."

"You're too logical, Liz. Just because he's had no religious belief since he left home as a young man doesn't mean that he's not scared now of dying."

"Oh, he was brought up in the fear of the Lord. And now that he is old and confronted by the unknown, he's frightened. How typical."

"He's an ignorant and superstitious man, Liz. He's very clever in manipulating money and using the power that comes with it. But otherwise he is not an educated man. He fears what he does not understand, as we all do."

"And he keeps his wife in the dark about her future. How despicable. Can you do anything about that?"

Hannah sighed. "I shall have to use all my wits to persuade him to make his will. It is unthinkable that a man with the enormous possessions he has should leave them unprovided for on his death. I think I know how I shall go about it."

She was thoughtful as she finished speaking. Elizabeth, watching her abstracted face, reached up to touch her cheek.

"My little goose girl," she said.

∿ ∿ ∿ ∿ ∿

It was early in the evening when Nell arrived at the door of her boardinghouse. The smart maid in the crisp uniform opened the door to her, grinning. Miss Rawles, she said, was upstairs waiting for her.

Daisy, at this hour! Nell climbed the stairs quickly and opened the door or her room. Not locked, she noted in passing as she stepped inside. Daisy, in a light dress, was dancing noiselessly around the room, humming to herself, not stopping when she saw Nell.

Nell took off her hat and threw it onto the bed. "What's up, Daisy?"

Daisy stood still. "Nothing. Why should there be?"

"It's not the usual thing for you to be here at this hour on a Wednesday."

"Oh, that." Daisy began to dance again. When she reached Nell she put her arms around her. "No. It's not the usual thing. But Aunt Edie said she'd be out till seven. I thought I'd take advantage of the fact. I told Elsie you were expecting me. I hope you didn't tell her you weren't."

"No I didn't. I'd have hurried home if I'd known you'd be here."

"Well, I didn't know myself till an hour ago. Don't you usually come straight home from work?"

"Yes, unless I run into Miss Beaufort. Do you know, she and her friend have leased a house over on A Street. I'm invited to their housewarming next Sunday. I said I'd come. You told me that you were going with your aunt to Annapolis that Sunday."

"Cousin Louise's wedding. Aunt Edie never lets me miss a wedding. She wants to keep the subject in the forefront of my mind."

"I think the housewarming will be more fun."

"Among a lot of greybeard professors?"

"Who said so? Miss Beaufort is expecting some of her old friends from the woman's rights groups to come. Do you realize, Daisy, that she has known all the famous women—Elizabeth Cady Stanton, Susan Anthony, Lucy Stone, Antoinette Brown—for years, long before they had any success in working for woman's rights? She is as much a pioneer as they are."

"You mean they are all going to be there?"

"Don't mock, Daisy. No, of course, I don't mean that. But there will be some women like that there. Daisy, have you ever heard of Mrs. Stanton's *The Woman's Bible*?"

"I have a copy."

"Daisy, you do?" Nell stared at her in astonishment. "Really you floor me sometimes. How on earth did you hear about it?"

"From Aunt Edie. Some of her friends talked about it. They think it is heresy—or blasphemy. Aunt Edie was so scandalized by what they said about it that I decided I'd get a copy."

"And how did you get it?"

"I walked into Lowdermilk's bookstore and bought it. The man who waited on me really was curious. He kept looking at me as he was wrapping it up but he didn't have the courage to say anything. I've got it hidden in my room now so that Aunt Edie won't see it. She knows I have books in my room but they are in French and she can't read them."

"Daisy, Daisy."

"Well, she would think the sky would fall if she knew."

"But all Mrs. Stanton is doing is demonstrating how the wording of the Bible has been used to keep women in their place. She is not attacking religion."

"I know. Aunt Edie hasn't read it. She wouldn't dare. She just knows it is dreadful because of what her friends say and also most of the preachers in town."

"The second volume will be out soon. Shall I get you a copy? I don't think the bookstore clerk will find it strange for me to be buying it. After all, I'm a librarian."

Her smile was mischievous and Daisy responded to it by coming close to her and putting her arms around her neck. They kissed gently.

"Why are you here, Daisy?"

Daisy gave a little shrug. "I had the chance and I was lonesome for you."

They kissed again. Then they released each other and Daisy sat down in the chair beside the bed. Nell's mind reverted to the housewarming.

"You know, I think Miss Beaufort is not as poor as she used to be. I've told you about how shabby her clothes were—very neat but patched. Well, she has a new skirt and jacket and her shirtwaists are quite fashionable. And her shoes are new, too."

"Perhaps she is just absentminded sometimes and puts on the wrong things."

"I don't think that is it. She is very sharp about things around her. For instance, the other day she asked me why I never wear that russet-colored blouse any more. She said it was so becoming. I told her I had got caught in the rain and it shrank. She has noticed you, too. She said she had seen you with me several times and she thinks you are a very pretty girl. Well, in any case, she has new clothes now and she and her friend have leased a house. They don't live in lodgings any more. So they must have more money."

"Has she explained?"

"Explained what?"

"Why, the change in their finances."

Nell laughed. "No. I don't think it would occur to her to talk about that. Scholars are not worldly people, very often. She is forgotten now but in the past she was quite talked about. I've told you that when she first published her book on the wandering singers, people said that she must have borrowed the work of a man, that a woman could not have done such a wonderful job. How outrageous! It is a wonder to me that she is not embittered. But she has a very sweet nature. Oh, Daisy, I wish you could come with me to the housewarming. She invited you, you know."

"You know that is impossible," said Daisy shortly.

$$\sim \sim \sim \sim \sim$$

January was almost gone and there was a trace of snow in the back garden outside the windows of the large room. The old house, built before the Civil War, had various features that spoke of a faded elegance—the blonde parquet floor, the bow window with its window seat. The gas lamps were turned low so that the guests were seen in a subdued radiance. Nell, looking eagerly about, saw Miss Beaufort sitting on a sofa beside an elderly gentleman with a white beard, his hands clasped on the gold knob of a stout walking stick—doubtless one of Daisy's greybeard professors, she thought.

Miss Beaufort saw her across the room and signaled her to come over, getting up as she did so. "Do sit here, Nell," she said. "This is Dr. Connaught, who wrote the textbook you undoubtedly used in college on the history of the Crusades. I must go and help Hannah. We will talk later."

The professor settled back on the sofa as she sat down beside him. He was a visitor to Washington, he said, though he came often. He was from Columbia University in New York he went on, observing her closely through his eyeglasses, his head tilted back a bit. His interest seemed to kindle when he heard that she was on the staff of the Library of Congress.

"It is a wonderful thing," he declared, "the moving of the Library into adequate quarters—into such a magnificent new, modern building after so many years of frustration. I am well acquainted with Mr. Spofford, the former Librarian. I know all his problems. You have no idea how difficult it was to manage the Library in its old quarters."

Nell murmured the expected assent. The professor's eyes were fixed on her. "I am glad to see," he said, "that so many able young women have had the opportunity to join the Library

staff. Oh, yes, I believe in opening doors for young women in
the intellectual world. It is unreasonable not to give an intelligent young woman the same opportunities as an equivalent
young man. Perhaps we shall have another Miss Beaufort in
your generation."

Nell, surprised and delighted, said, "Isn't Miss Beaufort
wonderful! It would be hard for anyone to equal her. I wish I
had known her as a young woman. You are an old friend?"

He looked at her ironically through his eyeglasses. "Oh, yes.
I have known Miss Beaufort a good many years. It is no lack of
gallantry to say that. In fact, I'll confess, I was a suitor of hers
at one time. I had the foolish idea that she would be interested
in retiring to a domestic life. Not that I would have required her
to abandon her intellectual interests. I was a graduate student
of her father's. He was a remarkable man, the first in this
country to teach according to the new methods pioneered in
the German universities, stressing the use of modern languages
and studying contemporary problems in the political and
economic spheres. Fortunately he was also a believer in
woman's rights. You might say that with such an unusual
daughter he could not be otherwise."

"There were no colleges for women then."

"There was one, I believe—what was its name —"

"Mount Holyoke."

"Yes, that was it and it was scarcely suited to her. I do believe she could have been a teacher there rather than a student.
She had a very thorough education with Dr. Beaufort. She was
always included when he held seminars for his students in his
house. There were a number of young men who were eager to
claim her for a wife. She refused because she said that the life
of a scholar suited her much better than that of a scholar's
wife. She was fortunate that her father supported her in this
belief."

"You were one of them."

"Yes. I was disgruntled at the time. I could not see why she
could not have combined the two—a scholar's life and being
my wife. But in the course of time I have realized she is right.
She knew I would insist on coming first with her in any

situation. It is not in a man's nature to think that his wife should not put him first."

"A man's nature?" Nell questioned boldly. "Or in our way of training boys and girls?"

He gazed at her for a moment. "Now that is a question I am not ready to debate. Perhaps you young ladies of this generation will be able to elucidate it."

"In any case, Miss Beaufort made her choice and she does not seem to have regretted it."

"At some sacrifice. When she started to earn her living when her father died, she learned the difficulties of the teaching profession for young women. Prejudice operated against them requiring them to be teachers only of children and girls, with no scope for intellectual activity. I believe that situation is improving."

"And nobody wanted to give her credit for her book on the strolling singers."

"Ah, you have heard of that! I can assure you that the idea, the research, the writing, were all hers. She began her work while her father was still living, using his personal library and materials he was able to borrow for her, since of course a woman would have no access to libraries otherwise. Finally, when she had completed the book, it was a question of whether she would be able to publish it. So, with the help of subscriptions from some of her friends, she was able to have it printed and distributed, using only her initials, so that it would be supposed to be the work of a man. Later, when the rumors began to spread that it was the work of a woman and she at last acknowledged authorship of it, there was such a furor that I believe she lost her teaching post over it."

"That is outrageous!"

He was amused at her indignation. "Times have changed, my dear young lady. They have indeed."

He glanced away and Nell, aware that his attention had been distracted, looked to see what it was.

He said, "Ah, I see that Madame Aurora is here after all."

Nell followed his glance. Miss Beaufort sat at one end of a long table decked with a fine white cloth and laden with a tea

service and bowls and small plates. Beside her stood a stout
woman wearing a voluminous skirt and a bright colored shawl.
Surely this must be Daisy's fortune teller. There could not be
two.

"The medium?" she asked.

A small smile appeared on his face. "That, I am told, is
incorrect. She is not a medium. She does not dabble in psychic
phenomena. She is a guide in the acquisition of knowledge
about the cosmic sphere. She does not tell you your fortune.
She teaches you to foresee your own. Or so I am informed. She
has gained a tremendous reputation in a very short while."

"Do you know her?"

"As Miss Beaufort's companion of many years, yes. Not as
Madame Aurora. This is a new manifestation of her gifts. She
has always been credited with psychic powers."

Nell, her attention riveted on the two women across the
room, saw that the stout woman was helping Miss Beaufort
serve their guests clustered around the table.

"They have known each other for a long time?"

"At least thirty years." His eyes, fixed on her, were quizzical. A hundred questions hovered on her lips but she suppressed them, warned by some sense of caution. He seemed
entirely friendly, yet some unspoken comment lay behind his
words.

She said, "I do not like the idea of someone preying on the
credulity of others. There have been so many exposures of
mediums lately."

"I think you misjudge her," he replied, picking up her
thought rather than her comment. "Madame Aurora has very
considerable intellectual endowments. Her avowed purpose is
to bring reason to bear on the subject of the evidences that
exist of phenomena that are outside the reach of our physical
senses. There are unexplained things in our lives—unexplained,
that is, by science as we now understand it."

"Are you one of her devotees?"

"No. I have enough to occupy me in considering the problems of historical research, which is my field. I don't believe
in dabbling and also do not think that anything will be gained
by dabbling in investigating psychic phenomena. Perhaps,

sometime in the future, when my interests shrink I shall bend my attention to the subject."

Nell saw that he was about to greet another elderly man who had been standing near them. She also saw that at the moment there was no one beside Miss Beaufort, so she got up quickly, making a polite remark to the professor, and crossed the room to her.

CHAPTER TWELVE

"Did you talk to her?" Daisy asked.

"No. I did not have a chance, except to say how-do-you-do when Miss Beaufort introduced us. A lot of people there were very curious to meet her. She had a group around her all the time. Everybody in Washington has heard about her."

They were in Daisy's room. It was the evening of one of Mrs. Head's dinner parties, followed by dancing, and the sounds of the music drifted up to them through the closed door.

Daisy, sitting in an armchair with her legs stretched out before her with her ankles crossed, said, "I've never talked to her. Once or twice I have met her when she has been here with Aunt Edie but all she does is nod to me. She has the strangest light grey eyes."

Nell, standing in front of her, replied, "It's such a funny combination—Miss Beaufort and Madame Aurora. You would not think that two such women would have much in common. But according to the professor I told you about, they've lived together for years."

Daisy said impatiently, "Oh, you and your Miss Beaufort! It's Madame Aurora I want to know about."

Nell gazed down at her uncertainly. "The professor seems to have quite a lot of respect for her."

"Did he say what she has done in the past? If he has known them for so long, he must know."

"Only that she has always had a reputation for psychic powers."

Daisy's glance up at her was half angry. "Do you mean that he believes in this sort of thing—in this hocus pocus that she's using on Aunt Edie and Uncle William?"

Nell said carefully, "He doesn't think it is hocus pocus. She

140

is not a fortune teller, he says. She is too intelligent for that sort of thing."

Daisy said scornfully, "She really does seem to be able to pull the wool over people's eyes. I suppose that means she is smart. It takes a smart person to fool smart people."

Nell's indecision showed in her face. "I don't know what to think of her. She certainly dresses in an odd manner—as if she wants to give the impression of being something of a fortune teller. And yet there is something else in her way of looking at you."

"Oh, she is funny looking all right. And I suppose it is done for effect."

Nell hesitated. "Daisy, perhaps you shouldn't condemn her like that. You say you have never talked to her."

"No, I've always avoided that."

"Then you really don't know what she is like, any more than I do."

Daisy shot her a satirical look. "You mean, I might succumb to her wiles, the way Aunt Edie has. Let's say I'm not anxious to run the risk."

"Oh, Daisy! There's a lot of difference between you and your aunt. I mean, you might find her an interesting person. The fact that she is Miss Beaufort's companion for so many years—she can't be stupid."

"I never said she was. What I don't understand is how she gets around Uncle William. He's such a curmudgeon. He's always been so proud of the fact that nobody can fool him. And he is absolutely ruthless. Even now, if you stand in his way, he won't hesitate to destroy you. He'll tell you so and it is true. He doesn't really like me, so I am careful not to be around him too much. I'm afraid of what he would do. He could make it impossible for Aunt Edie to have me here and that would make her very unhappy. She clings to me, Nell. I'm all she's got, she says. And now Madame Aurora seems to have him in her pocket. How does she do it?"

"He's old and probably losing his wits. She evidently knows how to manipulate him."

"Yes, but Aunt Edie can't do anything with him. She is really afraid to try and persuade him to do anything because she thinks it will only prompt him to do the opposite just to spite her."

"But why should he want to spite her?"

"He's very suspicious of people. The mere fact that she might ask him to do something would mean, to him, that she is trying to deceive him about something. She has always treated him with kid gloves—afraid to call her soul her own around him. And now this woman comes in and is able to lead him by the nose."

Nell, looking down into her distressed face, tried to comfort her. "I expect the reason is that your aunt has been so docile all the years she has been married to him that he suspects her when she shows any spirit. He probably thinks it means that she is expecting him to die soon. Madame Aurora, on the other hand, is different. She's a new person to him and she knows how to talk back to him. Besides, he's probably frightened and she uses that fear. It's pathetic how frightened some people get when they know they are going to die."

Daisy blazed. "I hate him! He knows Aunt Edie hasn't anything except what he gives her. He knows she is worried sick about what will happen to her when he dies. But he won't tell her anything. He enjoys tormenting her. She doesn't deserve such treatment. She has been a very good wife to him."

Nell said placatingly, "But don't you think he really will provide for her? It would be the normal thing for him to do. Besides, she will have her widow's portion. He probably thinks its silly for her to worry, so why should he reassure her?"

"You can't tell what he would do."

Daisy sat brooding and Nell stood beside her, yearning to reach down and kiss her, yet knowing that Daisy was in a rejecting mood. After a moment, Nell said, "Don't you think perhaps that Madame Aurora may be truly your aunt's friend?"

Daisy looked up at her unhappily. "What do you mean?"

"Well, I'm sure she knows what the situation is. If she can influence the Colonel, she may well use that influence on your aunt's behalf."

Daisy was again half angry. "That sort of person is only out for herself. You can't make me believe that she isn't. She knows just how to hoodwink somebody like Aunt Edie—make her believe she is her dearest friend."

"But suppose it was your aunt's idea that Madame Aurora should come and talk to the Colonel? How could she be here visiting all the time if your aunt hadn't arranged it?" Daisy's brooding gaze dwelt on her face. "That's rather calculating, isn't it?"

"Not from your aunt's point of view. Your aunt thinks that is the only way a woman can exercise any kind of power—by influencing a man. She must have come to the conclusion that she needed help with the Colonel so she invited Madame Aurora in. Now just think about it, Daisy. That's a reasonable supposition."

Daisy dropped her eyes, unwilling to challenge her. Nell knelt down beside her chair and put her arms around her. "Daisy, dear, don't be so unhappy. You know, there is something I want to tell you. When I was leaving the housewarming, Miss Beaufort invited me to come and see her next Sunday. She said there would not be anyone there except her friend —"

Daisy pushed her away angrily. She was in tears.

Nell cried in distress, "Daisy, what is the matter?"

"Oh, go ahead! Go and see your Miss Beaufort! Don't think about me!"

Astonished, Nell tried to put her arms around her again, but Daisy again pushed her away. Nell, half angry, exclaimed, "Daisy, you can't be jealous of Miss Beaufort! Why, she's more than seventy years old!"

"What's that got to do with it?" Daisy demanded through her tears. "That's all I hear—how wonderful Miss Beaufort is. You're in love with her, even if you don't know it."

Nell drew back a little, sitting back on her heels. She said seriously, as if recovering from a shock, "Daisy, you're very mistaken. I couldn't love anyone but you. You ought to know that. Oh, Daisy, please don't make yourself so unhappy! I know you don't have an easy time here in this mausoleum, but Daisy, all I'm doing is reaching out for something for both of us. Daisy, please look at me."

She raised Daisy's tear-stained face to kiss her. Daisy's resistance was gone. She leaned against Nell's shoulder.

"Oh, Nell, you've got so many things to fill your life and I don't have anything."

"Well, you've got me now. That's a good start. How's that for a little conceit? Anyhow, what I wanted to tell you is that Miss Beaufort and her friend want you to come with me next Sunday. Now do stop crying. Your eyes will be red and we have to go back downstairs."

Obediently Daisy wiped her eyes. Nell kissed their lids. Then she got up, pulling Daisy out of her chair. The music, downstairs, which had had stopped for a while, began again, a waltz. Spontaneously they put their arms around each other and began to dance. After a while they stopped and stood holding each other close.

"Oh, Daisy," said Nell into her hair, "We'll find a way out of this place for you."

"I don't want anything but you," said Daisy.

∿ ∿ ∿ ∿ ∿

The February afternoon was chill and grey. Daisy and Nell walked along East Capitol Street, catching their wraps around them against the cold wind. They had passed the grey bulk of the Library. The Capitol was at their backs.

"We turn at the next block," said Nell. Presently she added, "There, that's it, the small house between the two bigger ones."

They went up the walk to the front door and Nell lifted the knocker. "I suppose," said Nell, "there is someone here who can hear our knock. Remember, Miss Beaufort is as deaf as a post."

The door was opened by a young black girl in a white apron, who said nothing but stood back for them to enter. She still did not speak when Nell said, "Miss Beaufort is expecting us," but pointed to a hallway that ran beyond the staircase. Nell, remembering the house from her previous visit, led Daisy down it.

The door of the big room at the back of the house was open. They could see Miss Beaufort's head over the back of an armchair. She was obviously engrossed in a book. A Latrobe stove stood in the corner, radiating heat.

Nell, looking around for the maid, saw that she had not come with them. Nell stepped across the room in order to stand in front of Miss Beaufort. She waited for a moment till presently the woman in the chair lowered her book and looked up. A smile lit up her face.

"Why Nell! You're here! I had forgotten the time."

Nell drew Daisy forward. "Miss Beaufort, this is Daisy Rawles."

"How do you do?" said Miss Beaufort, gazing up at Daisy, still smiling. "I'm very glad you have come, Nell. Do take off your wraps and sit down. I'm afraid Willie Mae has not yet learned to take our guests' wraps at the door. But she is a willing child and will yet learn. Put your things there."

She pointed to a straight-backed chair nearby. The girls obeyed and then came to sit near her, facing her. She said to Daisy, "I must see your lips so that we may converse. Nell is used to me now. Deafness, you know, is a particularly trying disability. It does not seem to evoke the same sympathy as blindness, yet I think perhaps it is crueler, if one can make a choice in such things. It cuts one off so from people. But then if I could not read —"

Daisy, embarrassed by this forthrightness, murmured, "I'm so sorry!"

Nell came to the rescue. "Oh, no. For you blindness would be much worse."

Miss Beaufort said, "Well, we need not dwell on such a gloomy topic." She made a gesture to the book on her lap. "I have been diverting myself with this." She held the book up so that they could read the title, *The Authoress of the Odyssey*, by Samuel Butler. "It is newly out. He makes a most intriguing argument for supposing that it was not Homer, but a woman who wrote the *Odyssey*. He points out that much of the detail is what a woman would notice, a woman would remember—not the masculine mental landscape of the *Iliad*. I am especially taken with his rendering of Minerva, the goddess of wisdom. She is said, of course, popularly to be the daughter of Zeus, sprung from his head, in panoply, with a great shout. For after all wisdom must be claimed as solely a male prerogative. But in truth she was the parthenogenic daughter of Metis the Titaness, the daughter of Mother Earth, who presided over all wisdom and knowledge—this is what Hesoid says. Zeus swallowed Metis when she was pregnant. It was Hermes who guessed the cause of Zeus's headache and who persuaded Hephaestus to make a hole in Zeus's skull to release Athena or Minerva." She looked up again at Nell. "Such a typical maneuver of men, don't you think, to make sure that nothing valuable as far as the mind is concerned could be claimed by women?"

Daisy looked at her nonplussed, but Nell laughed. "It does take a long time for things to change where women are concerned, doesn't it?"

"Indeed," said Miss Beaufort. "Do you know, my dear, that the fiftieth anniversary of the first woman's rights convention in Seneca Falls will be celebrated this month, at the annual meeting of the Woman's Suffrage Association here in Washington? Mrs. Stanton will not be there. She says she is too old for such things but she is sending two speeches to be read. Miss Anthony will preside. In fact, there is a luncheon planned to honor her on her seventy-eighth birthday. Will you attend the meeting?"

"Oh, yes," said Nell. "I have arranged to take some leave so that I can do so."

"And you, my dear Daisy?—I cannot call you Miss Rawles." Daisy shook her head.

Again Nell spoke up for her. "It is difficult for Daisy to find the time. Her aunt has a very busy social schedule and she depends on Daisy."

Miss Beaufort continued to look at Daisy for a moment and then changed the subject. "You know, Nell, Susan Anthony was a teacher like myself, in her younger days. We attended some of the early teachers' conventions together. I remember at one of these —in 1853, I believe—she created a sensation by requesting and getting permission to speak. You see, my dear,"—she looked at Daisy—"in those days women did not speak in public gatherings. There were only men on the platform and only men voted, though they were outnumbered by women. Most of the women present were scandalized by her action—or pretended to be, saying this young Quakeress had shamed her sex and other nonsense, all for the benefit of the men. But she prevailed and succeeded in getting women teachers the right to vote, to speak and sit on committees. What it really takes is the courage to defy tradition. But that is something more than some of us can do."

There was a short silence before Nell said, "You certainly have seen great changes."

"Oh, yes. Why, in those days—I am speaking of forty years ago—in justifying higher education for girls, it was necessary to deny that studying mathematics and Latin would unfit them for their destiny as wives and mothers. Many men claimed to believe that teaching girls more than how to read and write would ruin their moral characters and indeed perhaps drive them insane. Oh, I see by your expressions that you think I am exaggerating. I assure you that is not the case. Even some physicians —all men, of course, since there were no properly qualified women at that time—declared that higher education would ruin a girl's health, give her neuralgia, destroy her ovaries and womb, make her hysterical and damage her nervous system. There were really no bounds to the folly that some men indulged in to prevent women from obtaining an education. They were afraid, of course, that educating women would make them independent. That is why girls' schools used to make so much of the fact that their purpose was to train young ladies in the domestic arts and the social graces. It was a disguise." She smiled suddenly at Nell. "There were no young women librarians then."

Daisy, not used to hearing such words spoken so plainly, was tongue-tied. Miss Beaufort's eyes lingered on her. Then she said, "You know, my dear, there were things we tried to do then to make young women stronger, healthier, in spite of the contemporary prejudice that required absolute passivity for respectable females. We tried to foster the idea of exercise. You young women now have benefitted from our efforts, because you think nothing of riding a bicycle, swimming in the ocean, or even playing golf—so I hear. But there is one thing you have failed to learn and that is that a tight-laced corset is one of the biggest hazards for a woman."

She paused and eyed Daisy's lace-trimmed dress, drawn in at the waist tightly so that her generous bosom was accentuated, her breasts swelling at the edge of the wide lace collar that spread over her shoulders. Nell, knowing that Daisy had made a desperate effort to escape from one of her aunt's afternoon teas to come with her, spoke quickly, "Daisy has a very small waist. She is not laced nearly as tightly as she looks to be."

Miss Beaufort watched her lips closely to grasp this statement, smiled and changed the subject. She began to speak of the history of the effort to gain the vote for women. When she paused, Nell said, "We don't seem to be any nearer than we were then. It's pretty discouraging. How can we have any real effect on the future unless we can vote?"

"And elect women to public office. But, you know, there is more to it than simply a right to vote. Mrs. Stanton never was deceived by that. She has spoken and written often about the fact that laws must be changed so that a woman can be more independent, in owning property, for example, and so less an unequal partner in marriage. A great deal has been accomplished but more remains to be done. Do you realize, my dear, how fortunate you are to be a young, independent woman now?"

"Oh, I do! But I want more! I want —" Nell hesitated.

Miss Beaufort gazed at her alertly. "You want personal freedom—the kind of freedom a young man has—political freedom, financial freedom, control over your own body—freedom from being told how you must dress, how you must behave, how you must pretend to hold certain beliefs, or you will forfeit the good opinion of society and become fair game for any man. Yes, I understand what you want. I have wanted it all my life. It is, I fear, another quest for utopia."

Nell said, half shy, yet eager to express her feeling, "People always say that women who take up causes—especially about woman's rights—are just frustrated women."

"My dear, women are always criticized—for doing too much, for not doing enough, for doing this, for not doing that. For some reason it is always open season when it comes to taking women to task for their shortcomings. No one finds the same need to criticize men in the mass."

Nell went on doggedly, "And if you are not married, then anything you do is because you're disappointed in life, because you've failed to catch a husband."

Miss Beaufort laughed. "You'd think men would be ashamed of the idea that they are merely the object of some woman's self-seeking. But instead it makes them complacent. Oh, I am very well acquainted with the attitude you speak of. My dear girl, one of the first things any self-respecting woman must learn is to discount the importance of male opinion, to free herself from fear of a man's disapproval."

There was another short silence. After a moment Miss Beaufort said, "Not only am I unmarried. I never wished for marriage. I have always thought of myself as very fortunate in not having to accept a man as the dominator of my life. But in our society such views as mine—I am agnostic, I do not subscribe to any form of religion, I believe a woman has as much right to such opinions as a man—do not make it easy for a woman to earn her living, to achieve respect for any gifts of mind she may have. It sometimes seems that most women are as much enemies of personal freedom for women as most men. Women can be the cruelest enemies of a woman who seeks another mode of life from that sanctioned by the narrow view of those who govern society. No doubt it is because they fear so greatly any disesteem that may attach to themselves by implication. Women are very vulnerable. They know that any woman can very easily become a pariah if she makes the least misstep and they fear to be seen as a friend to any woman who dares to invite criticism. I have seen this sort of tragedy even among the women with enough enlightenment to join organizations intended for the betterment of women. Any unmarried woman who does not at least pretend to accept gratefully a secondary position is suspect."

Her eyes were fixed on Nell and Nell felt the impact of something in them which lent a curious force to her words. She knows about me, thought Nell suddenly. She understands about Daisy and me. Involuntarily Nell looked at Daisy. Daisy was staring at Miss Beaufort.

None of them was aware that someone had come into the room. Madame Aurora came soundlessly across the parquet floor and laid a hand on Miss Beaufort's shoulder. Miss Beaufort looked up at her with a bright smile.

"Ah, Hannah! I'm so glad you've returned! You know both of my young friends."

Madame Aurora's light eyes moved first to Nell and then

to Daisy. "I believe I've met both of them."

Nell said at once, "Oh, yes! At your housewarming." Daisy remained silent.

Madame Aurora said, "Liz, I've had Willie Mae make some tea." As she spoke she gestured toward the doorway and the black girl came in carrying a large tray laden with a tea service and plates of small sandwiches and sweet cakes which she put down on the table near Miss Beaufort's chair. Madame Aurora began to serve the tea, handing the cups to Willie Mae to carry round. She was wearing a voluminous skirt of many gay colors and a white blouse cut low at the neck, with draped sleeves that hung halfway down her plump arms. Nell saw Daisy was scrutinizing her with attention, noticing the grizzled hair worn close to her head, the surprisingly youthful, unwrinkled softness of the skin on her throat and shoulders.

Miss Beaufort had reverted to her conversation with Nell. "You young women may feel that everything has been achieved now except the right to vote in national elections. How wrong this is. My dear, no woman is free unless she can do two things: deny the authority of religion, if she is not convinced of its truth; and decide what she will do with her own body—marry, or refuse marriage, live a celibate life or seek some other mode of fulfillment."

Nell saw Madame Aurora stand for a moment looking at Miss Beaufort, her tea cup in her hand, before she sat down.

∿ ∿ ∿ ∿ ∿

The keen north wind caught at Nell's and Daisy's skirts as they left the shelter of the doorway and walked back to East Capitol Street.

Daisy said, "I've never heard anybody talk like that before."

"I must say I haven't either. But isn't is exhilarating to hear a woman speak that way? She has freed her mind from all the fetters we think we have to accept."

Daisy shivered and drew her wrap closer about her. "What good does it do? It won't change anything."

Nell, feeling the euphoria created by Miss Beaufort's seductive voice draining away, objected. "Oh, but it will make a difference! If enough women speak their minds, people will have to listen. Daisy, a lot has been done in the last fifty years. As Miss Beaufort said, I could not be what I am now—why, we couldn't be doing what we are doing now, walking along this street together alone—if things hadn't changed during her lifetime."

But Daisy was stubborn. "Being able to vote won't make it possible for me to tell Aunt Edie that I don't intend to marry Hugh or anybody else."

"But it will make you more independent, Daisy. Every step that way is important."

"In theory, perhaps. But not for somebody like me." They walked along in silence for half a block. Then Daisy said, "You notice, Madame Aurora had nothing to say."

Nell said defensively, "What could she say? She was listening to Miss Beaufort just as we were. Did you notice she called her Liz?"

"And Miss Beaufort called her Hannah! That's a funny name for a psychic."

∿ ∿ ∿ ∿ ∿

Elizabeth said, as Hannah returned from the front door, "Such nice girls, love. Do you suppose they'll stick together?"

"They have some serious obstacles."

"You mean Mrs. Head, for one."

Hannah nodded.

"Daisy is a remarkably beautiful girl. I can see that her aunt would have plans for her—an advantageous marriage."

"Yes. Mrs. Head has spoken of that to me."

"And Daisy has ideas of her own."

"Daisy is very attached to her aunt, but she is not malleable. Perhaps it would be better for all concerned if she were."

"But what about Nell?"

Hannah picked up one of the remaining small cakes and popped it into her mouth. When she had swallowed it she said, "I'd like a bridge to use to reach Daisy. She is entirely dependent on Mrs. Head and she dislikes the Colonel. She dismisses me as a charlatan, one of many who have preyed on her aunt. She feels at a disadvantage because of all of these things and besides, there is her love for Nell, which she must hide. All this makes her uncertain of herself and unhappy."

Elizabeth smiled. "And there it all is in a nutshell, love." She sighed. "We have had difficulties, dear love, but at least we've not had to contend with others outside ourselves."

"No, we could sink or swim and nobody would have cared. It gave us a certain freedom."

"Yes, but I do feel a little sorry for these girls."

Hannah stepped over to Elizabeth and caught her head between her hands. "They must find their own path. Liz, we're in safe harbor now and I am going to see that we stay there."

V

CHAPTER THIRTEEN

In that month of February, 1898, the battleship *Maine* was blown up in the harbor at Havana, Cuba. In the following months the newspapers were full of the war with Spain, Colonel Theodore Roosevelt's Roughriders, Admiral Dewey and the battle of Manila Bay.

But on a humid July morning there was another item that immediately distracted many readers to something closer to home. W. T. Head had died at the age of 85, leaving an immense fortune—one of the greatest in the world, it was said—and no heirs but his widow. There would be, the newspapers hinted, a good deal of speculation about his personal history, the exact details of his wealth. A good many questions would be asked that could not be asked while he was living.

The newspapers carried accounts of his life, what was known about it, much of it guesswork. Nobody knew for certain where or when he was born, though probably this was in rural New England, on a starving farm that could not support a family, so that he had left for the frontier as a young man. He was known to have been in California before the gold rush. There were different explanations for his title of colonel. Some people assumed that it derived from the Civil War. But he had fought on neither the Union nor the Confederate side, for during that period he had been mining silver in Colorado, and like many of his associates had ignored the conflict. In the 1870s and 80s he was forming mining companies in Bolivia and Peru and another guess was that his title of colonel grew out of his actions during the War of the Pacific between these countries and their neighbor Chile. It was in these remote Andean regions, it was said, that he laid the foundations of his great fortune.

His name, to the public, was inextricably linked to silver. Before the silver mines were opened in the southwest of the

United States and silver was still rare and precious, he had commanded enormous power with the hoard of the metal he had mined in the Andes. Thus, in the 1870s when American greenbacks were redeemable in either silver or gold, it was said that he had amassed more millions. By the time silver became plentiful and most nations had abandoned it as a monetary standard, he had spread his financial net over many other sources of wealth and was unaffected by its decline. He was said to have laughed sardonically at the furor of those who wished to keep silver as a monetary standard, believing that this would provide the cure for all of the poor man's economic woes. Nevertheless, it was silver that everyone thought of at the sound of his name. His other financial dealings were hidden in a cloud of mystery.

One important source of this mystery was his fixed habit of dealing through agents. He himself never appeared in business conferences with other financiers, no matter how exalted. He never bought or sold anything himself. There were always other men who acted for him, who gave the explanations when these were called for, who laid down the terms for the transactions involving his assets. He also made a practice of never allowing any one of these agents to know what any other of them was doing. His right hand never knew what his left hand did.

So when he died, there were various men, several brokerage firms, an indefinite number of lawyers who each held knowledge of some part of his estate but none who knew what it consisted of in its entirety. Being prudent men, they all sat tight and waited to see what the next man would do, what sudden revelations would come to the surface.

In Washington, Hugh Carson waited until the funeral before revealing to anyone what he knew. He had expected to be besieged by Mrs. Head immediately but she made no move to talk to him. His uneasiness grew with each passing hour, but he called up all his stubbornness to maintain his silence. He saw Mrs. Head only from a distance. She was sweetly subdued, obviously saddened yet resigned as was normal for the widow of so old and ailing a man to be. He was struck by the fortitude that must be necessary to keep up this appearance of unconcern and his uneasiness became acute.

The funeral, attended by all sorts of strange people from out of town as well as by personages from the Washington official and social scene, was in the morning, in Rock Creek Cemetery. This fact was the obvious result of Mrs. Head's family connections. Otherwise there was no knowing where the Colonel might have been buried.

In the afternoon there was a reception at the house and Hugh was aware of the curious eyes of many of the guests roaming over what was visible of the Colonel's possessions and also of the scarcely veiled rapacity in the eyes of some of the financial men who had come from New York, men involved in the Colonel's multiple enterprises. Much of the attention was focused on Hugh himself and he was relieved when the last guest had left.

∿ ∿ ∿ ∿ ∿

He arrived on the doorstep of the Colonel's great house the next day and sent in a message by the doorkeeper to inquire whether Mrs. Head would see him.

Mrs. Head received him in the room called the library since on one wall was a glass-fronted case that held gold-embossed uniform sets of Shakespeare, Dickens, Byron and Tennyson, and the walls were closely covered with paintings, some by new American artists and some copies of famous pictures in the Louvre. She was sitting in an armchair next to a table on which stood a lamp with a large, many-colored glass shade. Hugh noted that she looked pale. That was scarcely surprising. What was more surprising was the degree to which she kept her good looks, in spite of everything. He knew she was in her fifties, but even now in circumstances of strain she seemed like a woman ten years younger. Of course it had been her apparent youthfulness that had captured the Colonel fifteen years before. He had wanted a young and personable wife but he had also wanted a woman capable of appearing to the best advantage as a wealthy matron. He had married for respectability. There was no doubt about that. Marriage to a sweet young girl would not have served his purpose. Edith Rawles had had the good fortune of combining all the requisites.

When she saw him, in spite of her evident fatigue she

brightened at once—her never-failing response to a social demand. "Oh, Hugh! How kind of you to come and see me!"

"It's no more than I should do, dear lady." He laid a thick packet of legal. papers down on the table. "I expect you are anxious to learn how the Colonel left his affairs. The first thing I must tell you is that he did leave a will." He paused and looked at her to note her response.

"She murmured, "I believe so."

He was puzzled by the quiet certainty with which she said this. It was obviously no surprise to her. How, he wondered, had she learned this? Surely not from the Colonel. He said, "This is something that has concerned me very much in the course of the last two years, ever since the Colonel had his stroke. I have indicated to you before that it was almost an incredible situation, that a man with his enormous wealth should make no effort to provide for his estate upon his death. I have explained to you before that, although as his widow you would be well provided for in case he died intestate—the law assures you your widow's portion—it would be much better if he declared his intentions in a will. In fact, it would be downright scandalous for a man of his position to die without specific provision made for the inheritance of his goods."

He paused again and Mrs. Head nodded.

"You do not know of any heirs who may come forward?" She did not reply and he went on. "His will names you his sole heir. He has not even made provision for the usual charitable bequests or gifts to servants. The will states that he leaves all details in such matters in your hands." Again he looked at her closely. "Mrs. Head, there is one very strange statement in his will. I was not present when he drafted the instrument. It is brief and he dictated it to someone else —" He paused to look at her questioning, but she shook her head.

"I know nothing of this, she said, "only that he made one, naming me."

"I see. When I read it I asked him why he inserted it. In fact, I remonstrated with him—pointing out that it could raise doubts. But he brushed my objections aside—said it was all lawyers' claptrap" — Hugh became a little pink in the face at the recollection — "and that was as far as he would go. But I did persist in questioning him on this one statement." He referred to a paper he held in his hand. "He says, 'If any person should come forward and claim my estate or a portion of it as my son, I here and now declare him an impostor, who is on no account to receive any share of my property.' Mrs. Head, have you ever heard of a son?"

For a long moment Mrs. Head did not respond. Then she said, in a voice that showed that she had difficulty in speaking, "My husband never mentioned to me that he was ever married before or that he had children."

Hugh contemplated her. "He was, however, well along in years when he met you. There was a good portion of his life already spent by that time. So, unless he told you about it, you cannot really know what prior connections he may have had."

Mrs. Head's expression hardened. "He never referred to his earlier life—to anyone. It was a matter we never discussed."

She has closed that door, thought Hugh. "Well, we shall, of course, have to give notice in the newspapers of the probate of his will. Considering the enormous amounts of money involved, there are bound to be people who will come forward to press a claim. That is something we must be prepared for. I do wish we knew more about his antecedents."

Mrs. Head made no reply. She sat quietly. Was she stunned? he wondered.

Her silence put him at once on the defensive. "I am very sorry, Mrs. Head, that I was not able to give you even a general idea of what the situation is before this. Beyond the fact that the contents of his will were confidential—he made a point of telling me that I was to disclose to no one—to no one—what its terms were. Beyond that fact, there was the possibility—indeed, the probability that he might revoke it or change its provisions. As you know, he had for years rejected the very idea of making a will. He had a superstitious feeling that by making a will he would hasten his death. In fact, I am sure he was convinced of that in his last conscious moments."

Mrs. Head still did not respond. He thought, after all, she is a woman. She does not expect to understand the workings of the law. She was being addressed by a trained man, a

trustworthy man, who accepted his duty as a gentleman to protect her from the sordid, the incomprehensible.

Warming to his task, Hugh said, "But this question of a son.
The fact that he referred to one so explicitly raises a doubt
about his existence. I tried to question the Colonel about this.
Was he a widower when he married you? Or a divorced man?
Divorce in California was not difficult even fifty years ago. Or
perhaps this son was not legitimate, merely acknowledged."
Catching himself up, he added hastily, "Forgive me for mentioning these unpleasant matters, but it is of the first importance that I should clarify the situation."

Mrs. Head said bleakly, "I have never known anything about
his early life. I've always assumed that whatever was in his past
that he did not like to remember he shut away and I had no
wish to revive it. I never asked questions."

He understood the implications of what she said. She had in
that distant spring of 1884, decided to seize the opportunity
that the Colonel's offer provided for a life of ease and respect as
a married woman—the achievement of a woman's natural goal
which she thought had passed her by. She had not wanted to
look too closely at what the past held. And the Colonel perhaps
had not wanted to, either, as she said. What was buried could
stay buried. Until the situation created by his death had un-
covered it.

Hugh said regretfully, "It is a pity that you can cast no light
on his past. None of his remaining associates have much knowledge of him as a young man. He would never brook any inquiry
from anyone. You alone perhaps could have elicited some information."

"I cannot help you. He would have been angry if I had referred in any way to his life before he married. He never spoke
harshly to me, but I've seen him very angry with others. I
avoided arousing him at all costs."

The soft finality with which she spoke caused him to take up
his papers reluctantly and place them back in his briefcase.
"Then there is nothing more that we can do than wait and see
whether anyone comes forward to make a claim."

Mrs. Head sat for a while after he had gone. A certain rebelliousness did flicker in her heart at this relegation of herself to

the status of a cipher. If it had not been for Madame Aurora and the information she had gained from her, her resentment would have been greater. As it was, she gave thanks for the small amount of reassurance, at least, that the seer had given her.

∿ ∿ ∿ ∿ ∿

They sat at breakfast in the sunny back room off the kitchen. A thunderstorm during the night had cleared the air and the morning was fresh. Elizabeth said, "So Mrs. Head has known all along that the Colonel did make a will. You told her."

Hannah wiped the egg from her mouth. "I not only told her. I saw to it that he did make one. I also told her that it was best to allow that young man, the lawyer, to believe that the Colonel acted as a result of his persuasions. He is a well-meaning young man and quite honorable. I said that she should not mention the fact that she knew of the will to him."

"She is to appear innocent of any part in the matter."

"Yes. Mrs. Head has never taken part in any financial dealings. If she were to be understood to be involved in prompting the Colonel to make a will, it might be assumed that she used her influence and that its terms favored her unduly for that reason."

"But does he have any other heirs?"

"I imagine that there will be many people who will come forward to claim some relationship with him. It is an enormous estate."

Elizabeth finished off her toast and jam. "Poor Daisy. She is engaged to be married to the lawyer, isn't she?"

Hannah nodded. She was obviously preoccupied with something else. "There is something ahead for us that troubles me. I don't know just what it is but I have a sense of danger."

"Us? Danger?"

"Yes. I see an aura of violence forming about us. And we have not had anything to do with violence—I have not since I met you."

She was gazing at Elizabeth, whose mind went back instantly to their first meeting. Hannah then had come from the violence

of war into a peaceful setting. "Do you mean bodily danger?"
"I do not know. It is a sense of menace—not only to me but
to you, too."
"And to do with the Colonel?"
"He was a man of violence. Violence dwelt in his nature. It
was in abeyance while he was living and I knew him. But
now —"
"This seems very strange, love."
Hannah did not answer her but sat wrapped in a cloud of preoccupation. Elizabeth said nothing further but watched her.
Hannah's eyes were fixed on space and she seemed no longer so
evidently present in the room as she had been. Presently she got
up from the table and went out of the room. Elizabeth heard
her go down the hall to the room where she received her clients.
She heard the door close.

Elizabeth sat on alone. Something was amiss with Hannah,
she realized. Obviously the problem, whatever it was, was connected with the Heads. Early in their intimacy she had adopted
the habit of not questioning Hannah about her thoughts and decisions. Hannah had a curiously imperative air of command that
sometimes lay in abeyance and sometimes came suddenly to the
fore. She had found herself accepting this dominion. It was a
part of Hannah she did not understand but found herself unwilling to reject.

There was always this strange business of Hannah's psychic
sense. Back in the days when they were both at the seminary,
Hannah had acquired a reputation—spoken of only in confidence and not openly admitted—for psychic powers in foreseeing events in the lives of others. It had had its effect on the
teachers and even on the Principal. She played sometimes, as
entertainment of an evening in the drawingroom, at telling fortunes, reading palms and cards. In spite of the lightheartedness
of these episodes, there were times when Hannah seemed beset
by genuine foreshadowings of future events. In such cases, after
they had left the gathering and returned to their own quarters,
she seemed to go into an almost trance-like state of removal
from her surroundings. Hannah said these were not trances. She
never had the feeling that she had left her body, as some
psychics claimed. But she was at these times rapt away into a

state of clear light when she seemed to see through the surface of things to an inner, pervasive meaning. When she spoke thus, Elizabeth made no comment.

Now Elizabeth realized that Hannah had reached a climax of inner stress. For months she had been aware of Hannah's pre-occupation with some unnamed struggle. A year ago they had reached the nadir in their efforts to maintain themselves. Anxious herself, distressed that she could no longer do anything that would bring them income, she had refrained from question-ing Hannah, from pressing her for explanations. Hannah, she knew, had some plan in mind. It involved first the offering of psychical advice to those who sought such guidance for their day-to-day affairs. It brought in enough money to keep them. Then it had led to the arrangement with the Colonel, which plainly had greatly increased their income. But there was some-thing further now that troubled Hannah. There was some source of uneasiness under this surface which had grown to alarm with the Colonel's death.

She wanted to go down the hall and find Hannah in her room and try to comfort her. She resisted the impulse. Hannah would not be able to respond.

ᴐ ᴐ ᴐ ᴐ ᴐ

Hannah sat in her consulting room and brooded. She disliked coming away from Elizabeth when they could have sat together, talking in the desultory half-sentences that had become the habit of their thirty years together. But there was too much that she did not want to talk about with Elizabeth just then.

It was true, what she had said to Elizabeth. She felt an atmo-sphere of menace invading their lives and she knew she was responsible for it. Her intention, in becoming Madame Aurora, was to provide for them. This she had done. The way then had opened for greater fortune: Mrs. Head's interest and then the Colonel's invitation to speculate. She had felt the thrill of success, the rush of self-confidence that more money brought. His death—looked-for but nevertheless sudden—had put her in a precarious position. His transactions with her had been kept in the greatest secrecy. Would anything of them come to light in this new situation? She must be alert. It would take all her wits and resolution to find her way through the labyrinth that involved this new affluence. And she passionately intended to keep this more secure, easier way of life—more on Elizabeth's account than her own.

She sat very still and concentrated her mind on the problem. There was a key to the matter and she must find it. Yes, that was it. With the Colonel's money came the threat of violence. But how? And whence? Her sense of it was so strong that it was as if there was a presence in the room with her. No. Whatever came, must come. It was there. But she would not give in to it.

Her mind seemed suddenly illuminated by the past—those many years ago, when she and Elizabeth had each so quickly found the mirror of herself in the other's heart. She remembered Elizabeth then—to her contemporaries a hopeless spinster of forty, to herself a radiantly handsome woman, vigorous in mind and body, joyful in spirit. She remembered Elizabeth speaking of her book, how her eyes sparkled, how her voice rang with her pleasure in this world she had recreated in this dark patch of history—yes, like a mother describing the beauty and brilliance of her child.

Hannah sighed and stirred in her chair. There had been an aura of foredoomed failure about Elizabeth's book. She had felt it at the time and had been unable to convey her feeling to Elizabeth in the face of Elizabeth's elation at its completion and publication. In her inner consciousness she had seen it as a bright jewel obscured by a dark cloud. She remembered making a determined attempt to tell Elizabeth this but coming upon her with a copy of the journal in her hands containing the first enthusiastic praise, her cheeks aglow with pleasure, Hannah's heart had failed her and she had remained silent.

And then the weary business of the controversy. At first Elizabeth had been amused by the furor, but that brave-spirited response had been worn down by the increasing bitterness engendered in the world of learning and finally their own little corner of it at the seminary. The Joves of learning thundered. This could not be the work of a woman. There were no such beings as women scholars, only female pedants, unsexed creatures who depended upon the learning of men collaborators. Who, it was demanded, was the hapless man whose work had been stolen by M. E. Beaufort? No doubt he was dead and unable to defend himself.

Well, it had all gone by now—the active years that followed when they had been respectable vagabonds. Living here and there, travelling the breadth of the country while Elizabeth lectured for the Lyceum Bureau on the ancient Greeks and Romans, on Chaucer, on Shakespeare, on the poets and artists of the Renaissance—journeys by train night and day through all kinds of weather to large cities and small towns. In spite of the hardships there had been an exhilaration in the freedom and variety of these years. And then came the years of decline, when Elizabeth's deafness overtook her and their income shrank.

And then there came this resurgence of vigor and success in herself. But burdened by this sense of evil—yes, evil, in the contact with the Colonel. Somehow or other she must shelter Elizabeth and their future from this menace. First she must know whence it came. She rejected the idea of taint on the money from its source. Money had no character, no moral nature. It absorbed no goodness or badness from the hands through which it passed. But there was such a thing as a quality of evil or good that was attached to a human soul. The one might gather violence, danger, pain, to itself. Another, calm, peace, balm. There were people whose natures caused an atmosphere of spiritual peril to surround them that sucked into itself anyone unwary enough. The Colonel had been one such. There were those who, in their ignorance and fear, would say that his spirit lingered nearby after his death, ready for revenge on those who had anything to do with his possessions. She dismissed the idea yet she felt that he had left behind some remnant of himself, of the powerful impress of his personality, that now threatened the peace and harmony of her and Elizabeth's household.

As she thought this she shivered with the strength of the feeling of danger nearby. She looked about the room as if to assure herself that no menace lay close at hand.

She said to herself, in exorcism, There is only one presence in this room. The presence of good. No evil can enter here. Good dwells here. Whoever enters here is conscious of the one divine presence, that of good. This room is filled with peace and harmony. No restless or discordant thought can enter here. No fear can enter here.

She sank back into her chair, spent.

CHAPTER FOURTEEN

Elizabeth put down the morning paper and looked across the table at Hannah. "Have you seen what it says here about the Head estate?"

Hannah, with a swiftness that belied her bulk, got up from her chair, her skirt swishing about her, and came around the table to look over Elizabeth's shoulder. The caption at the top of the news column said, New Developments in the Head Estate Case. She read further: A man had come forward who declared that he was the son of W. T. Head, the millionaire silver magnate. He stated that he claimed the whole of the estate as the only legitimate heir.

Hannah said softly, "So that is it."

Elizabeth, aware that she had spoken but unable to hear her, looked up at her in perplexity. "Did you know of this, love? How can it be? Mrs. Head is the heir under the will, is she not?"

Hannah seemed not to hear her. Her eyes were fixed on the newsprint. She read the column to the end and then straightened up. Elizabeth saw that her eyes were brilliant.

"What is it, love?"

Hannah looked down at her. I see what it is now. I see the shape of what I have been expecting."

"You knew about this man?"

"I know about the man he is trying to impersonate. Have you finished with this paper, Liz? I want it."

"Yes, of course. But tell me, love, what is this all about?"

"I can't because I don't know. But I understand now what has been threatening. The Colonel did have a son. He told me about him. But the man is dead long since. This explains the phrase the Colonel put in his will, warning against such an interloper. I expect I shall be in touch with Mrs. Head." She folded up the paper and went out of the room.

ᵥ ᵥ ᵥ ᵥ ᵥ

The man calling himself the son of W. T. Head came to the great house on Sixteenth Street on a bright, hot morning. He was a tall, broad-shouldered man of indeterminate age, with a square-jawed face and firmly closed mouth. His skin was weatherbeaten and slightly pitted, as if he had spent most of his life under a scorching sun and in a relentless wind. There were crow's feet around his watchful eyes and his hair was grey. He stalked into Mrs. Head's drawingroom like a man who would not tolerate any hindrance.

She watched him come into the room, paused for a moment before sitting down and glanced half-fearfully around her as if seeking some support.

He said, without waiting for her to speak, "I am Warren Head. I am Colonel W. T. Head's son."

Mrs. Head, sinking into one of the high-backed armchairs, said, "I have received your letter. I have agreed to see you privately against the advice of my attorney."

He said brusquely, "That's right, ma'am. I said I was coming to see you alone. I have no use for lawyers."

She gathered all her strength. "Nevertheless, you must realize that I—and my attorney—do not accept your claim. I have never heard my husband speak of a son."

There was a glint in his eyes. "I don't admit anybody's questions, ma'am. I'm who I say I am. You'll have to try to disprove that. You won't succeed."

His insolence roused her to anger. "I beg your pardon, but you are mistaken. You will have to substantiate your claim. Do you have documents?"

"All in good time, ma'am. My mother was W. T. Head's wife. I was born in California. I grew up in the mining camps. A hard life, ma'am, for a woman, for a child. It taught me to fight for what's due me."

"Your father did not support you?"

"He made himself scarce when I was a kid. Went to South America. That much my mother learned. My mother brought me up as best she could—taught me to fight my way and get my just due."

"It seems to me that you have been rather a long time in claiming your inheritance. Why did you not approach the Colonel himself, while he was living, if he was your father?"

Her soft voice seemed to make him angry. "Damn it! Do you suppose I haven't tried before this? He's tricked me out of it more than once. Now he's dead he's not going to get away with it again. You had better watch out for me, ma'am!"

His truculence seemed to stiffen Mrs. Head's determination. "Please remember where you are. I am not accustomed to being sworn at. You're not in a mining camp now."

Her manner checked him. He made an effort to be formal.

"You must understand, ma'am, you're speaking to a man who has been wronged. I don't take that sort of thing lying down." He paused and looked around the big room. "This is a pretty fancy house, all right. Never saw him in a place like this."

Mrs. Head's disgust showed. "I believe you were frightened of my husband. You would never have brought forward this claim to him. Whatever you sought from him, it was not on the basis of being his son."

His anger flared. "What do you know about it? God damn it! I'll make you believe it! I'll not let anybody ride over me."

"Why do you come here to see me? If you think you have a claim, you should approach my attorney. I have nothing to say to you."

He said arrogantly, "I wanted to see what you looked like. I wanted to see what kind of a woman would marry that old devil." He paused to leer at her, his eyes blazing with hatred. "You were not his wife—you're not his widow. My mother was still alive when you thought you married him!"

Shock and anger brought a flush to Mrs. Head's pale face. "How dare you say such a thing! You are despicable! What you say cannot be true!"

He smiled in triumph at her consternation. "Oh, yes. I can prove it. You're afraid, ain't you? You wouldn't have seen me otherwise."

Mrs. Head's voice trembled but she replied resolutely, "When I received your letter, saying you were his son, I was very much

surprised—and incredulous. But out of respect for his memory
I wished to give you a chance to speak for yourself —"

The man laughed loudly. "Respect his memory! He'd like
that! That's the last thing he'd want, for me to come into his
money. But that's just what I'm going to do—take all of it. No,
ma'am! you thought you'd buy me off with a handout, didn't
you?"

Mrs. Head got to her feet. "If you don't leave this house immediately, I will call my servant."

He turned away, saying insolently, "Oh, no need for that. I
just wanted to let you know where we stand, you and I."

He walked away to the door, where he paused for a moment
and glanced back at her. Without another word he went out.

～ ～ ～ ～ ～

Daisy, dressed for tennis, stood in the hall outside the drawingroom, alert. The sound of a loud, arrogant man's voice had
stopped her on the way out of the house. She had heard angry
men shout like that but never in her aunt's drawingroom. She
stood still and listened. She did not hear her aunt's voice, but
then Aunt Edie spoke softly. She wondered, should she go in?

But before she could decide, a tall man walked out of the
room. He stopped in front of her as if astonished, apparently so
engrossed in his own feelings that he was nonplussed to find
anyone there. He stared at her, his eyes slowly examining her
flat straw hat, her high-necked tucked shirtwaist, her straight
white skirt caught in by a wide black belt around her waist. His
glare was that of someone who had never beheld such a vision
before. She stared back at him. Some exclamation seemed
about to burst from him but instead he muttered something
and, ducking his head, stepped past her toward the front door.
Before he opened it, he turned again and gave her a look of concentrated hatred. She stood for a moment more, transfixed by
it.

Then she sprang forward and entered the drawingroom. She
saw her aunt sitting in the armchair, her head bowed, a handkerchief to her eyes. "Oh, Aunt Edie, what is wrong? Who was
that man?"

Mrs. Head lifted her eyes brimming with tears. Daisy dropped down on her knees beside her. "Oh, Daisy! He is a dreadful creature!"

"But who is he and why did he come here?"

Mrs. Head tried to gather herself together. "He says he is William's son. He had written me a letter, saying this, and that he wanted to come and see me. I said he might."

"Uncle William's son! Why, I never knew he had a son– or that he was married before he met you. Is he—illegitimate?"

The sound of the word from Daisy caused Mrs. Head to stop and look at her for a moment. But she said, "William never told me he had a son."

"Then this man is an impostor. Hugh said that there would be all sorts of people coming forward with a calim against Uncle William's estate. But why did he come here? Why didn't he go to see Hugh?"

Her aunt was looking down at the floor. "Because he said he had to see me."

"Did you tell Hugh about the letter?"

"Yes, I did. He did not want me to see the man. He said that I should let him deal with the matter. But I felt I owed it to William —"

"Aunt Edie! But you knew there wasn't a son!"

Mrs. Head looked at her sorrowfully. "There is a son mentioned in the will."

Daisy stared at her in astonishment. "Oh, Aunt Edie!"

"Yes, it is true. But William specifically cut him off from inheriting."

"Hugh knew this all along and did not tell you?"

"He says it was to save me anxiety. And also William made him promise not to tell anyone the contents of the will, even me."

There was disdain in Daisy's voice. "How like him! But then you deliberately decided to see this man anyway?"

Mrs. Head gave a little sigh. "Honey, I've known about this for some time. I knew William made a will before Hugh told me. Madame Aurora had already told me."

"Madame Aurora? How did she know?"

"Why, I don't suppose he would have made a will if she had

not persuaded him. He was afraid, honey. He was afraid he would die if he made a will."

"Well, he would have anyway."

Mrs. Head seem undecided. "I don't know, honey. He thought it would hasten his death. Perhaps it did."

She looked so unhappy that Daisy put her arms around her. "Oh, Aunt Edie, honey! That's not reasonable! The doctor said he would have another stroke at any time and that it would kill him."

Mrs. Head did not seem convinced but she said nothing.

"Anyway, how did Madame Aurora persuade him to make a will?"

"I don't know. She had a lot of influence with him. He respected her in a way he did not most people."

Daisy gazed at her doubtfully. "Did she do it for you?"

"She said it would not be right for her to act for me, because it would be breaking William's trust in her."

"Pshaw!"

Mrs. Head looked at her in disapproval. "Daisy, you've picked that up from Nell. You know I don't like it."

"I'm sorry, Aunt Edie. But why must everybody be so careful about being honest with Uncle William? He never hesitated to deceive anyone if it was to his advantage."

"Daisy! You must not speak that way! Besides, he is dead now —"

But Daisy was not repentant. "It is true, Aunt Edie. But Madame Aurora. What will she get out of it? Did he leave her some money?"

Mrs. Head was offended. "No. She is not mentioned in the will. She refused to let him give her a legacy."

"How do you know she did?"

"Why, she has told me so. Oh, honey, she is a remarkable woman. I know he would never have written a will without her, if she hadn't made him see it was necessary for him to do so— not just for me but because of all the great financial interests he had."

"Then, if she was able to make him do something he didn't want to do, she had more influence on him than anyone I ever heard of. I'd like to know how she managed it." Daisy thought for a moment. "Of course, I expect she worked on his fears. He was as superstitious as anybody could be. That's probably it. She knew how to use his fears against him."

Mrs. Head was angry. "Daisy, I won't have you talking that way. He was a very hard man. That I don't deny. Madame Aurora must have been able to find a way to bring him to his senses. Hugh says it would have been downright scandalous for a man in his position to die without a will. She was able to convince him of that."

"But this man who was here."

"William says in his will that if somebody comes and says he is his son, he is not to be believed."

"Of course, an impostor. Don't you believe Uncle William? He wouldn't put such a thing in his will if he didn't mean it."

Mrs. Head hesitated. "Daisy, William always treated me well. He never spoke harshly to me, as he did to other people. Yet I realize that he could be cruel—and unjust. That is partly why I told this man to come and see me. Daisy, it would be very unjust if he was really William's son and William disinherited him."

Daisy stared at her increduluously. "Aunt Edie, you can't be so soft!"

"Daisy! That's not a nice way to talk to me."

"I'm sorry, honey. But, really, you mustn't be taken in by somebody like this."

"How do you know what he is like?"

"Why, just looking at him —. I met him face to face when he was going out. You said yourself he is dreadful."

"I was upset. It might be just because he's upset that he acted the way he did."

Prudently, Daisy shifted her approach. "Madame Aurora must know about this statement in Uncle William's will. Does she know about the letter you had from this man?"

"Yes, she was here when I received it. She said that I shouldn't see the man. She says he is dangerous."

"Well, then, surely you shouldn't have let him into the house. If he wants to make trouble, Hugh should deal with him."

"I won't receive him again. But I'm very worried."

"Well, even supposing he is William's son, he has been disinherited. So that is that."

"He says he is going to contest the will. And —"

"And what?"

But Mrs. Head put her hand over her eyes and refused to answer.

∿ ∿ ∿ ∿ ∿

Elizabeth sat by the open window, enjoying the breeze from the river that sprang up at this hour every night, refreshing the humid warmth of the day. She watched Hannah fidgetting with the dishes of their evening meal which still were on the table.

"What is it? Tell me, love. You're very unsettled. Something has been troubling you very much these last few days."

"It is something I have not wanted to upset you with."

They both knew that this was a confession—that Hannah needed reassurance.

"Well, tell me. It concerns Mrs. Head. She has been threatened by this man who claims to be her husband's son."

Hannah nodded. She came in and sat on a love seat near Elizabeth's chair. For a while they were silent. Then Hannah said,

"He came to see her the other day. Now he has been to see the lawyer. He says his name is Warren Head—that was the name of the Colonel's son. He declares that he is contesting the will, on the ground that it was made under undue influence. He says this is proved by the words the Colonel inserted, to the effect that if someone comes forward and says he is his son, that man is an impostor.

"Does he disinherit his son?"

"That statement is the only reference to a son. He does not otherwise acknowledge having a son."

"Did he to you?"

"Oh, yes. He told me about his son. He was positive that he was dead—long since dead. It was against my advice that he put that phrase in. The will is so simple that this statement gains in importance by that fact."

"But whose influence, love? I know there have been many cases in which a husband excludes his children and leaves all his property to his second wife. That always leads to a contest between the widow and her stepchildren. Does this man accuse Mrs. Head of causing the Colonel to disinherit him?"

"I suppose that is the gist of his claim. But Mrs. Head knew nothing of the will except what I told her. That can be shown. She could not have influenced him."

"Then, whose influence, love? The lawyer's? Or yours?"

"Mine, of course. Everyone knows that I saw and talked to the Colonel more—much more—often than anyone else in his last months."

"Yes. But you are not mentioned in the will. You have told me that. You do not benefit from his will."

"I was very careful to see that the Colonel did not include me, though he said he wanted to. I had a very strong feeling that something like this would arise and I did not want to be mentioned. But of course this man will say that I influenced him to make the will in favor of Mrs. Head—that I acted on her behalf, at her instigation."

"So that you would be rewarded by her."

"That is doubtless what his argument will be. On the contrary, I have made it very plain to Mrs. Head from the beginning, that I will accept nothing from her. She understands, though now in gratitude she wishes to make me a gift, a substantial gift. You see how impossible that is."

"It seems unjust, considering the extent of his estate."

"As I've told you before, when Mrs. Head first approached me for help in dealing with her husband, I told her that I could not play the part of her agent. If I did that, I could not convince the Colonel that I was not her cat's paw. He was very fierce on the question of being manipulated. He was fond of her after his fashion, and he really preferred her to inherit his property. In fact, the reason he married her, rather than some other woman, was that he was convinced that she had no designs on reforming him, on interfering in any way with him. He saw her as just a charming, thoroughly genuine lady, who would give him respectability and who was too naive, too reticent to feel anything but gratitude to him for rescuing her from impecunious single blessedness."

Hannah broke off to grin at Elizabeth. Elizabeth laughed.

Hannah was serious again. "But he hated the very idea that

even she might try to influence what he did. He would never tolerate any sort of interference. I think he always had that feeling and that it grew stronger as he got old and sick. So you see why I was careful to let him know that I was not Mrs. Head's agent. I would have lost my influence with him if I had not done so."

"But Mrs. Head? You will accept nothing from her?"

"No." Hannah was thoughtful for a moment. "There is more to this, Liz, than merely the challenge to the will. He says that he can prove that Mrs. Head was never legally married to the Colonel—that his own mother was still alive when the Colonel married Mrs. Head. That would mean that, unless Mrs. Head can disprove this, she will not even get a widow's portion. You can imagine, also, how devastating this will be to Mrs. Head."

"But, love, it cannot be true."

Hannah shrugged. "I don't know. All I know is what the Colonel told me about his son—that he was the child of a woman the Colonel married in California fifty years ago, that as a young man this son came to seek him in South America, where he was mining silver, in competition with other men. I believe the Colonel said the woman was then dead—according to the son's statement. From what the Colonel said, these mining ventures must have been a lawless, violent business, far away from civilization in the high Andes. The son was a weakling and he despised him. Then the son made the mistake of being persuaded by some of the Colonel's enemies to act as a spy for them and give them information of valuable sites for mines which the Colonel had prospected and also about the donkey trains carrying silver down the mountains, so that they might be waylaid. There was an ambush and the son was killed—possibly at the Colonel's deliberate order. So you see, he was certain the son was dead. But what about the woman? She would be about seventy, I suppose, if she is alive."

"Dear me, love, what a situation! Does anyone know of this except you?"

"Some of the Colonel's associates must have known about it at one time. But he had outlived most of them by the time he died. I don't know whether any are still living. I have the impression that most of them are dead, or beyond remembering anything of the past. He quarreled with everyone at one time or another. But there is always the possibility that one or two may be found."

"Is that what the lawyer will do?"

"I suppose he must set about inquiring to see if there is any truth to what this man says." Hannah paused for a while and Elizabeth watched her face. Finally Hannah said, "I am uneasy about the lawyer's inquiries."

"Why, dear heart?"

"For what he may uncover. You remember, Liz, that the Colonel amused himself in his last weeks by giving me money to use on the stock exchange."

"Oh, yes! We're sitting here in luxury right now because of that, aren't we, love?"

Hannah saw Elizabeth smile as she glanced around the pleasant room. "Of course. I do not want anyone to learn of these transactions if it is possible to keep them hidden."

"But there was nothing fraudulent about them!"

"Oh, no, that's not it. But there is nothing to show, no one to testify that this was just what I have told you—a kind of game the Colonel played with me, which produced profits for me."

"I see. The human instinct to see evil where perhaps it does not exist."

Hannah nodded absently. "Up to the last transaction I would perhaps not have much trouble justifying my actions. The sums, though large to the average person, were not large to the Colonel. He made his profit. I made mine. Our transactions were always in cash. He had a safe in his room. He kept large sums of money in it. I sometimes wondered about that young man who was his personal attendant. He must be an honest person, since he must have known about the safe and of course realized that the old man was pretty helpless."

"And how did the Colonel get this money, love?"

"When he wanted money, he sent to New York, to men with whom he dealt in banking matters. He had a wide range of business associates. No one would ever dare to ask him what he was doing with it. He was notorious for never letting anyone know the full extent of any of his dealings. He kept the details of his affairs to himself. I came to be able to divine much that went on in his mind but I was careful not to let him know. He would become angry—frightened, I think, really—and suspicious and secretive for days if I let something slip."

Hannah paused for a moment while Elizabeth watched her face in the lamplight. Then she went on.

"At the end, a couple of days before he had his final stroke, he gave me a very large sum of money—in cash, as usual, large bills. He was dead before I could do anything with it. You know, I must be careful in dealing with Wilmot, the stock-broker. He acts for me in placing the money I have to invest. But I must not arouse his curiosity about the size of the invest-ment I want to make. I must allow him to think that I am only reinvesting profits. So I could not act at once in regard to the whole sum and I had not made up my mind how to proceed when I heard of the Colonel's death. The money is still in my hands."

"What do you propose to do with it?"

"I do not propose to return it to the estate. These sums he handed over to me were trifles in his eyes. More than once, lately, when I have brought him his share of the profits from an investment, he would push the whole lot over to me and tell me to take it. He didn't want to be bothered with it. When he gave me this last sum, he said, 'There, there is your legacy.' I have refused steadfastly to allow him to mention me in the will. He must have had some warning that his end was near. He said, 'Don't be a fool and let anybody know about it.' But it is an un-easy thing to have the money in my hands under the present circumstances."

Elizabeth said thoughtfully, "I see that it is. No one can know about it? There is no trace of it?"

"I am not certain of that. I know that he obtained the cash from men in New York and kept it in the safe in the wall of his room. I suppose he must have paid that young man well to over-look that. But who sent him the money and whether any record was kept of it, I don't know. He said not. He told me at one time that he had many uses for money which he did not divulge to anyone—I am sure the bribing of public officials was one of them. He bought men as a matter of course when he needed their acquiescence in some scheme important to him. He said he always made sure that nobody kept tabs on him—that is the way he saw it. He had an intense desire for obscurity in his affairs. He would not put up with anyone's surveillance, even in an innocent way."

"This is worrisome, love. You cannot know what this man who claims to be his son may know, can you? Or the lawyer?"

"No. I have no means of learning that except through Mrs. Head."

They sat on silently in the moist warmth of the river breeze coming through the window. In the garden below there was the sound of katydids and occasionally the call of a nightbird.

Hannah said, "Liz, we have had a hard time most of our lives. This isn't a world made for women like us. It has been an uphill battle to stay afloat very often —"

"But, love, we've had each other! How thankful I am that we have been able to be together through all of it. Think of what it would have meant if we had not. For me, at any rate, it would have been a miserable existence."

Hannah did not answer her at once but reached out her hand to cover Elizabeth's as it lay on the arm of the chair. Presently she said, "It was ordained for us, Liz. I know you do not always agree with me, but things do not happen haphazardly. Sometimes we earn the episodes of our lives, good or bad. Sometimes they come to us from another source."

Elizabeth said readily, "I know that your philosophy is teleological in nature. You believe in an ordered cosmos. How can I— or anyone—say you are not right? But whatever the source, I give thanks—and to whom? I realize the ambivalence of my feelings—that I have you, that I have had you, all these years. And now, through your efforts, we are at least comfortable. We lack nothing important."

"Except assurance for the future. But you never look to the future, do you, Liz?" Hannah was smiling at her. "You take less care for it than I, who am supposed to be able to foresee it."

Elizabeth leaned over and tapped her cheek. "You shouldn't tease. Yes, I accept the poet Horace's dictum, *carpe diem*, for, as he says, 'Even while we speak, Time, the churl, will have been running. Snatch the sleeve of today and trust as little as you may to tomorrow.' I have you now, my dear love, this very night, this very hour, this very moment."

"And I you, sweet Liz."

They sat again in silence for a while and Elizabeth said, "Let us go to bed, love. It seems a little cooler now."

They went through their usual routine of closing the windows of the downstairs room, checking the bolts on the doors. Hannah gathered up the clutter on the table and carried it out to the kitchen to be dealt with by Willie Mae the next day.

Elizabeth was already in their big front bedroom when Hannah reached it, sitting in the rocking chair, taking off her stockings. She looked up when Hannah came in.

"Have you seen Mrs. Head, love, since she was visited by this man who claims to be the Colonel's son?"

"No. She has not indicated that she wants to see me. I have wondered what this means."

"She must be distressed—especially if doubts are being raised about the legality of her marriage to the Colonel."

"Yes. I am sure that is so. I cannot decide why she does not get in touch with me—whether she is upset or whether she is ashamed to be involved in such a sordid matter and does not want to see anyone. Of course, it may be otherwise—that she feels her situation has changed so much—her new status as an extraordinarily wealthy woman in her own right—that she does not wish to keep up her former associations."

"Oh, no!" Elizabeth exclaimed, standing up to remove her petticoat. I should hardly think that of her, from what you've told me about her. Perhaps she would like to see you but is waiting for you to come to her. You must risk a rebuff, dear love, out of kindness."

Hannah nodded and came to help her out of her chemise. She stood for a moment holding Elizabeth's spare white body between her hands. Suddenly she said,

"Yes, you like this nice house and this comfort and I shall see that you do not lose it. We shall have money, too, for your new book, and with it we shall erase what happened with the first one. I will do it, Lizzie. We will not be defeated this time."

Elizabeth, feeling the tension in her fingers against her skin, said quietly, "What is it, love? There is something more that is troubling you. This man?"

Hannah nodded.

"Are you afraid of him?"

There was a tone of reluctance in Hannah's voice. "Yes, I cannot say just why, except that there is an aura of violence surrounding him. He holds violence in himself—as the Colonel did. He attracts violence. He visits it on others. It is as if there is an angry spirit in pursuit of him, driving him on in spite of himself into violent action that could be deadly for himself and those about him."

"It sounds as if you are speaking of Nemesis."

"Perhaps there is something of that. I feel that he brings the threat of great danger."

"He draws the lightning to us?"

Hannah's shrug was more a shiver. She took her hands away and started to undress.

As Hannah got into bed beside her, Elizabeth said, "What do you intend to do, love?"

"I don't know. I must go a step at a time, as I am led." She turned out the bedside lamp and lay down beside Elizabeth, her lips close to Elizabeth's better ear. "Whatever it is, I must not back away."

"Take care, my love."

"I will. Please do not worry, Liz."

Elizabeth felt her sink down more closely in the bed. Very soon, she knew, Hannah would be asleep, deeply and quietly asleep, without the musings that would keep Elizabeth herself awake for a while. It was a marvelous gift that Hannah had—to lay aside the day's preoccupations so that she could at once drift away into the contentment of peaceful sleep. When she awoke Hannah would be instantly aware of the least sound, the presence of anything strange. Whereas, she herself, locked into her almost silent world, was left to rehearse, to imagine, to recapitulate.

Elizabeth turned herself so that she could put her arms around Hannah. Whenever she did this in the warm closeness of their bed, she was flooded with an enormous wave of tenderness, of reaching out to seek the Hannah that was truly hers. In her sleep Hannah would respond in a half-conscious reaching, as if through the layers of unconsciousness she knew Elizabeth was there and seeking her. Elizabeth's long, narrow hands sought the smooth, moist skin of Hannah's haunches. She pressed herself against the ample softness of Hannah's breasts. In her sleep Hannah's lips moved to kiss her.

CHAPTER FIFTEEN

They turned their bicycles into Connecticut Avenue. The summer was on the wane, even though the August sun was hot. There were dry leaves already blowing along the gutters, a foretaste of the autumn. They rode abreast. One of her cousins, a senator, had obtained for Nell the privilege of play on the tennis courts of a private club. She and Daisy had taken advantage of it in these dog days when the city was half empty of its winter throng.

Daisy said, "You see, she can be very stubborn. She can get an idea like this into her head and there's no getting it out. I know. I've been through this sort of thing before."

Nell steadied the racquets she carried across the handlebars. "Do you mean that she'll give in to what this fellow wants? Won't that cause a lot of trouble? How can she, really? Your uncle left an immense fortune. I doubt if his lawyers and business associates would allow it."

"Nobody seems to know just how big Uncle William's estate is or just what it consists of. He spent his life keeping people in the dark. It will take years to sort it all out. This man is very bold. First he said he would contest the will. Then he said he'll prove that Aunt Edie was never really married to Uncle William —"

"That she is not his widow."

"That she is not his widow. He has been to see Hugh to make these threats."

"But making threats won't amount to anything. Anybody can make threats."

"Well, but he says he will go to law over it."

"He'll have to prove what he says. That sounds to me like a tall order. What does Hugh say?"

"I've talked to Hugh. Really, Nell, Hugh puts me out of

patience. He's such a dunce sometimes. He speaks to me as if I were Aunt Edie. I have to pull him up short and remind him I'm not so behind the times. Then he gets sulky. But I've been able to get most of the details."

"Surely this statement about your aunt's marriage is nonsense. It is outrageous! What can the man mean?"

"He claims that when Uncle William married Aunt Edie, his first wife, this man's mother, was still alive. So Uncle William was a bigamist."

"The important thing is, can he prove it?"

"I don't know. Nobody knows much about Uncle William's early life. The man claims to have proof. I suppose he would have to present that proof to a court."

"Documents, I suppose? I can tell you that it is pretty difficult to produce documents of that sort for California fifty years ago. They're likely to be forgeries."

"That is what Hugh says. Hugh thinks Aunt Edie has been frightened by this man and that she is ready to give in to his demands just to avoid notoriety—that this is blackmail. It is true that Aunt Edie is suffering tortures over the newspaper accounts. In her world no decent woman is ever mentioned in a newspaper—unless it is to describe her dress at her wedding or something of the sort."

"But surely she would not hand the whole estate over to him just because she doesn't want to be mentioned in the papers!"

"Of course not. I don't suppose she could if she wanted to. But she has some idea that, if what the man says is true, he should have a share."

"But he says he wants it all."

"Hugh says that is just a way of bargaining. He can be bought off with much less. He thinks the man is making this outrageous claim as a prelude to compromising on some sort of settlement. He says he is sure the man has no delusions about winning his case in court, that he is bluffing. He just wants to frighten us. And he has succeeded with Aunt Edie."

"Well, then, let him bluff away."

"Yes, but, you see, Hugh is wrong about Aunt Edie. She really does have scruples about doing the man out of his birthright, if he is who he says he is. If he is Uncle William's son, he should share in the estate. So it is not just that she is frightened.

She really thinks she should give him a fair hearing."

"Even though he is vile enough to accuse her of not being a properly married woman, even though he wants to strip her of her own self respect. Really, Daisy!"

They rode on for a while before Daisy replied. A cab crossed in front of them at a street intersection and they maneuvered around the horse.

"You know, Nell, the fact is—and I've just realized this—Aunt Edie isn't as unaware of Uncle William's true character as she has always made out. I wonder about that. While he was alive, she never showed that she thought he was anything but a completely honorable man. She acted as if she had never heard of the stories everybody tells about him. But now she has as much as told me that she knows he could be very unjust, that he did things that were not honorable, that he was ruthless with people who stood in his way, regardless of their rights. This is the reason she is in doubt about this man who claims he is Uncle William's son."

"Do you mean that she contemplates making some sort of private arrangement with this rogue? Daisy, that would never do. He would just be encouraged to blackmail her further."

"That is what Hugh says. He insists we must treat the man as an outlaw." They wheeled along for another block. Then Daisy said, "Nell, this man comes from California. That is, he says he was born there and his mother lived there till she died. Do you suppose you could find out something about him from people you know there or your parents do?"

Nell broke into merry laughter. "Oh, Daisy! You Easterners! I wouldn't know anybody who would know anything about such a creature—some rascal from the mining camps! California is a very big place—a pretty empty place still. We've got a lot of shady characters. After all, think of all the scalawags that went out there to find gold and silver—like the Colonel. But my parents would not have anything to do with such people."

"Don't make fun of me, Nell. I just thought maybe your father could find out something about the Colonel's first wife— if she really did exist."

Nell said more soberly. "I don't think so. From what I understand, when the Colonel left California he was a pretty obscure character. Nobody would take any notice of whether he was married or not—just another mining camp itinerant. And afterwards he was able to conceal the details of his early life, from what the newspapers say. They say he has even outlived most of his enemies."

Daisy did not reply. They had reached the tennis courts now and their attention was taken up with getting ready to play. Nell was aware that Daisy's thoughts were not altogether on her game. She was usually the better player, making use of her greater adroitness to offset Nell's greater strength and reach. Today Nell won without difficulty.

At the end of the first set they stopped for a rest. There was a bench in the shade of a plane tree in a quiet corner of the court and they sat down to cool off.

Nell said, noting the brooding look on Daisy's face, "You must do your best, darling, to persuade your aunt to give up this idea of hers. It is not reasonable."

Daisy was slow to reply. "I've told you that she is very hard to budge when she becomes convinced of something like this." Daisy paused for a moment, the brooding look on her face growing more marked. "It would be easier for me if I didn't sympathize with her."

"Sympathize! Daisy, you can't be so foolish! You don't for a moment think she can be right."

"Oh, I don't mean about the man. I saw him. He glared at me when he came out of the room after talking to Aunt Edie. I've never seen such a dreadful look on anybody's face." Daisy shivered. "It was as if he hated me personally. I suppose he just hates the house and everybody in it because it isn't his. No, that's not what I mean. I do think he may be crazy—a little crazy. People do get crazy when they become obsessed with something, don't they?"

"Yes, they do. That's all the more reason not to have anything to do with him. He sounds really dangerous."

Daisy nodded. "Yes. Hugh says the same thing. But what I am talking about is something else. Nell, I know what it is to wrestle with something that is on your conscience—to have to decide what is really right and wrong. That is what is bothering

Aunt Edie. She can't convince herself what the right thing to do is. She would rather be deceived by this man than take something away from him that is rightfully his."

"That can't possibly be, since he is a thief."

"But she doesn't know for sure. We all don't. Except, perhaps, Madame Aurora."

"Madame Aurora? You mean, she can look into a crystal ball or whatever it is she does to learn the truth?"

"No, of course not. I mean, she was with Uncle William a lot. Aunt Edie says that the only reason he made a will at all was because she persuaded him to—whatever Hugh may think. I think he may have told her the truth."

"Oh. Why doesn't your aunt consult her, then?"

Daisy was silent for a moment, drawing a pattern in the dust at her feet with the handle of her racquet. "I don't know how much Aunt Edie confides in Madame Aurora. You see, Nell, there is something deeper involved. I know—though Aunt Edie probably doesn't know that I know—that she is uneasy—has always been uneasy about having married Uncle William. Oh, the reasons she did it are all perfectly all right. If she had refused him, everybody would have said she was out of her mind. And you can say it was a very good bargain. He wanted to marry a lady and be respectable and she needed a husband and money. But I know that it has been on her conscience that she made that bargain. If she had loved him, if he had been the sort of man she had always expected to marry, it would have been different. But this was a pretty cold-blooded affair. Uncle William never made any bones about it. And he lived up to his side. So she tried to pretend, all the time he was alive, that he meant more to her than he did, that he was a different kind of man who was just maligned by his enemies and other envious people. But now it is hard to shut your eyes to what Uncle William was and did. And she is overwhelmed by the whole thing. She can't bring herself to face people when she knows what's in their minds, what they have been reading in the papers. I don't blame her. I'm just so sorry that she has to feel all this now." Daisy relapsed into silent brooding.

Nell, knowing this side of Daisy, did not say anything but

watched her with sympathy. This was a Daisy she had come to recognize, even if she did not understand her. Sometimes when Daisy was unusually quiet—she was never very talkative—she had come to realize that Daisy was examining her own motives, her own actions, the moral quality of what she did. Daisy, who seemed so even-tempered, so compliant with the mood of her companions, so ready to fit in with someone else's opinions, was in reality a person of strong principles. She rarely brought them forward into anyone's view. What she really thought about anything was often a mystery even to Nell.

Two white-clad young men, spying them, came over to talk. Nell recognized them as frequent visitors to Mrs. Head's draw-ingroom, attracted by Daisy. Outwardly Daisy lost her moodi-ness and entered into the lighthearted banter with which they showed their admiration of her. Come and have some lemonade in the club, they said. The father of one of them was a member.

∿ ∿ ∿ ∿ ∿

That afternoon they were fortunate enough to be able to finish the afternoon in Nell's room. The Sunday quiet pervaded the boardinghouse. They threw off their clothes to gain the transient coolness of a little breeze that came in the window. Holding each other in their arms, they allowed the pressure of the outside world to recede. Through the months that first spontaneous, irresistible reaching out for each other's body had matured, as their love sensitized them to the touch of each other's hands. Nell had learned the tender places of Daisy's magically smooth-skinned body, the gentle, deliberate stroking that brought her sometimes reluctant desire to the surface. Her own was always more ready, more eager. She had grown used to waiting, holding back her own impatience, for Daisy's tautness to relax into a dreamy welcome.

But now Nell was aware that there was still some part of Daisy withdrawing from her. Suddenly impatient, she asked, "Daisy, what is the matter? Are you worrying about what we are doing? Do you think this is something for which you will be punished?"

Daisy's half-lax body stiffened under her hands. "Wrong? What do you mean by wrong?"

"You were talking about your aunt. You said you understood how she could be unhappy because she could not decide what was right, that she worried about what was wrong. Are you that way? You said you sympathized with her. Are you unhappy because you and I are here together, joined this way, satisfying each other's desire?"

Daisy sank back softly into her arms. "Oh, no. Nothing I do with you is wrong. Are you upset because you think my religion would get in the way? Well, don't be, because I know when I am doing wrong and I've never felt that way about you and me."

Well, sometimes, when you don't seem to be altogether here with me, I wonder. You go to church every Sunday. I thought —"

"Shush. I don't accept anyone's idea of what is wrong but my own. I have my own understanding of what God requires of me and He does not require that I should deny you. If I've made a mistake, I'm ready to pay for it. You should always be ready to take the consequences of what you do, you know."

"Does that mean that you think you must pay for what we are doing? Is that why you hold back sometimes?"

Daisy raised herself to lean over her and look down into her face. Nell saw an odd little smile on her face. "Is that what you think about me? No. I don't think what we do here in bed is wrong. We are given the capacity to love. We should not deny it, if it brings harm to no one else, if it does not infringe on any bond we have otherwise undertaken. I have never undertaken any bond with anyone except you, Nell, nor will I ever. There is no substitute for the way we express our love. It is not a sin. It cannot be. But, my darling, you cannot go through life without earning your right to behave as you think you should. It is not something that is handed to you. And you cannot pretend that you give the responsibility for what you do over to someone else, you can't abdicate your responsibility, saying, I won't do this because someone or some institution says I may not."

Nell looked up into the blue eyes hovering above her. "Daisy, I couldn't love anyone else the way I love you. It seems so terrible that we cannot be openly what we are, cannot show our love for each other the way men and women can. It is a dreadful thing that we must hide as if what we do is something sordid, unhealthy. By some miracle, I found you. When I look back now, I see that I thought I was so well-off, with a career I liked and being as independent as I am, but now I know there was a hollow place in the middle of my life, which I was trying to fill up with busy, worldly things. Oh, Daisy, suppose we had not met!"

Daisy subsided on top of her and murmured into her ear, "We don't have to conjure up horrors."

Nell relaxed to welcome the weight of her body. You don't set out to think of these things, she thought, searching gently around Daisy's smooth flanks. Love can teach you a great deal which you can learn so effortlessly. It would be possible to go through these motions with someone else. She supposed some married couples did, hiding their sensuality behind the smooth mask of propriety. But then it would be a mechanical thing. Only Daisy's body, Daisy's hands, Daisy's breath hot on her cheek, could rouse this warmth of desire that came as if by itself. She tightened her arms around Daisy.

After a while Daisy with a sigh rolled away from her and lay gazing at the ceiling. "If we could just go on like this, without thinking of anybody else. These are such brief moments, when I can think just about you. It is really very hard, Nell, to love you like this, especially when I know you're impatient because we are so seldom together alone. But you must make do, just as I do."

Nell leaned over her, kissing her cheeks, her eyes, joining her mouth to hers. "Oh, darling, I'm just unbelievably fortunate to have found you! I'm not complaining, really. How can I?"

They clasped each other again in a close embrace. Then abruptly Daisy sat up. "It's almost five o'clock. We'll have to get up. Aunt Edie will be looking for me."

She got up from the bed and stood beside it, her arms raised to sweep her heavy hair up into a bun on top of her head. Nell seized her and fondled her generous breasts, kissing her nipples. Daisy, laughing, pulled her off the bed.

They dressed quickly. Nell was aware that in the few minutes since they had ceased to caress each other, Daisy's anxiety had returned. Her kisses were absentminded when Nell tried to revive their playfulness.

"Not now, honey," Daisy said, gently pushing her hands away. I've got to think about Aunt Edie. I must try to think of some way to reassure her."

Nell helped her fasten her dress. Watching Daisy's face she pondered whether to say what was in her mind. At last she decided.

"You know, there is someone I think could help."

Daisy looked at her, waiting for her to explain.

"I know you'll probably object, because you don't like her. But I do think she might help. I mean Madame Aurora."

Daisy did not show surprise. "I don't think I want to ask her. I am suspicious of her."

"Why? I know you think that she is a charlatan, that she is just out to make money by working on people's fears. But I've come to believe that she is not that, that she does have some sort of gift. Miss Beaufort thinks so, and she's nobody's fool."

A faint smile appeared on Daisy's face. "Isn't Miss Beaufort what the lawyers call a prejudiced witness? She would hardly criticize her friend to you, would she?" Daisy grew more serious. "I am uneasy because she has had such a lot of influence on Aunt Edie—and on Uncle William. I suspect someone who is so successful at getting people to eat out of her hand."

"She hasn't done your aunt any harm. In fact, she has done her a very good turn, if it is true that she persuaded your uncle to make a will when he would listen to no one else. And not only that, but a will leaving everything to your aunt. It looks as if you ought to be grateful to her."

"You mean, without her, Aunt Edie and I might be turned into the street as paupers. Well, I could always rescue us by marrying Hugh."

"Daisy." The hurt sounded in Nell's voice.

Daisy put her arms around her. "Oh, it's only a joke!"

"It's too close to being possible to be funny."

Daisy sighed. "I know you don't like jokes like that. I suppose I don't either."

"Anyway," said Nell. "Madame Aurora still comes to see your aunt often, doesn't she?"

Daisy was thoughtful. "As a matter of fact, I don't believe she has come to the house for some time. She used to come almost every day. Aunt Edie couldn't live without her. But lately—I've wondered about that, in the back of my mind. You know, Aunt Edie won't see anybody. She seems to be too ashamed to want to face people. Not even Madame Aurora."

"Well, then, you had better suggest that your aunt send for her. Maybe you could talk to her privately, about what is worrying you about your aunt."

Daisy looked at her closely and said ironically, "That really would be inviting her in, wouldn't it? I've no doubt she would take over. And then if it turns out that she is victimizing Aunt Edie —"

"Daisy, I don't really think so. She has been a good friend to your aunt."

Daisy brooded. "You see Madame Aurora often, don't you?"

"No. But I see Miss Beaufort often. She works at the Library every day. She's working on her second book, you know, the one that is to outshine her famous first one. Oh, I do hope she is able to finish it and get the recognition that was denied her before. Daisy, it stands to reason that Madame Aurora must be an unusual woman to be Miss Beaufort's companion for so many years. You mustn't be prejudiced against her."

"Oh, perhaps I'm not being reasonable. But sometimes I wonder if I am the only one who is skeptical. You should hear Aunt Edie's friends. They speak of Madame Aurora as the wonder of the age. She is practically a goddess. They all have some story to tell about her, how she has saved them from disaster by predicting the future, or solved some terrible problem with her advice. They really do believe in her. She must have a remarkable power of persuasion."

"She does, Daisy. She allowed me to join one of the parties of people who gather at her house every so often. You remember the house, where we went to have tea with her and Miss Beaufort? Well, the room in front, which we did not see that afternoon, is fitted up for her parlor. That's where these meetings are held and she sees people privately there, too."

"Well, what's it like? Full of stuffed owls and spectral lights flitting about? Does she go in for table turning and ghostly rappings?"

"No, she does not. She doesn't believe in that sort of thing any more than you do. Her ideas are different. She says we all have the capacity to govern the course of our lives, if we can learn to understand the forces that govern the world. I'm not sure I follow everything she has to say but she isn't a crazy woman or a charlatan. She has a very logical mind. Do talk to her, Daisy."

"Well, I'll see. But she is such a funny looking creature."

"You'll forget that when you talk to her."

CHAPTER SIXTEEN

Mrs. Head hurried across the Turkey carpet. "Oh, Madame Aurora, how relieved I am to have you here!"

Hannah gave her a keen glance and let her lead the way across to the cluster of chairs where they usually sat.

For a moment Mrs. Head's social aplomb seemed to desert her and she was silent. But then she said, "I have missed your visits so much. Yet I hesitated to ask you to come."

"And why?"

Mrs. Head's hands fluttered for a moment. "I have been so much discomfited by—by—this dreadful publicity about William. I have not wanted to see anyone. It is painful to me to have—all this talk—by all sorts of people — It is as if I have been stripped of all privacy—a dreadful business —"

Her eyes filled with tears and she dabbed at them with a lace handkerchief. Hannah said soothingly. "I quite understand. It is a very trying time for you. And a situation into which you have been pitched without warning. Dear Mrs. Head, you know that you can always call upon me if there is any comfort I can give you."

Mrs. Head wept quietly for a moment. "Yes, yes, I know I have your support. But for a while I have been stunned. This is a trial I never envisioned."

Hannah said softly, "We must all face things sometimes that are beyond our experience. This will pass. Oh, I am afraid that people will talk about the Colonel and his affairs for years. After all, his estate is one of the largest ever recorded in this country and money—large masses of money—has a fascination for the average person. But that is something that you must accustom yourself to. You must learn to withdraw yourself from association with this talk. It is really nothing to do with you.

Your spirit is on another plane. It is not concerned with violence, strife."

As Hannah's bell-like voice flowed on, Mrs. Head began visibly to relax. After some minutes, when Hannah had ceased to speak, she raised her head.

"Oh, Madame Aurora, what peace and balm you bring to me! If you only knew how I have suffered in these last weeks!"

"Yes, my dear lady. I was aware that you were troubled. Messengers of the spirit told me of your distress. I knew that before long you would send for me. There is a particular problem disturbing you, isn't there?"

"Oh, yes." Mrs. Head paused as if gathering her wits together. Then she began, timidly, "You have seen, haven't you, these accounts in the papers of a man who claims to be my husband's son and says that he is entitled to all his property."

Hannah nodded.

"He goes further than that. He—he accuses my husband—he declares that — "

Hannah watched her efforts to state the unwelcome fact but did not speak to help her.

"— that my marriage to William was not valid—that his first wife—the woman this man claims as his mother—was still living at the time William married me." She was overcome and raised her hand to cover her eyes.

"Dear Mrs. Head, you should not let this distress you. We should not assume that this is the truth and if it is not, then it is beneath your contempt. He will have to prove his assertions. He must present documents and establish their authenticity. I doubt very much that he can present witnesses—credible witnesses—to support his claim. He has been to see you?"

"Yes. He speaks as if he has no doubt—as if no one can have any doubt—of the truth of his statements. Oh, Madame Aurora, he frightens me!"

"Yes, of course. It is his intent to frighten you, to bully you into accepting what he says. Does he in any way resemble the Colonel?"

Mrs. Head took thought for a moment. "Really, I cannot say. He is a big man, like my husband. He is very much weathered, as if he has indeed led the life he says he has. I can believe that he has known a great deal of violence —"

"In fact, he could well be the sort of man your husband was when younger. And the documents he presents? Has he been to the lawyer, to Mr. Carson, with them?"

"Yes. Hugh tells me that it will be difficult to prove the authenticity of these documents. At the time he says his mother was married to William the records of marriages and births in California were not well kept and many have been lost since."

"There, you see. All he can do is raise a doubt. You have no reason to suppose that this man is anything other than someone who has been attracted by the newspaper accounts of the Colonel's fortune and, having learned some of the details of his early life, has made a bid for a share. I am sure Mr. Carson has received other equally unfounded claims." Hannah paused for a moment. "It would interest me considerably to know how this man learned of the Colonel's son. He did have one. He told me at one time the details of the son's death. And as you know from the statement the Colonel inserted in his will, he anticipated that someone might come forward with just the claim this man has. Most of the Colonel's early associates—all of them, I think we can say—are dead—for some years. This man must have picked up some secondhand story. Or perhaps in the past he has had dealings with the Colonel and is now seeking revenge."

Mrs. Head rested her cheek on her hand. "Yes. Hugh tells me much the same thing. I know I should not allow this imputation to trouble me so. I cannot believe that William would have deliberately deceived me. Unless he thought at the time that his first wife was dead and in fact she was still living."

"I assure you that is not the fact. The woman he married in California was dead before the events in which his son died."

Mrs. Head looked up quickly. "You are sure of that?"

"Certainly, from what the Colonel told me. There was no need for him to tell me anything but the truth."

Mrs. Head settled back in her chair and sat silent as if in thanksgiving. Hannah said nothing but waited.

Presently Mrs. Head said, "My dear Madame Aurora, I must confess something to you that is very private, very intimate—to you, who understand so well what is in my heart. It is something I cannot speak of even to my niece. When I married my husband, I knew I must accept him for what he was. I did not know a great deal about him. He refused to discuss his previous life with me. He said I must take him as he was and I did. It became my duty then to be loyal to him in every way, to close my ears to criticism of him, to deny all knowledge of the rumors about him that reached even me before our marriage. I—I did what I believe most women would have done in my place—refused to see what I did not want to see or listen to what might disturb my tranquility. I knew also that I must walk very carefully with him—not to arouse his anger or his vindictiveness—oh, yes, I was well aware that he would not hesitate to crush me as he would anyone else whom he suspected of disloyalty to him. And I know this deliberate choice of attitude of mine has earned me the reputation of being very naive, very ignorant of reality. But, dear Madame Aurora, I am not blind. I am not such a fool as many believe me."

"I would never believe you that, dear friend," Hannah murmured.

"Ah, I know how kind you are! To the outward eye it appears that I have had very good fortune, without having to pay for it in any way. That is not so. There has been a weight on me all these years."

Hannah looked at her squarely. "I have known that you have carried a weight for many years, from the first time I met you. But after all, as you say, your decision to accept the Colonel's offer of marriage is nothing more than would have been expected of any woman in your position."

"But, you see, though I tell myself that and though others assure me of the same thing, I feel that I have betrayed myself. I do not cast aspersions on William. He has gone to his reward and he must bear the consequences of his actions himself. He was, within the limits I have indicated, a good husband to me. I do not complain of him. It is myself who am to blame. If I had felt for him any true fondness, if I had loved him in spite of what I knew of his character, then I would not be troubled. I might have known that I had made a mistake, but it was not a mistake of conscience. Oh, do you understand me?"

She turned her eyes beseechingly on Hannah, "Of course, of

course. But you chastise yourself too much. He had his reasons for marrying you, which were just as calculated as your own. And he understood yours. He was under no illusions. The Colonel, you know, could not bear to think that there was any part of the world that he could not conquer. He conquered the financial world. He was a hidden power in the political world. He was determined that he would conquer the world that always rejected him, the world you represented. Through you, he had at least the outward semblance of success. No, you should not distress yourself so. He was not troubled in the least by your private opinion of him. He wanted only your public acceptance."

Mrs. Head shrank back in her chair. "How I wish I could take your advice to heart. What has tormented me in these last weeks is the feeling that now I find my happiness, which is based on something false, is destroyed by —"

She faltered, and Hannah supplied for her, "You fear that this man's appearance represents in fact a retribution that you must make. That is very wrong, my dear friend. That is not what would be required of you under any just system of spiritual values."

She waited to see what effect her statements had. Mrs. Head seemed intent on her own line of thought. "Now that William is dead, I must not do or say anything in disparagement of him. Nevertheless, I feel that I must act more for myself. I owe no one else the obedience I did to him as his wife." Mrs. Head grew more agitated as she spoke. "I feel very strongly that I must not be party to some grave injustice which William may have committed. What if this man is indeed his son, in spite of all that William himself said to you? This is something that must be cleared up."

Hannah spoke sharply. "There has been no injustice. The Colonel gave me the full account of his son's death. It is not a nice story. I do not wish to repeat it, if it is at all possible to avoid that. I tell you plainly that the Colonel's son is dead, violently dead, the result of treachery against his father. This man cannot possibly be that son. He is, I am sure, a violent and dangerous criminal. It would be folly for you to have anything further to do with him."

Mrs. Head looked uncertain, as if she wished she could surrender her own intransigeance and succumb to the other woman's authority, yet hung back. "You are quite sure of this?"

The faintest smile appeared on Hannah's face. Do I ever, dear Mrs. Head, assert something I am not sure of?"

"Oh, no! No! I meant no disparagement. It is merely that —"

As she hesitated, Hannah supplied, "It seems too easy a solution to your dilemma. That's it, isn't it? Well, this time you can accept the easier path. You have no duty towards this man. I also warn you, with all the strength I can, that you are in danger from him—physical danger, I mean. I see a cloud of elemental force about him, a primitive savagery, ungoverned energy." She passed a hand over her eyes. "I cannot see clearly through that cloud. It is dense and menacing."

Mrs. Head sat poised in her chair, her eyes fixed on Hannah, half-mesmerized by the intensity of feeling in Hannah's voice. "My husband told you a great deal about himself, I know. Did he give you any details about his son's death?"

"I have told you he gave me a full account. I do not think that the Colonel would wish me to relate to you what he told me. Nor to anyone else, for that matter. But I can say in general terms that this episode occurred in South America twenty-five years ago. His son allied himself with his father's enemies—those were lawless times in wild country. I need not tell you more, because I think you know how implacable your husband could be when he thought he was betrayed."

Mrs. Head sat silent, as if paralyzed by the force of what she said. Hannah went on. "I don't think it wise for me to dwell on this. Please accept what I say and ease your mind."

"Yes, I shall try to do that." She settled back in her chair with a little sigh.

"You must remember that we mortals are made of two elements—the spirit and the body. When the body dies, the spirit lives on and, freed from the body, grows in wisdom and grace. The realm of the spirit is beyond our cognizance. We can contribute to the wellbeing of the spirit by our actions and good intentions while we live in our bodies. Well developed spirits endow us with clear, confident thoughts while we live on this earth, which is but a speck in the universe. But there are people whose spirits have received little care or consideration. They are dominated by ideas of violence. They tend to disrupt those with whom they have dealings, especially those who are not on the alert. The cloud of thoughts that surround such people can be seen and felt by astute, trained minds. People in the old days spoke of demons. People like this man with whom you are dealing are demons, in this sense. There is an attraction between like spirits. You know that your husband lived a life of violence. Through this attraction, this man has been led to attempt to wrest from you what your husband acquired through violent means. I feel a menace directed toward you from him. You must recognize him as a dangerous man. You must take care how you deal with him. You must give the essential grace of your own nature the opportunity to combat this menace—to send it away from you."

Mrs. Head sat bowed in her chair. "Yes, yes, dear Madame Aurora. I shall try to follow your advice." She reached out and took Hannah's hand. "Oh, don't desert me! I feel you are the only one on whom I can depend."

"Of course, of course," Hannah said soothingly.

∿ ∿ ∿ ∿ ∿

Daisy stood in the long window that lighted the vestibule, waiting. Madame Aurora had been with her aunt for more than an hour. She could have joined them. Aunt Edie had not told the servant that she was not to be disturbed. But Daisy hoped for a private moment.

Then she heard the voices of the two women. Her aunt came out of the drawingroom first. It was obvious to Daisy that she was distraught and her goodbye to Madame Aurora was brief as she turned away at once and went up the stairs. She heard her aunt say as she did so, "Dear Madame Aurora, I shall hope to see you tommorrow," and the portly woman standing at the foot of the stairs murmured, "Certainly."

Daisy watched as Madame Aurora stood looking up the stairs after her aunt. Then she turned with a swift swing of her full skirts. She stopped abruptly on her way to the front door when she saw Daisy. She stood still, waiting, without speaking.

Daisy stepped forward and said resolutely, "Madame Aurora, may I talk to you?"

The pale, enigmatic eyes widened in a brief response. The heavy woman stood perfectly still, her hands folded. She said then, "Of course. I believe I know what you want to speak about. You are troubled about your aunt. You have reason to be."

Daisy looked at her with a slight frown. "She depends on you very much. I am glad you have come to see her again."

"In the past you have not approved of my visits, have you?"

Daisy blushed. "I —"

"Never mind. We need not talk about that. The important thing is that your aunt is greatly distressed—about all the publicity about your uncle's death—about this man who has come forward as a claimant to the estate."

"Yes. I am sorry, Madame Aurora. I realize now that you are a very good friend to Aunt Edie. Please forgive me. She is upset and I don't think she is able just now to think straight about the situation. Has she told you that she feels that she must give the man the benefit of the doubt? Just in case there is some truth in what he says?"

Madame Aurora nodded. The necklaces around her neck twinkled in the subdued light.

"I am sure he is an imposter. I have only seen him once, but I'm scared of him."

"Yes, he is an imposter and a very bold one. You are right to be apprehensive. I have tried to impress on your aunt that she must not have any more dealings with him." She paused for a moment and looked full at Daisy. "I have access to powers that are able to give me absolute knowledge of his nature, his intentions."

She watched as Daisy absorbed these remarks. But Daisy passed by what she said. "Uncle William must have told you many things that he never spoke of to anyone else. So I am sure he told you something about this man. He never told Aunt Edie about his life before he married her."

"After all, he must have felt that there are many things in the world that a lady like your aunt would not understand."

That's delicately put, thought Daisy. "I expect she didn't want to know about them. I'm afraid Aunt Edie thinks that what you don't know can't hurt you. That is dangerous, isn't it?"

"It is an unwise assumption. But it is understandable that your aunt should want to pass over some things about her marriage. Now, however, the world at large is talking about the Colonel and it is difficult to ignore things that have till now been safely buried."

"It's like burying your head in the sand. I hate that. I think you should always look things in the eye—not try to deceive yourself, to make yourself believe something because it is more comfortable to do so."

Madame Aurora said in a kindly voice, "You are a young woman. You have grown up in a freer world than your aunt's. You must be sympathetic to her."

Daisy said vehemently, "Of course I'm sympathetic to her! That is why I told her that she should ask you to come and see her."

Madame Aurora's light eyes widened briefly. "Ah, that was it! Well, I believe it has been to her advantage to have me here. I have spent the last hour assuring her that this man cannot possibly be the Colonel's son, that she should abandon any idea of giving in to him."

Daisy exhaled a long breath. "I am very grateful to you. She won't listen to me. Oh, I don't mean that, exactly, but she is not convinced by anything I say. I think she has more confidence in you. I am glad to have talked to you."

Madame Aurora bowed her head and turned to go toward the door. "May I give you one bit of encouragement? I can assure you that this man will not succeed in what he is doing. But he is dangerous. That you must remember."

Daisy gazed at her for a moment. "I'm sorry that I don't believe in prophecy."

Madame Aurora gave a little shrug and walked away.

∿ ∿ ∿ ∿ ∿

"The problem is," said Hannah, impatiently pushing away

her dinner plate, "that girl has no real confidence in me. She persuaded her aunt to send for me because she is genuinely concerned about her and knows that I have gained a certain ascendancy over her—for my own benefit, of course. She has come to respect me but she does not like me."

"All very understandable, my love," said Elizabeth, picking delicately at the chicken that remained on her plate. "You know, of course, that wherever there are large amounts of money, there are suspicious relatives."

"Of course. But she is an intelligent girl. I think she is capable of taking a broader view—if it were not for the fact that the conventions of her religious faith have hampered her."

"Really!" Elizabeth looked up in surprise. "But how is this, dear heart? I understand from Nell that Daisy *is* quite religious, unusually so for a young woman. But you've sometimes told me that truly religious people are easier to reach. They are naturally more open to the spiritual view of things."

"That is not what I meant. Yes, Daisy may well be genuinely religious—that is, spiritual values count more with her than material. But the formalities of her church cause her to close her eyes to the pervasiveness of spiritual beliefs. You're familiar with that, Liz. You've talked often enough of the strait jacket into which churches force their communicants. Don't you remember how you felt about that back in the days when you were teaching in schools where we were required to observe the formalities of religious services regardless of our own wishes?"

"Of course I remember, love. You mean that Daisy refuses to give any credence to your ideas because she wears the blinders of her traditional beliefs. That, as you know, was always the basis for my aversion to churchly people—the narrowness of mind they cultivate. However, I do wonder about Daisy. She seems a very honest person, from what Nell tells me, and by no means of limited outlook."

Hannah frowned. "I know that to be so. No one will ever persuade Daisy to pretend what she does not believe. Nor will she hesitate to tell you when she disagrees with you."

"That is a refreshing thing, my love, though apt sometimes to be wounding."

"Ah, Liz, I know you think my feelings are hurt because of her attitude towards me. But there is more to it than that. I do have a special friendship with Mrs. Head. She depends upon me because she feels I am the only person in whom she can confide. I am truly her friend."

"But you find it hard to convince Daisy of this."

"I think now Daisy accepts the fact that I am not going to hurt or deceive her aunt. She is devoted to her, but she sees the weaknesses of Mrs. Head's character. She realized that her aunt is unhappy now because she was not true to her own nature in the past, when she accepted the Colonel as her husband, for mercenary reasons."

"But, my love, she did only what women have been trained to do for centuries—achieve respect and comfort for themselves by attracting the interest of a suitable man. I'm sure everyone in her circle at the time applauded what she did—and envied her her chance."

"Ah, yes—a suitable man. That's the crux of the matter, I suppose. The Colonel was not the sort of man Mrs. Head would as a young woman consider a suitable man. There are natures more scrupulous than most, who suffer a form of self-loathing for doing something that, though it may be applauded by others, violates their own basic principles. Mrs. Head is in a special dilemma. Her married life has been reasonably happy, at least on the surface. She has no complaint about how she has been treated. But it had an uneasy foundation. She had ever to be watchful that she did not provoke her husband into showing the side of him that she did not wish to see, that would remind her that she had deliberately closed her eyes to his true character. And of course now part of her distress is a feeling of guilt at her relief at the fact that he is dead. You cannot say that money cures everything so far as Mrs. Head is concerned." Hannah paused and Elizabeth saw in her face the distaste she felt. "How can a woman spend a lifetime in such subservience?"

"Dear love, you cannot compare the Mrs. Heads of this world to you and me."

Hannah sighed. "Yes. You see the problem, though, don't you, Liz? Only Daisy and I understand Mrs. Head's inner struggle. Yet we cannot be true friends."

"Cannot, love?"

"She is so much the product of her world."

Elizabeth's smile was faintly ironic. "You forget Nell, don't you, dear heart? Their friendship is not platonic."

Hannah cast her a surprised look. "Has Nell —?"

"Oh, no. Nell would be too much embarrassed—and cautious—to speak of such a thing, even to me. But Nell is transparent. She cannot conceal her ardor. It glows in her eyes when she speaks of Daisy. And Daisy does not strike me as being a cool young miss, for all her fashionable clothes and lady-like manners. I think her too full-blooded to follow entirely a decorous path through life. And as you know, my love, I've had considerable experience in teaching girls."

CHAPTER SEVENTEEN

For the rest of the summer the newspapers were filled with the affair of the Colonel's will. It was a subject that absorbed many people, if only because of the vast sums of money in his estate. There was a great deal of confusion concerning his holdings in siver mines, railroad stocks, ranches in the far west, business connections outside the country. Many men who had had dealings with him for the first time, now that he was dead discovered that what they knew of his affairs was only a fragment in a great puzzle. It would be years, the lawyers said, before all these matters could be untangled.

And on top of that was the question of the challenge to his widow's right to inherit the whole of this imperfectly catalogued wealth—and even to her right to be called his widow. The challenger threatened court action. He said he would attack the will as having been written under undue influence. He would prove that Mrs. Head was never legally married to the Colonel. He even stated that he would name the seer, Madame Aurora, as the person who had brought influence to bear. This in itself was a prime topic of gossip. She was well-known. Her psychic powers had always been the subject for a lot of debate. Now it would be seen just what the truth was.

One Sunday afternoon Hugh Carson came to the Sixteenth Street house to see Mrs. Head. He wanted, he said, to bring her up-to-date on the progress of affairs. She received him in the drawingroom, as usual. She was, he noticed, looking rather worn and sad. He was sorry for that, but at least she had ceased, in the last few days, to talk about the possibility that this impostor had some basis for his claims. He did not know why she had given up the idea—or whether she had in fact done so. But he was uneasy about this sudden abandonment of a fixed idea.

They talked for a while about some of the latest reports of

the accountants and officers of several of the Colonel's companies. Or rather, he related these to her, without confidence that she understood in the least what he was saying. More than once he had reflected that possibly her lack of concern about the great wealth that was now hers alone arose simply from the fact that she did not grasp its magnitude or the power it gave her. Now her responses were low-voiced, as if it was an effort for her to speak at all. The panels of stained glass that trimmed the big windows glowed and threw a pattern in color into the room. He had never liked them. Often a patch of red or green would light upon someone's face, erasing personality and creating a grotesque mask.

Finally he said to her, "This man who is threatening us —" he used the "we" and "us" when he talked to her, with a vague feeling that in this way he was able to reassure her, that she was not alone, that he shared the burdens placed upon her — "I'm very much inclined to think that he is not acting alone. Probably he has accomplices—others who are in this game with him, to share the spoils. He is certainly not the Colonel's son."

Mrs. Head contemplated him for a moment. "Madame Aurora has convinced me that he is not William's son. She tells me that William described to her in detail when and how his son died, years ago, in South America."

Hugh looked at her alertly, like a dog picking up a scent. "Is she prepared to state this in court?"

Mrs. Head stared at him, astonished. "Madame Aurora? Would she be required to speak in court?"

"Well, from what you have just told me, it looks as if she would be the best witness we shall have to refute this fellow's claims. I am afraid we must be prepared to treat this attack as a serious matter, however flimsy we think his allegations are. He came to see me, to tell me he is instituting suit. I am inclined to believe that he is not alone in this. He spoke as if he is acting alone, but he seems to be such a rough character, a real ignoramus, which makes the think he has been hired by some of the Colonel's enemies who have armed him with information and documents. If this is the case, there is no telling how many public officials and men in important business concerns they have bribed and intimidated into helping them. He is a cat's-paw, I believe for such a combine.''

Mrs. Head looked up at him in horror. "Oh, Hugh? How can that be?''

Hugh said firmly, as if admonishing a fearful child, "Dear Mrs. Head, we're sitting on a powderkeg, really. You must realize that the Colonel's estate is so huge that it arouses the cupidity of some very greedy men. They will not be satisfied to let you inherit it all. Some of them will go to court on all kinds of pretexts—I have been served notice of a number of suits already. That is legitimate. Some of them may have a good case. The Colonel's affairs are so complex that there may be legitimate claims relating to some aspects of his holdings. Only time and the courts will tell. But this man is another matter. We have to think of the worst aspects of the situation so that we are not taken by surprise. I thought first that this was a simple case of blackmail—that this man intended to frighten us into paying him off with a sum of money to avoid publicity. Now I think there is more to it.''

Mrs. Head sat silent. He waited patiently, aware that she was probably bewildered by the picture he presented. Presently a sound caused him to look over his shoulder across the big room. Daisy was walking towards them. She came to a stop by another of the tallbacked chairs and leaned on on its back. She said nothing.

He turned back to Mrs. Head. "You see the importance of Madame Aurora's statements.''

Daisy exclaimed, "Madame Aurora! What has she got to do with this?''

"Your aunt has just told me that she declares that the Colonel told her about his son—the details of his death. She can give us information about the date of his first wife's death. I want to have her in court, when this fellow's suit is heard.''

Daisy looked at him in alarm. "Good lord, Hugh! Don't you realize what that would mean? Absolutely everybody would be in an uproar! Don't you realize what a notorious person she is? We would lose every shred of privacy.''

Hugh, annoyed at the chiding note in her voice, snapped, "That would be better than losing the estate, wouldn't it?''

Daisy looked at him soberly. "There can't be any chance of that, can it? Not from this man's claims?''

"No, I can't say I seriously think he has a leg to stand on. But I won't have my hands tied. If I say she has to come on the witness stand, she'll have to. I'll have her subpoened."

This time Mrs. Head exclaimed in horror, "Hugh! This is dreadful! You cannot treat Madame Aurora like that."

"I? It's not I who have created this situation." He paused for a moment. "Besides, I don't think she would mind it at all. She is used to being in the public eye."

Mrs. Head stared at him in anger. Daisy thrust in. "Hugh, I think you are going too far. I don't think she will help you if you try to bully her."

"She'll certainly do what she can to help your aunt, if she is really her friend. Don't you realize that this man is making three serious allegations. One, that he is the Colonel's son. Two, that your aunt cannot inherit the estate as the Colonel's widow —" he hurried by this without a glance at Mrs. Head— "and three, that the will was made under undue influence and the person who used that influence was Madame Aurora, at your aunt's behest. I tell you, we can't avoid publicity. I have seen the papers he is filing. What we must do is scotch his attack at the very beginning and the best way to do that is to have Madame Aurora testify to what the Colonel told her."

Daisy protested. "But Madame Aurora is not mentioned in the will. She does not benefit by it."

Hugh smiled mirthlessly. "So what does that imply? According to this fellow? That she acted on Mrs. Head's behalf, in the expectation that she would be rewarded by Mrs. Head."

The big room echoed with silence. After a while Hugh said in a quieter voice. "I'm real sorry, Mrs. Head, to have to put it all so baldly. But there it is. Do you think I can get an interview with Madame Aurora? Perhaps if I can lay the matter out to her, she will see that she must help us."

Daisy looked at her aunt. "Do you think she will see Hugh, Aunt Edie?"

But Mrs. Head had placed her hand over her eyes and made no response. Daisy said, softly, "Aunt Edie, I think you had better go upstairs and lie down for a bit."

Her aunt made no protest when she took her arm and guided her towards the door. In the doorway she stopped and said to Daisy, "I'll be all right honey. You talk to Hugh."

Daisy stood for a moment watching her go slowly across to the big staircase and climb the steps. Then she came back to Hugh, who was briskly putting his papers back in his briefcase. "Couldn't you have been a little more careful? she upbraided him.

He was annoyed at the disdain with which she seemed to treat him these days, and yet anxious to propitiate her. "Well, I don't know what else I can do. I have got to warn her. Look here, Daisy, if she had to deal with these big lawyers in New York, they'd be a lot harder on her. It's just lucky that the Colonel liked me and put me in charge of his personal affairs."

"Yes, but don't you realize how upset she is at being talked about all the time—about all this business in the newspapers? You know, Hugh, she has old fashioned ideas about that sort of thing."

"Yes, I understand that. I sympathize with her. She is a real lady. But, Daisy, I can't change the situation. You know, don't you, that the court is likely to call your aunt as a witness. She will have to go on the stand and give her side of things."

Daisy looked at him in dismay. "Hugh, I don't really think she could do it."

"Well, if you could arrange for me to see Madame Aurora, perhaps we can forestall that."

Daisy moved away from him through a band of highly colored light.

∿ ∿ ∿ ∿ ∿

He had not known exactly what to expect—a dimly lit room with strange figures and cabalistic designs on the walls, the smell of incense. When he arrived on the doorstep, he found it perfectly ordinary—an old square house set back from the street. Inside it was pleasantly furnished, in no particular style. A young black girl took his hat and motioned him to go across the vestibule to the door of a room that took up most of the front part of the house. He knocked and a deep-toned woman's voice asked him to come in.

Again he did not know exactly what to expect as he entered

– a gypsy woman in a fringed shawl with large rings in her ears. The room was dimly lit but on the table was a lamp with a multicolored glass shade that cast a good light onto the woman who sat there. She was not young and she was portly. The dress she wore—he saw only the upper part of her body—was cut wide at the neck, with full sleeves that reached her wrists. It seemed to be of an East Indian silk in many hues. On the hand with which she gestured to him to sit down, she wore a broad ring with an opaque dark stone.

"Mr. Carson," she said, "welcome."

"Madame Aurora? Thank you." He sat down opposite her and placed his briefcase on the floor beside him. He looked up to see that her eyes, pale in the lamplight, were fixed steadily on him.

He said briskly, in an effort to establish a businesslike tone, "You are aware, I know, why I have come to see you."

She inclined her head. It was a big head with closely dressed grizzled hair. "Yes. You come as an emissary from Mrs. Head. She is threatened with a lawsuit by someone who disputes Colonel Head's will."

"Yes, that's it. We've never met, Madame Aurora, though I know you were frequently with the Colonel. We must have just missed each other many times."

This time she inclined her head but said nothing. There was something unacknowledged that nevertheless lay between them. He had always mistrusted the Colonel's choice of her as a confidante. He knew that Daisy influenced him there but there was also his own contempt for the sort of superstitious fear that led people to come to seers. He knew the Colonel had been superstitious. No doubt this woman had used that fact to influence him. But she did not seem to have gained anything for herself from it. This puzzled and baffled him. Surely there must be some private understanding between her and Mrs. Head and if so, he had better find out what it was before the whole thing came out in court.

Her voice reminded him that he had become preoccupied.

"You wish to question me about the Colonel's statements to me."

"Yes. You are named in the complaint filed by this man as the person who used undue influence in causing the Colonel to make his will."

"I am named there, yes, and this man's intention is to show that Mrs. Head, uneasy about her situation and aware that she was not legally married to the Colonel, conspired with me to persuade him to make a will in her favor."

Hugh could not resist a short laugh. "You have it in a nutshell. You are convinced that this man is an impostor?"

"Yes."

"Because of what the Colonel told you about his son?"

"Yes, and for other reasons."

"Other reasons?"

"I have, Mr. Carson, a source of information that is not available to the ordinary person. My spiritual guide keeps me apprised of many important things."

"Oh." Hugh's distaste was obvious. He said sharply, "Of course, you understand that such—information—from such a source would not be admissible in a court of law."

"I am not concerned with that."

"Oh, but we must be concerned with it, Madame Aurora. Your evidence is crucial. It was only to you that the Colonel spoke of his son. Can you give me the details? Mrs. Head has spoken of the matter only in the most general terms. Could there be any mistake about the son's identity?"

"None at all. The son went out to South America to join his father in the silver mines. He was not invited by the Colonel to come. But he did so, telling his father that he had left California because his mother had died and he thought he could do better for himself by joining his father. I am sorry to say that the Colonel had a poor opinion of the young man's capacities. The son became dissatisfied with his life there and was seduced by some of the Colonel's enemies with promises of great wealth. There was a local war going on at the time over claims to silver mines. The Colonel was always an unforgiving man. He saw to it that his enemies were wiped out in an ambush and made no effort to exclude his son from the massacre. He told me he saw his son's body after the fight and thus was assured that he would no longer have his treachery to fear. That is a pretty certain answer to claims made by this impostor, isn't it?"

Hugh was silent for a few moments, half mesmerized by the throaty timbre of Madame Aurora's voice, by the seductive quality of her manner of speaking. Finally he said, "Yes—if this statement can be established beyond a doubt. It seems to settle the question of the legality of Mrs. Head's marriage. Have you any information about the date of the death of the first wife?"

"Only that the Colonel said his son had come out to join him, leaving California because his mother had died. On her deathbed, he said, she had urged him to go and see if he could find his father and get him to help him get started in life. The Colonel was not prepared to do anything more for his son than he would do for any other young man who proved useful to him. He would not brook any disloyalty."

"A hard man. What year was this?"

"Sometime in the 'Seventies. The Colonel went to South America shortly after the Civil War."

"And he married Mrs. Head fifteen years ago—in 1883. There was no doubt that he was a widower at that time."

"None at all."

"And now," said Hugh, "we come to the specific question I have to put to you: Are you prepared to go into court and state that the Colonel said this to you?"

Madame Aurora did not answer at once. The silence in the room drew out so long that it began to affect his nerves. There was after all a peculiar atmosphere in the room. Daisy had told him more than once that he was too stolid, too immune to the less obvious influences that people and occasions might have on him. He had not questioned the truth of her observation. He had accepted the idea that he was more or less impervious to nuances of meanings and feelings. He felt that this was a strength. It preserved him from vacillation and perhaps from falling victim to deception. It kept him from being distracted from the really important things with which he had to deal. When he said this to Daisy, she had looked at him with that funny expression that he had seen on her face often, as if she doubted that he understood what she meant.

He glanced across the table. There was no sign that Madame

Aurora was about to answer his question. Normally he would have repeated it, demanded that she pay attention with a responsible reply. But he could not see her eyes now. She had leaned back in her chair. He found himself drifting off into his own thoughts again. Perhaps what Daisy meant was that there were ways of conveying meanings without the use of words. He was used to listening carefully to what people said to him, trying to judge how much credence to place in what they said, how well-informed they really were about what they were telling him, whether they were deceiving themselves into believing what they wished to believe. This was part of his growing experience as a lawyer—learning what to retain of what people put forward and what to discard. He had never considered that in such situations people might be using some less obvious method of influencing his own thought. It now occurred to him that Madame Aurora's silence, some wordless emanation from her, was having a decided effect on his response to her.

In fact, the silence in the room was not just silence. It began to have the somewhat eerie, spirit-filled quiet that he associated with church. Sometimes he went to communion with Daisy early on a Sunday morning. He felt little attraction to religious contemplation. Mysticism, religious ecstasy in any degree rather put him off. He mistrusted such feelings, suspecting whether they were genuine. Of course he did not really think that people like Saint Francis of Assisi or Saint Theresa were not true mystics. But they had lived in a more primitive age, before scientific knowledge had brought its clear light of day onto the phenomena of the physical world. Daisy baffled him sometimes. Of course, he approved of her regular observance of religious forms. It was appropriate for a woman to be concerned with the higher things in life and church-going was evidence of this. It helped to define her status in the world. Occasionally he had had misgivings. Daisy seemed to take it all a little too seriously. When he sat in the pew next to her, watching the acolyte light the candles on the altar, surrounded as the two of them were by a handful of mute, motionless people obviously wrapped in their own thoughts, he had a feeling that Daisy was far away and that he could not follow her.

He brought his attention back to Madame Aurora. The light

of the lamp once more fell on her face, which was impassive. The smooth, plump cheeks, the lids of the downcast eyes, the grey hair parted in the middle of her forehead—there was an absolute repose here that struck him as uncanny. His instinct was to speak in order to break up this strange quiet that seemed to threaten him. But he found he really did not want to do that. He waited.

Madame Aurora said, "I do not see in the future the projection of any aura that might be interpreted as representing a courtroom, as myself in any such situation. Nothing comes to me indicating that a court of law, judicial proceedings, interrogation before a judge, lies in the future for me. No warning comes to me that may be seen as that."

Hugh was annoyed. "I'm afraid that I do not put any dependence on psychic phenomena, Madame Aurora. It is very certain that a suit has been brought which will be heard in preliminary session three weeks from now. My question is whether you will be prepared to come into the witness box and describe the statements made to you by the Colonel?"

This time she did not take so long to answer, but she did not speak immediately. "I see no purpose to promising something that is not going to take place."

"That means you refuse to testify?"

"I did not say so."

"But you will not commit yourself to speak out." He was impatient.

"I do not foresee that I shall be called to do so."

He was exasperated. "All right. Let's say you are called upon to testify. Are you sufficiently certain of your facts to state them in court under oath?"

"They are not my facts. Yes, of course, I am willing to repeat what I have told you to anyone to whom it is appropriate for me to speak. Your oaths mean nothing to me."

"Oh, I see. But so far as you are concerned, your statements represent the truth of the matter. That is, you are convinced that the Colonel was telling you what he believed the truth to be. Of course, this man's claims cannot be disproved by hearsay evidence. What we want is for you to tell the court that the Colonel did make certain statements to you that will give us a clear case against this impostor."

"They were the truth as the Colonel saw it. I am sure he was speaking the truth to me. The concept of what is the truth is always open to question."

Hugh took a deep breath. "Well, I don't think we need debate the philosophical basis for the concept of truth. All I need to know now is whether you are ready, if you are summoned to appear as a witness, to state that the Colonel gave you this information about his wife and son and that his mind was clear at the time. You realize your consent will be very important to Mrs. Head."

Madame Aurora did not respond.

He pressed her. "I do have your undertaking on this?"

For the first time she showed a slight impatience. "Mr. Carson, Mrs. Head's financial interests are not threatened in any way. There is no substance to this man's claims. I see no sign that her material wellbeing is in jeopardy. Therefore, I am not concerned about her in that way. What I do feel is a very strong sense of violence emanating from this man."

"What do you mean by that?"

"I can only tell you that she should not have anything to do with this man. He is dangerous."

"Well, I think we are all in agreement there. But if you mean he may attack her physically—what would he gain by that?"

"I don't know. I receive messages that he is unbalanced, ready to take revenge for fancied wrongs. Perhaps he has convinced himself that what he says is true—that he is indeed the Colonel's son, unjustly stripped of his inheritance. I see something further —" She held up her hand so that he saw the lamplight shine on her palm. For a long moment she was still and he sat joined with her in the compelling silence. After a while she sighed and he noticed that she looked tired. "There is a confused picture that appears to me. But I do not think that Mrs. Head is in danger."

Hugh stirred restlessly in his chair. "I'm afraid I cannot credit spiritualist warnings —"

She swept away his words. "You are mistaken in this. Unfortunately, so many unworthy people have used false phenomena—crude devices—to deceive the credulous that now the whole subject is suspect. Let me assure you that there are forces beyond our ready comprehension. Because we do not understand them does not mean that they do not exist. Those of us who are more sensitive, more open to these emanations from the astral world, are aware of that fact. Most people are so immersed in the loose, vague, dense cloud created about them by their emotional impulses that they are sealed off from the clearer vision that is created by their thoughts. We have shut out our own access to the ancient wisdom, the laws and formulas that in ages past have given some the power to see what lies beyond the moment. We have discarded all this as ignorant superstition, believing that our science will explain everything. We shall discover in due course that much of what we gain through the advancement of scientific knowledge is in fact this ancient wisdom, which has until now been intuitively known by a few. Take heed of what I say."

Hugh sat still. The atmosphere of diffused strength that he had sensed when he had first come into the room and which seemed to emanate from the woman opposite him, now grew thick about him. He wanted to brush these words of hers aside as an impediment to what he had come to do. But the persuasive effect of her voice gave him pause. Whatever she said, there was a powerful effect in the sound of her voice.

"Well," he said at last, "certainly I shall heed your warning about this fellow. Your feelings agree with mine. I want to tell you something further. I've been more or less convinced that this man is not acting alone. He is the cat's paw for a group of the Colonel's enemies. Do you have any information that would corroborate this idea?"

"There are others about him with whom he is at odds."

"Ah, then it is true! Now if we can only discover who they are!"

"That will be unnecessary. He is at odds with these associates. The conflict is of his own making. He is now acting on his own. If you tried to find these men, they would deny all connection with him."

Hugh looked at her with a slight frown. "You mean, he is now acting independently?"

"And contrary to them."

"So, he has decided to doublecross his partners. There is no honor among thieves, they say. But will they allow him to take the plum from them?"

"It will not come to that."

Hugh shook his head and reached for his briefcase.

CHAPTER EIGHTEEN

Daisy said, "You must be very careful how you talk to Aunt Edie. Her nerves are badly shaken by all this business."

She and Hugh were sitting side by side on the glider in the glassed-in porch, full of great ferns in wicker baskets, that overlooked Sixteenth Street. She preferred sitting here to anywhere else in the house because she could escape from the overpowering ornateness that otherwise surrounded her. The big green plants were a welcome change from the massive furniture, the marble statues, the great mirrors, the myriads of paintings, bibelots, vases that filled the big rooms. Perhaps, the thought glanced through her mind now and then, Aunt Edie would, as soon as possible, move away from here into some more comfortable place.

Also she was less likely to be intruded upon here. She knew the reason why. The porch was just off the big room that had been the Colonel's, where he had spent almost all his waking hours. Nothing in it had been changed. His wheelchair was set against the wall. The rack holding his pipes still stood on the side table. So strong had the impress of his personality been that those who lived in the house could not believe that he was really gone. Even her aunt avoided entering the room—a recrudescence, she supposed, of the family tradition of ghostly visitations in the old houses on the Eastern Shore. If the Colonel's shade ever came to haunt, it was here that you would expect it to appear. The room had been cleaned and aired, yet it was still impregnated with the old-man smell that had been characteristic when he sat there every day, brooding over this final defeat brought about by his body's collapse. This had been the habitation of his body. The fearful felt it to be still that of his spirit.

Daisy's attention came back. Hugh was answering her. She

heard the note of conscious patience in his voice. "I am as careful as I can be. But I can't change the facts. We have to make some sort of rebuttal to this man's charges. We can present the facts about your aunt's marriage to the Colonel—the date—and we can attack the authenticity of the documents he is presenting. I think they are all forgeries that won't stand up in court for one minute. But it will be a lot more conclusive if we can have Madame Aurora's evidence about the statements the Colonel made to her. She can say what he told her about his son and about the approximate date of his first wife's death."

"You've talked to her? She agrees to do this?"

"I found her difficult to deal with. She doesn't refuse to testify but she insists it isn't going to be necessary. This business will all pass, she says, without the need for anyone to go to court. She says she knows this through supernatural means. You realize how frustrating I found that, Daisy."

He expected her sympathy. Daisy did not answer at once.

He went on, "I can't put any stock in all this moonshine about omens and foretellings."

"I would not discount her altogether, Hugh. She's an unusual woman. Oh, I don't say you have to accept her prophecies. But she does seem to have a gift for knowing things before they happen."

Hugh frowned at her. "Now, look here, Daisy, you've changed your tune. You used to complain about her influence on your aunt. Has she got around you now?"

"I've changed my opinion, if that is what you mean."

"He did not look pleased. "Well, I thought you were too sensible to be affected by that kind of person."

"What kind of person do you think she is? She's a very intelligent one and I know now that she is a real friend to Aunt Edie. We all have our foibles, Hugh."

"I'd say this—ah—trade of hers is more than a foible. It is a very astute game."

"But it's not a game with her, Hugh, not entirely. She really does think she is gifted with some sense beyond hearing and seeing."

Hugh seemed uncertain how to take her statement. "Well, just because she is convinced of this herself doesn't make it any more reasonable. Besides —" He gave her a keen glance — "I would never have expected you, of all people, to accept that sort of thing. You're a good Episcopalian. You shouldn't be dealing with—with —"

"Witches and sorcerers." Daisy smiled at him. When he did not answer, nonplussed, she said, "Hugh, you don't have much faith in anything, do you?"

He was angry. "Now look here, I've never questioned anything of that sort. I just don't have time to think about religion and philosophy and all that kind of thing."

"When you marry me, you think, you can leave all that to me to take care of—see you into heaven on my own recognizances. You can't do it, Hugh. I'm not going to marry you."

He stared at her, dumbstruck. Then he said, "Oh, that's just how you feel right now. You'll change your mind."

Anger made the color come into her face. "Hugh, whenever I tell you I don't intend to marry you, you act as if I was feeble-minded, not responsible for what I say. I mean it, Hugh."

But she could see that her arrows did not penetrate the shield of his self-confidence. She sighed and gave up the effort. She said instead, "Hugh, I know from my own faith that there are things beyond what we see and hear. This world is not everything. Madame Aurora is mistaken about some things, I believe, but she is right when she says our physical world is not all there is. We do have a destiny that is not encompassed by our earthly life."

Hugh looked uncomfortable, as he always did when someone raised questions beyond the scope of his own professional world. He changed the subject. "Let's get back to reality. I want to warn you about something we haven't talked about before. It is very likely that your aunt will be called upon to testify in court."

"Hugh! She couldn't possibly do that!"

"Well, we have to be prepared for this."

"Even if Madame Aurora testifies?"

"Yes. You see, part of the problem is that Madame Aurora is the person this man accuses of using undue influence on the Colonel. And since she doesn't benefit under the will, he is going to say that she did this for Mrs. Head's sake and that Mrs.

Head promised her a reward to do this."

Disgust appeared on Daisy's face. "What a miserable thing to say!"

Hugh shrugged. "He's a miserable creature. You don't think she was acting on your aunt's behalf?"

"Well, yes, I think she did persuade Uncle William to make a will. It was what he should have done long ago, if he hadn't been so superstitious. But Aunt Edie didn't *hire* her."

Hugh thought, It would have been the sensible thing to do, given the circumstances. But aloud he said, "Most people will assume that there was some sort of collusion between your aunt and Madame Aurora. You know, Daisy, people who don't know your aunt personally will look at her simply as a very lucky woman who married the Colonel for his money and saw to it that it didn't escape her at the end. You have to remember the kind of reputation he always had and everyone will take it for granted that everybody connected with him is of the same stripe." He suddenly broke off. "I hate to be talking to you all about this, Daisy. This sort of thing isn't a fit subject for a girl like you to be involved in."

Daisy's anger burst forth. "Hugh, I'm a grown woman. I've got some brains. I know what goes on in the world. And do you think that living with Uncle William didn't open my eyes to a lot of things? He could keep a lot from Aunt Edie because she did not want to hear about it. But I learned a lot from reading the newspapers. Aunt Edie doesn't like newspapers—except for the society news. But I keep up with things."

Hugh looked as if he did not approve of this. But he prudently let the matter lie. Instead he said, "I suppose I can persuade the court to let me read a statement from your aunt. I'm sure Judge Barrett—I think the case is coming up before him—will be sympathetic. He understands the sort of woman your aunt is—a true lady. But there is something else that Madame Aurora said that I should warn you about. She thinks this fellow is crazy—crazy and violent. I shouldn't doubt it. She thinks your aunt should be careful and not have anything more to do with him."

"As far as I know, she has no intention of letting him come into this house again."

"Well, just see to it that she doesn't. Now, I'd better be going. I've got a lot on my hands."

He stood up and reached for his briefcase. He waited for a moment, hoping that she would relent and give some sign of affection. But she did not look at him, simply wishing him goodbye.

He strode off down Sixteenth street, headed for the trolley. He liked to walk as much as he could, seeking opportunities for the exercise that he knew he needed and seldom had time for. Walking gave him the opportunity, too, of mulling over thoughts without interruption. Daisy was very often in them. Of course he understood that women, especially young pretty women, were unpredictable. Their whims and caprices were to be endured for the sake of their company and he would never begrudge Daisy hers. But these days Daisy was certainly in a mood. In fact, it was a mood that seemed to have been growing and becoming more constant through the past winter and summer. He wished she would treat him with greater friendliness— sometimes she seemed downright cranky. But he supposed all this would pass in due time.

When she was his wife—he was certain that this was something that would eventually come about—she would, under his steadying influence, become less moody. He could not really call her flighty. No, she wasn't flighty. It was simply that occasionally she seemed withdrawn, far away in her own thoughts. He was a little in awe of the sternness with which she responded sometimes to something he said. He approved of that streak of austereness in her, which he stumbled over every so often. It meant that she would be a woman who would not be easily swayed by casual friendships. He wanted a wife who would be uncompromising on important matters, whom he would be forced to respect, even when he wanted his own way. That was what a really good woman was for, to keep a man up to the mark.

There was only one thing about Daisy that really worried him. Sometimes she seemed to know more than she should about some things that should be a mystery to a young unmarried woman. He wasn't against the modern young woman, educated, independent, ready to speak her mind. He would not want to spend a lifetime with an empty-headed woman who was unable to understand the problems of his own life. Daisy suited him fine there. He was in favor of votes for women. It was ridiculous to say that women would be any sillier than some of the male voters he had observed in political campaigns. He drew the line at women getting involved in the dirty side of politics, though. He would not even mind if Daisy did as she sometimes threatened to, went to college. He was willing to wait while she did so. Of course, anything like that would be out of the question once they were married. She would have plenty to keep her occupied then in her home and family. She would not have time or inclination for other things then. No, he would not want to change Daisy. But sometimes she made him uneasy by understanding more than he expected her to, about public affairs, the seamy side of politics and business dealings, the relations between men and women. He did not like to deal in his legal practice with women who were experienced enough to question his decisions. He would not want Daisy to be like that. She read a lot, he knew. It was her favorite recreation and though she wasn't a great talker, she was thoughtful. When she was his wife, he would be able to control to some extent what she read.

He had reached the trolley stop. He took out his watch and noted the time. He had another hour before he saw his next client. In the meantime, he had better be giving his attention to the Head case. Now, this business of Madame Aurora —

～ ～ ～ ～ ～

In the next week or so there was a lull in the popular attention given to the Head case. August was almost at an end and September had signaled its approach with unusually cool nights. Two weeks would elapse before the court would be in session. In the meantime the struggle between Joseph Pulitzer and William Randolph Hearst to outdo each other in Yellow Journalism occupied the readers of newspapers.

"It's a relief," Daisy drawled, stretched out on Nell's bed with her shoes off, "not to see the Head estate in the headlines on the front page."

Nell, standing by the window, watched the glow in the

western sky where the sun was ready to set behind the bulk of the Library building. They had eaten dinner at the boarding-house table—a rare occasion now, for Daisy was seldom able to leave her aunt alone in the evenings.

Nell said, "I suppose it's especially a relief to your aunt."

"Oh, Aunt Edie never reads the newspapers—she never has. She thinks they're full of all sorts of things a nice woman wouldn't want to know about."

Nell laughed. "Well, she's probably right. But that hasn't saved her from being involved in a very unpleasant business. You can't shut your eyes to what goes on in the world, Daisy."

"I suppose most of the time you can pretend it isn't there— especially if you are careful where you go and what you do. For instance, she would never approve of your going out on the street by yourself after dark."

"You mean, like tonight?"

Every so often Nell worked irregular hours. For a year now the Library had stayed open until ten o'clock at night for the benefit of the many readers who came to take advantage of these fine new facilities. There was still much to be done to bring the collections into proper order in the new building, to modernize the Library's service. Nell enjoyed this occasional extra stint in the reading room. It was a change from her usual work. Of course, the men on the staff were usually assigned to the night duty but she had insisted that she be given her share of it. Women, she explained to Daisy, should not be favored in such situations. That only gave the men a further weapon in saying that women could not be their equals in responsibility and therefore in pay.

"Of course," said Nell, "I don't have a husband, like some of the women, to come and fetch me and shepherd me home after dark. But then I don't have a husband who expects me to be waiting with dinner ready for him when he comes home."

Nell's eyes had twinkled brightly when she said this. Daisy had looked doubtful.

Nell reassured her. "Oh, don't worry! There really isn't any danger. This is a quiet part of town. Why, Miss Beaufort often stays until the reading room closes. I walk home with her. You know that she lives just a step away from here."

So sometimes Daisy came to Nell's boardinghouse in the early evening and stayed through dinner until Nell was ready to return to the Library. This marked a change in her aunt's life, one that brought great relief to Daisy. Mrs. Head no longer entertained in the evenings. She shrank from mingling with people she suspected of feasting on the scandal of the Colonel's affairs, on the aspersions cast on her own status as his widow. In vain did Daisy say that she was undoubtedly mistaken in regard to most of her social circle, that certainly the best of them were sympathetic to her and indignant over the Roman circus the newspapers were making out of the case. But Mrs. Head apparently remembered with more clarity than Daisy suspected the sort of gossip and relish of gossip that was typical of Washington society. It was a sort of mourning, Daisy told Nell, mourning on her aunt's part more for her loss of reputation than for the Colonel.

"Of course, she wouldn't be entertaining just now in any case. But she refuses to see people even on an informal basis. That worries me, because she just sits and mopes, unless Madame Aurora comes to see her. And that is another thing. People will say that if Madame Aurora comes to see her so frequently, this shows they were in a plot together over the Colonel."

"Well, it's all ridiculous," said Nell. "No reasonable person would hold your aunt accountable for what the Colonel did, especially before she married him."

"That's not it. It is the idea that she married a man who can be talked about in such a way."

"Still, she is not responsible for him."

"Yes, but don't you see? She can't cut herself off from him now, just because he is dead. He was her husband. She can't join his detractors. She must be loyal to him and the only way she can do that is by ignoring what is being said. That is easier if she doesn't see people."

Nell shook her head. "It's beyond me. I think she should just go along doing as she always has."

"You mean, brazen it out. Aunt Edie could never do that."

But for Daisy this cessation of social activity was a boon, especially on the evenings when Madame Aurora came to visit and she was free to come to Nell.

Daisy stretched, looking at the ceiling. Nell, gazing at her fondly, said, "Have you been practicing on the typewriter?"

"Yes. Most of the afternoon. Miss Cohn let me do a letter today. She said nobody could tell that she hadn't done it herself."

"Oh, Daisy! I think this is wonderful! Not that I want you to have to work all day in an office, but it is a useful thing to do. Lots of girls earn their living now that way. Miss Cohn is certainly a good sport."

"Yes. I must be a nuisance to her very often. There is so much to do in Hugh's office—he and his partners are terribly busy. I'm not paid, of course, and I expect I hinder as much as I help. But she is very goodnatured about it—partly, I suppose, because she thinks I'm engaged to Hugh, so I'm no real threat to the other girls and it will please him. I'm not a threat to anyone but not for that reason. You know why I want to be able to use a typewriter. One of these days I am going to get an assignment on a magazine and I want to be able to work fast."

"Yes, I know. It's the modern thing, really, Daisy—the typewriter. You could get one of your own."

"You mean, I could get Aunt Edie to buy me one—they're very expensive. But I don't want to explain to her what I'm doing. She would not like it."

Nell made an impatient sound. "All these obstacles," she said.

"It's Hugh who bothers me. I don't think it was a good idea for me to ask him to let me come to learn to type in his office. He thinks it gives him an advantage and of course he would not have agreed except that he thought he was indulging a whim of mine—his future wife. I would not have asked him except that I couldn't think of any other way I could do it without telling Aunt Edie."

"Does he annoy you?"

"Oh, no, not if you mean, does he try to kiss me and all that. He knows that makes me mad. He'd like to kiss me, of course, but he puts up with it because he thinks that's the way a well brought up young woman ought to act. After all, *he* thinks he is engaged to me."

Nell asked stiffly, "Haven't you told him you're not?"

"Till I'm blue in the face, but he doesn't believe me. He

thinks I'm just being a typical woman—making him think I'm too much of a shrinking violet to acknowledge the fact." Daisy sighed. "I don't think I'll ever convince him."

Looking at Nell from under her eyelashes she saw the expression of half-angry disgust on her face. How hard it is, she thought, to tell even Nell the exact state of her feelings. She had never intended to marry Hugh—or any man. It was wrong of her to let the situation with him develop as it did. But then, before she met Nell, it hadn't really mattered much to her how she spent her time or with whom. She had drifted along, from childhood through adolescence, docile, acquiescent to what was expected of her, by her mother, by Aunt Edie, and then by a series of young men who had culminated in Hugh. She had been mildly content through it all. But there was a part of herself which she felt deeply was her own and this part she never displayed to anyone. Moments when she was alone this private self absorbed her attention—in bed at night, in church, when she could be free of intrusion.

That private self was not concerned with what went on around her in her daily life. A good part of the time she struggled with the religious faith that seemed instinctive to her. It dewlt in the cadences and phrases of the *Prayer Book*, it was embodied in the communion service, but it was something of its own, not susceptible to interpretation by anyone else. Its development had gone on from the serene, secure belief in God and the angels of her childhood. In adolescence she went through a period of turbulence, buffeted by the awakening to the fact that there were people who seriously doubted the very basis of her faith, and there were those who, doubting, observed its forms for the sake of social compliance. Her aunt, she soon recognized, was among those whose conformity was based on nothing stronger than a tacit acceptance without examination of what they had inherited. She had emerged into adulthood with an unshaken belief that God existed, that there was a vital force that governed her life and the universe, no matter how much these beliefs were impugned by others. She had thought a great deal about the nature of God and had arrived at the conclusion that neither she nor anyone else could with authority declare what God was but that God's existence and power was unassailable. It was God who spoke personally to her in ways that she found it impossible to convey to anyone else. This must be a mystery that no one could know until death, the death of the body, brought knowledge and light into a dark and puzzling world.

She was amazed when, on the only occasion when she had talked to Madame Aurora it had suddenly struck her that this odd woman held a vision very like hers, though their outlook seemed diverse. She had tried to explain this to Nell, who was astonished, but being Nell, set the thought aside for further consideration.

When she had tried to explain to Nell her inner thoughts, Nell had been puzzled. She had said, "My parents are both scientists, Daisy. They do not accept anything that is not susceptible of proof by scientific means. They believe that in this age of science, religious beliefs have been proven outmoded, the remnant of a more primitive age. Man has outgrown these childish stories. Oh, I don't mean that they deny the existence of true religious feeling. They know it exists in some people. But they brought me up to question everything, to think of religion as something that has been used to keep people in servitude—like the slaves before the Civil War or to keep women in their place, as Mrs. Stanton says. I must admit I do not have what you have—a real belief in the life of the soul, here on earth and beyond death. But don't cast me out, Daisy. I don't want to be cut off from you, now or ever."

They had left it at that and this difference did not seem to come between them even in their most intimate moments.

She came back from her reverie to hear Nell say, "It's a nuisance, this narrow frame of your life, Daisy. Between your aunt and Hugh, there's hardly room for me."

Daisy looked at her crossly. "That's not so. Of course I can never desert Aunt Edie. She clings to me and I do love her. You'll have to put up with that. It is not the same with Hugh. I don't love him. He'll have to learn sometime or other that I mean what I say when I say I won't marry him."

"I see."

Daisy caught the note of resentment in her voice. "I can't help it, Nell. I can't change things." She smiled at her ironically.

"You know, I could say, why did you have to come into my life? I'd have settled for Hugh and that would have pleased Aunt Edie and everybody would have been happy."

Nell looked at her angrily. "Would you?"

Daisy got up from the bed. "Oh, don't pay any attention to me, Nell! I feel so divided sometimes." She stepped across the room and putting her arms around Nell's neck, buried her face in her shoulder.

"Oh, Daisy, Daisy! Don't get so upset. You mustn't let all this affair get on your nerves this way."

Daisy took her arms away but made no effort to leave Nell's embrace. She wiped her eyes. "I'm over it." She seemed suddenly aware of the time. "Oh, Nell, you'll be late!"

Nell glanced at the little gold watch that hung from a pin fastened to Daisy's shirtwaist. "So I shall. Come on! I'll walk you to the trolley stop."

They walked along East Capitol Street in the fading light of the sunset behind the Capitol dome. As they walked past the great bulk of the Library building looming even larger in the dusk, Daisy said, "It is pretty deserted here at this hour."

She glanced around at the wide spaces of street and pavement and grassy park. Nell, more used to the scene, also glanced about them but said nonchalantly, "It would be hard for anyone to hide, except for those bushes. Here's the trolley, Daisy. Good night, my darling."

She waited until she could no longer see the white of Daisy's shirtwaist aboard the trolley. Then she turned and walked up the drive to the wide flight of granite steps that led to the terrace in front of the Library's great doors. The cavern-like entrance under the steps shone with the yellow light that beamed out from the doors on the ground level. She greeted the guard at the door and walked inside.

VII

CHAPTER NINETEEN

Hannah came into Elizabeth's study and put her hand on Elizabeth's shoulder. Elizabeth, absorbed in writing, looked up at her in surprise. Hannah was smiling but in her eyes was an unusual brilliance. Elizabeth felt in her grasp a current of energy. She had seldom seen Hannah in such a state of scarcely suppressed elation.

"What is it, love?"

Hannah held a paper in her other hand, a legal document, it seemed to Elizabeth. Hannah gave it a little shake.

"You didn't realize that our lease was to be up in a few weeks, did you, Liz, and it was uncertain that we could renew it?"

Elizabeth sighed. She looked around the pleasant room, lined now with bookcases. "Oh, dear. You should have warned me, love. It will be a wrench to leave this."

"It is the nicest place you've ever had to work in, isn't it? Your books all at hand, space to spread out your papers."

"Yes. Luxury we have never been able to afford before—not in all my life, dear heart. But at least I've had it for a year."

Hannah put her arm around her shoulders and pulled her head against her breast. Elizabeth could feel her laughing silently. She drew away enough to look up into her face.

"What is the joke?"

"It is no joke, Liz. We're not moving. This is now our house. We've bought it."

"Bought it! Dear love, you have bought it?"

"Yes. I decided that, even if we could renew the lease, there would always be this uncertainty coming around each year. And you have everything you want here—the Library is only two streets away. If you need to travel anywhere, we'll have our own place to return to—to our own belongings, which we shall no longer need to carry everywhere on our backs wherever we go."

Elizabeth contemplated her exultant face for a moment. "Yes, sweet love, this is a demi-paradise. But how has it been achieved? At what sacrifice?"

"None." Hannah was still smiling, her eyes still alight. You need not be so unbelieving, Liz. We may, in fact, call this the Colonel's legacy."

"Ah!"

"I could not wait because of the lease. The owner of the house was not sure he wanted the notoriety that came with housing Madame Aurora. I said, very well, I shall buy it from you. I'm afraid I paid a little more than I should have. But he knew he had the advantage. His greed overcame his disinclination to deal with me. I was, you see, in a position to give him the entire amount without a moment's delay. He was not prepared for that."

Elizabeth was smiling now. "I should have liked to have observed the scene, my love."

Hannah grew more sober. "However, I must be careful. We must not make any further show of affluence. I hope, in fact, that our purchase of the house will not reach the ears of the newspapers. You remember, Liz, there is all this question of how I am to gain from the Colonel's will, since I am not named there. If people hear that we have a sudden prosperity, they will be convinced that after all I have a special understanding with Mrs. Head. You know that that is not the case. You know that the Colonel gave me the money before he died. But I do not want to be required to explain and justify myself. I have been very successful in dealing on the stock exchange and we have a good store of money put away, which I shall not tamper with. All we need do now is wait for this threat to clear up—the threat to the Head estate."

"Marvelous, dear love! Marvelous!"

∿ ∿ ∿ ∿ ∿

The September night was damp and cool. The smell of earth came in from the narrow garden in front of the house. Hannah, as she sometimes did, sat in her consulting room, wrapt in thought. In almost two years she had achieved a good deal. What was needed now was patience and vigilance to get through this period of danger.

In talking to Elizabeth she had minimized the danger, which she felt increasing as the time grew near for the court hearing on the claim by the man who said he was W. T. Head's son. She realized now that the inevitable result of that hearing—the discrediting of his claim—would only increase the menace from him. The man was obviously unbalanced. If he lost—and certainly he must—what revenge would he try to take?

The sense of this growing menace dwelt strongly with her now. Something, she felt, was coming to a climax. Several nights before, Elizabeth had returned from the Library shortly after ten o'clock, accompanied by Nell Purcell. This was unusual, for Nell, in walking home with Elizabeth, left her at the garden gate and the sound of its click would tell her that Elizabeth was home. She had been alarmed, because that night, like this one, had been filled for her by a strong foreboding. She had tried to brush aside the feeling. It did not, she was sure, relate to Elizabeth herself. She had thought of Mrs. Head. But surely Mrs. Head, in her great house, surrounded by servants, could be in no danger. Yet when she heard Elizabeth's voice at the door, saying good night to Nell, a wave of panic had swept over her. She had hurried out of her room to greet Elizabeth.

Elizabeth had closed the outer door and stood removing her hat. She looked up in surprise at Hannah's wild stare.

"Why, dear love, what's the matter?"

Hannah's alarm ebbed away. "Are you all right? Has anything happened?"

Elizabeth gazed at her curiously. "So you were conscious of it? No, there is nothing the matter with me. But something did happen earlier this evening."

"Who was it?"

"Daisy. But she is perfectly all right. Don't be alarmed, dear love."

"Tell me."

"Well, it could have had far worse consequences. This is an evening when Daisy was visiting Nell at her boardinghouse. She walked with Nell back to the Library. Fortunately Nell did not go on at once into the building when they parted. Therefore, she observed this man preparing to attack Daisy and prevented him, with the help of one of the Library guards. Nell sent for Mrs. Head's carriage—there are telephones in the lobby of the Library, as you know—and sent Daisy safely home. She was not hurt, only badly frightened. No, they did not catch the man. He ran away in the dark. I decided not to come home and tell you then. The affair was over. But I've been speculating all evening about how you would view this. It quite interfered with my reading."

Hannah followed her upstairs to their bedroom. A spirit lamp stood on a side table and she lit it and made them a cup of chocolate, while Elizabeth got ready for bed.

She said, as she poured the chocolate, "He was, of course, the man who claims to be the Colonel's son."

Elizabeth paused in dropping off her petticoat. "Why are you so certain?"

Hannah put the two cups down on the nightstand. "Because I have been expecting him to make some move against Mrs. Head."

"But why Daisy?"

"He saw her once. He knows who she is—Mrs. Head's niece. She embodies for him all that he feels he must have—all he thinks he has been unjustly deprived of. He is mad, Liz. That young lawyer—Hugh Carson—has an idea that this man is the cat's-paw for a group of the Colonel's enemies, that he has been hired to put forward this claim. But I do not agree. If that was ever the case—it may have begun that way—he has long since been repudiated by them as too dangerous. Because he has convinced himself that his story is true. And now he begins to think that perhaps he will not succeed—everyone says so—and the injustice of it, from his point of view, is driving him to violent action. He could not get at Mrs. Head. Mrs. Head does not walk about the streets alone at dusk."

Elizabeth stood still, her nightgown in her hand. "You are very logical, as usual. But then he is indeed very dangerous. What should we do?"

"There is nothing we can do until he makes another move."

Hannah came over to lift the flannel nightgown over Elizabeth's head. But for a moment they paused, Hannah's hands gently stroking Elizabeth's spare white body. Elizabeth shivered and they kissed.

∿ ∿ ∿ ∿ ∿

That had happened a week ago. Since then, at her request, Elizabeth had ceased to go to the Library in the evenings. Instead she spent the hours after dinner in her study at the end of the hall. Her new book was nearing completion and she was absorbed in it. Hannah, seeing the brightness in her eyes, knew she was savoring ahead of time the revenge she would have when the world should know that M. E. Beaufort once more challenged the scholarly fraternity. This time successfully, for the world had changed in the last twenty years and women could no longer be discounted. Hannah thought fondly back over the years. They had had their trials, but they had survived them together. And now —

The sound of the front doorbell brought her abruptly back to the reality of the room where she sat. She waited, poised for the sort of visitor who sometimes came unheralded to consult Madame Aurora. The peal was not repeated so she supposed Willie Mae had gone to see who it was. Presently there was a knock on her own door.

She felt a warning hesitation and did what she seldom did, got up and walked to the door to open it without a preliminary response. There was no light in the corridor and she saw at first only the silhouette of a man. Then as she stepped aside the subdued rays of the lamp on her table showed his features—a man above her own height, burly, with a weatherbeaten face, his eyes for the moment blinded. There was no sign of Willie Mae.

He said, "Madame Aurora," and she nodded and stepped back to let him come in. With an effort of will she turned her back to him and walked back to her chair at the table behind the lamp. When, having sat down, she looked up, she saw that he had followed her and stood waiting, his hat still in his hand. She gestured to the chair opposite and he sat down.

But not before, she noticed, he had looked around the room

as if he was seeking for an enemy. This was perhaps a habit learned from experience, she thought. For she knew—and had known even before she had opened the door to him—that he was the man who had attacked Daisy. She sat looking at him across the table, in the shaded light of the lamp.

At first he seemed not to focus on her. The uneasiness he had shown when he came into the room seemed to intensify. He can't expect to find anyone hiding behind the furniture, thought Hannah. He has come to confront me, in my own house, in my own room, because here he thinks I will be alone, that what we say will have no hearers. She watched as he sat in silence, his jaw working.

At last she said, in her deepest, quietest tone of voice, "You have come here to talk to me about the Colonel. You are not his son."

"How d'you know who I am?" There was a note of savagery in his voice, as if he barely suppressed a seething rage.

"Your identity was announced to me before you came into this room."

Again he looked wildly around. "Who told you? That girl who opened the door—I told her to go away. She ran away down the hall. I frightened her."

"I have no doubt that you did. But I was expecting you."

He glared at her intently. "What do you mean by that? How did you know I was coming here? I didn't know where I was going, an hour ago."

Hannah, fencing with him, said, "There are messengers that you know nothing about, messengers who are at my service."

She was pleased to see the alarm that flared in his eyes. He tried to hide it with bluster. "You don't fool me with that kind of talk. You're just a fortune teller—like those gypsies over there on the other side of the Capitol, sitting on the sidewalk looking for customers. Only you are a little sharper. You know how to go after people with real money, like that old thief— that damned old murderer —"

"Your father, you say."

He fell silent. She could not read the expression in his eyes. He had reared back so that his face was not in the lamplight. She said, "You know that the Colonel was not your father.

You have invented this story because you want his money—and you want to revenge yourself on him. You believe that he has done you an injury."

There was a strange grimace on his face in the shadow. "That old bastard is frying in hell right now, so he can't deny what I'm saying. Dead men don't tell tales. But I'm alive and I can tell the world plenty about you."

Hannah hesitated only a moment. "What can you tell the world about me?"

He leaned forward. "I can tell 'em you're a fraud. I can tell 'em that woman hired you to scare the old devil into making a will that gave her everything. You charge pretty high fees for your services, don't you?"

This time Hannah deliberately waited before answering. "So it is blackmail you have come here for tonight? You have no evidence to support what you say. Tell me, did you know the Colonel's son?"

He sat back. His eyes were full of suspicion. "Think you can catch me, don't you? What do you know about his son?"

"A good deal. The Colonel told me about him in detail, including the fact that his son came out to join him in South America because his mother had died in California. That was years before the Colonel married his present widow."

She was surprised that the man opposite made no immediate attempt to refute what she said. He seemed submerged in his own thoughts. Presently he began a rambling speech.

"I know what I know and I'm going to tell it to the court. I'm going to tell them how you talked the old devil into making a will. He'd always said he wouldn't do that for anything. He said that when I first knew him back in Colorado. We were mining silver there. He said if a man made a will, he would die, sure as shootin'. The Devil was just waiting for you then. He said he wasn't going to die. He knew how to get around the Devil. If you watched out for the omens —"

"Making a will was an omen?"

"You bet. You tempted the Devil when you made a will."

"And you say this was back in Colorado—when?—just after the Civil War?"

He suddenly flared at her across the table, thrusting his face into the lamplight. "What are you trying to get at?"

"You can't very well be his son, then, can you? If you were with him in Colorado at that time. He never saw his son after he left California, until he came to find him in Peru."

"He told you a pack of lies!"

"His son was a child then."

"I know what I know! You can't throw me off!"

"I may not be able to," said Hannah calmly, "but I expect the lawyers in court will be able to."

She was silent and she looked at him keenly across the table, her eyes gleaming in the rays of the lamp. "The Colonel wasn't the only man afraid to die. When you get the Colonel's money, what do you propose to do with it? If the Devil is helping you, what are you going to have to pay him?"

The sharp thrust of her quiet voice reached him and caused him to jerk upright in his chair.

"I ain't going to die for some time. I've waited too long for this. I'll do what I damn please with that money."

"You were afraid of the Colonel, weren't you? As long as he was living you made no effort to get your revenge, did you, because you were sure he would win in any kind of battle. He had the Devil on his side. That's what you thought. And now you think you have the Devil on your side. He's got the Colonel. He's likely to get you now. What are you going to do when you meet the Colonel on the other side? You always sniveled to him here on earth. Are you going to be bolder there?"

She could see his eyes full of a dawning fear. "I'm not the only man who was afraid of him. He'd have your life, your soul, if you crossed him."

"As you learned, when you betrayed his son to him."

The fear in his eyes became rage. "God damn you, you bitch! Don't you know I came here to get rid of you? I'm going to see that you don't get to tell your piece." He leaned across the table towards her and she drew back in her chair. She could see no sign of a weapon about him but his hands, powerful, rough-skinned hands, worked in the light under the lamp.

She said quietly, "I don't think so. I have protection here that you cannot see. Yes, you were the one who went to him and told him that his son had become a spy for his enemies.

You expected to be rewarded. You never received that reward. The Colonel would never forgive betrayal nor the instruments of betrayal. After all, a betrayer cannot be trusted, can he?"

The man swore under his breath, muttering to himself. When she could hear him, he was saying, "I couldn't stay in the mines after that. He saw to it that nobody would hire me for anything, stake me for anything. I left Peru hungry in my guts for revenge on him."

"You drifted back to the silver mines in the southwest. But by that time there were too many ahead of you. You never struck it rich and when you did have a little money you drank it up. You were afraid to go near the Colonel. You kept away from him because he became the Devil to you, who could seek you out anywhere."

"Did he tell you all this?"

"Perhaps. But then you saw in the paper that he was dead. You brooded about him, his fortune, about his silver mines. Why shouldn't you have your revenge now, when he could not pursue you?"

She was watching him closely and she saw the uneasiness in his eyes turn slowly to fear—like a horse about to shy, she thought. She pressed on.

"The newspaper accounts mentioned some of the men who had been the Colonel's enemies. Perhaps some of them would seize the power when the Colonel died. You thought this might be your chance, so you got in touch with them, reminded them of what you had done in Peru. They did not welcome you. Then you threatened them with blackmail—that you would expose the story of their warfare with the Colonel. They spurned you."

He stared at her without speaking, fascinated. She waited again. The room was very quiet. Its closed windows, thickly carpeted floor, heavy door produced a silence that pressed on eardrums. The clear restricted light of the lamp cast the rest of the space into shadow in which objects were only half-seen. It was a calculated effect that she found useful in working upon the nerves of those who came to sit opposite her at the table.

She went on. "But after you had seen these men, had talked to them in their sumptuous offices in Wall Street, substantial men in expensive clothes, staring at you over the cigars in their mouths, out of bold eyes—as if you knew nothing of them when they had been like you, rough characters in filthy shirts who had spent their days prospecting for silver in desert wastes among hostile Indians, peons—you went back to your room in a dirty lodging house on the East Side of New York. You sat in that room—you did not have even the few dollars to pay another day's rent—and you thought how you could make them pay for the scorn with which they had treated you. Then a vision came to you. It lighted up that dark room in the shadow of the elevated trains. It exploded in your head. You knew how you could get your revenge against them and against the Colonel, how you could get all that silver you'd been digging for all those years. You saw it all in front of you—the piles of silver, the power it would give you. You had your plan. It was laid out before you like a map. All you had to do was follow your demon. It was a demon, wasn't it —?"

He suddenly roared. "Stop it! You she-devil! How'd you get there? How'd you see this? Where were you?"

Hannah leaned forward into the lamplight so that he could see the smile on her face, the brilliance in her eyes. "Do you think you could kill me?"

His eyes were full of terror, panic-stricken. For a moment she was daunted, looking into the eyes of madness. But she pulled herself up short before the feeling could dominate her. She did not cease to return his stare, even for an eye-blink.

He shouted, "Where'd you come from? Who are you?"

"That you can never know. Yes, you do know that there are spirits all round you. They are coming closer—they're pressing round you —"

He leaped up from his chair. At first she thought he was going to attack her and she shrank back. But he switched around to search the gloom of the corners of the room, as if he expected to see shapes moving within it. He turned away from her and ran toward the door.

And at that moment she thought of Elizabeth. Where was Elizabeth? She had lost track of the time. She did not know how long she had been locked in combat with this man. Elizabeth would have heard nothing. Even when the man bellowed the sound would not have penetrated into Elizabeth's study, reaching her deaf ears.

Hannah jumped up from her chair, pursuing the man. He snatched the door open and ran through it into the darkened corridor. She saw then where Elizabeth was, framed in the door of her study, roused by a sense other than hearing.

She started to speak, "Hannah —" She stopped, astonished.

The sound of her voice drew his attention. He swerved from his path to the front door and turned towards her, looming over her.

A great force of pent-up anger and energy burst in Hannah. With the clarity of a fierce white light she saw him as the destroyer, the destroyer of them both, at this the culmination of their lives. This flash carried her to him almost before he reached Elizabeth. Even as she seized him by the back of his collar he had struck Elizabeth down. But her grip caused him to rear backwards, striving to fling her off, glaring at her over his shoulder. By the light of the ceiling lamp she saw his eyes gleaming in rage and then suddenly in terror as he gazed at her. With a roar he pulled out of her grasp and ran for the front door. Snatching it open he fled out into the darkness, bellowing in fright.

Hannah leaned down to Elizabeth, lying on the floor. "Liz, are you hurt?"

"I don't know. What a dreadful man!" She leaned on Hannah as Hannah helped her to her feet. "No, I'm not hurt. Perhaps bruised. What did he want, love? I thought he was going to strangle me."

Hannah, still breathing heavily, felt over her body and then caught her in her arms, moaning, "Liz, Liz."

Elizabeth kissed her on the neck, under her ear. "Don't be so upset, dear heart. He was your madman, wasn't he? Suddenly she laughed. "I saw your face, love, over his shoulder. What an avenging fury! I would have fled too, if you had been after me."

They stood apart. Elizabeth examined her face. "But, dear love, how extraordinary! I have never seen you lift your hand in anger to anyone."

Hannah muttered, "You, of course. He was not to touch you."

CHAPTER TWENTY

"The point is, love, shall we inform the police?"

Elizabeth sat in the sunshine that came into their breakfast room. Hannah paced nervously about. Elizabeth had amazed her at the coolness with which she had taken the attack. They had agreed that they would not call the police before they went to bed. Hannah had locked and barred the doors of the house and closed the windows. She was sure the man would not return, at least that night.

Elizabeth had been remarkably calm. She had in fact slept most of the night, as if nothing had happened. Hannah had been sleepless, assailed by a storm of conflicting psychic currents. The deep foreboding that had gripped her during the last few weeks seemed to have dissipated. In its stead was a fluctuating sense of unease, like shallow waves of a sea washing over the sand at the shore's edge. She had sought unremittingly, through the hours of darkness, sitting up in bed listening to Elizabeth's even breathing, to understand what this new development meant. Was there some other, more subtle danger in store for them?

Now she stopped in her pacing to attend to Elizabeth's question. Elizabeth went on to say, "Of course, really, we should have notified the police last night. They would have had a better chance of apprehending this man. Where do you suppose he has fled to? You know who he is, so it won't be a question of searching for an unknown assailant."

Hannah said with sudden decision. "I shall not go to the police, Liz. We want no notoriety over this affair. We shall stay out of the limelight."

Elizabeth, watching her lips, replied. "Ah, yes. I understand. But are we in no further danger from him?"

Hannah thought for a while. "I have a strange feeling. The

danger has passed, for us. But I feel strongly that there is a sphere of violence near us. This affair is not concluded yet, Liz. The police, however, are not our answer to it."

"As you say, my love," said Elizabeth and turned her attention to the newspaper.

~ ~ ~ ~ ~

Daisy stared at Nell in outrage. "You mean, he broke into the house and attacked them?"

"Not quite that. He pretended to be somebody who came to consult Madame Aurora. She frightened him, apparently. Evidently she guessed that he was highly superstitious and believed in ghosts, so she used his own fears against him."

"Ah, she knows how to do that! Have they informed the police?"

"No. They do not want to be in the newspapers. Madame Aurora would be quite a sensation in the newspapers."

"I suppose so. But, still, how do we know what he will do next? He must be crazy."

"Oh, I don't think there is any doubt of that. But Miss Beaufort says that Madame Aurora is not concerned. She seems to think they're not in any further danger. You know, Miss Beaufort is wonderful. She was in her usual seat in the reading room this morning. I hadn't any idea of what had happened to her last night till she told me—as cool as a cucumber."

"Oh, yes, your wonderful Miss Beaufort. Oh, never mind me, Nell! Yes, of course, she's remarkable."

The September day was hazy with the belated warmth and they were strolling together under the trees in the Capitol grounds in Nell's lunch hour.

"And imagine Madame Aurora," said Nell, enthusiastically, "going after that fellow like that! There aren't many women who would be so brave—and at her age!"

Daisy was thoughtful. "Do you really think she has psychic powers, Nell?"

"I don't know. I've never put any stock in such things. My parents always insisted that every phenomenon we encounter on earth can be explained by scientific means. If we don't

understand how something happens, it is because we haven't
yet conquered all the laws of the universe. This is the age of
science. We've made enormous strides in understanding our
world." She paused for a moment. "You know, when I raised
this question once with Miss Beaufort—I'm always pretty careful because she is very sensitive about Madame Aurora—she replied that perhaps someone like Madame Aurora is able to grasp
the essence of something intuitively which may in the future
come to be understood empirically. It is true, you know, that
there have been many inventors and scientists who have grasped
a principle that it has taken years to demonstrate by practical
means."

Daisy glanced at her. "You don't believe in miracles. Miss
Beaufort doesn't. Madame Aurora says miracles can be explained by the laws that govern the universe beyond our ken."

"And what do you say, darling?"

"That God is the answer. No matter how you explain phenomena, as you call it, you can't explain to me, at least, how it
all began. Yes, granted all your scientific discoveries. I don't
deny them. We don't live now the way we did even a hundred
years ago and we keep learning new things every day and one
discovery leads to another. But when did it all begin? Even if
you talk about other universes—you've told me about your
parents' theories, as astronomers, that our universe is only one
of many—even if you say life was a spontaneous explosion of
some sort—there must have been a time and a place and some
substance to explode."

"I wonder what Madame Aurora's idea of that is."

"Oh, she knows there is a divine power behind everything.
She just sees it as different from what I see. And she believes
that it is knowable, that we can learn from it, that we can apply
it to our own lives."

"Have you been talking to her, Daisy?"

"Oh, yes. When she comes to see Aunt Edie, we usually have
a talk."

"Do you believe, then, that she can really foretell the
future?"

"Well, she doesn't really claim that, you know, Nell. She says
she simply tries to understand the current of events to come."

"About this man, then. What is going to happen when she must confront him in court?"

"She says that won't happen."

∿ ∿ ∿ ∿ ∿

Each morning, while she sat at breakfast, Elizabeth read *The Washington Post*, which Willie Mae brought in to her from the doorstep. On this particular morning, her egg and toast disposed of, she unfolded the paper and glanced at the headlines. Her exclamation made Hannah look up, to meet her eyes gazing at her in disbelief.

"Well, what is it, Liz?" Hannah was used to an intermittent stream of comments as Elizabeth read her way through the paper, caustic or amused remarks, especially on political issues. This sudden exclamation came as a surprise, for it was followed by silence.

Elizabeth said then, "It is unbelievable! Hannah, this man— what is his name? The man who burst in here night before last."

Hannah jumped up from her chair and came around the table to look over her shoulder at the newspaper spread before Elizabeth. She read the headline: Challenger of W. T. Head's Estate Found Dead. She read on quickly. The police had been called to the lodging house where the man lived and had broken down the door to his room, discovering his body sprawled on the bloodsoaked bed, his throat cut. The straight-edged razor used for the purpose was found on the floor where it had apparently dropped from his hand.

Hannah, feeling sick at her stomach, was aware that Elizabeth was looking up into her face inquiringly. "So that is it," she murmured.

"What did you say, my love?"

Hannah shook her head.

"Do you think it can be true that he killed himself? Would not it be more likely that someone else killed him?"

Hannah returned slowly to her chair and sat down. "He was very frightened when he left here."

Elizabeth gave a short, mirthless laugh. "He was indeed! The police say that he had been dead for some time. Which would mean that he went from here to his room and cut his throat."

"Oh-h-!"

Elizabeth, looking across at her in a mixture of surprise and concern, said, "There is no need for you to feel compunction, my love. Imagine what would have happened if you had not been so resolute. Why, we—at least not both of us—would not be sitting here now."

Hannah did not answer but sat brooding.

Elizabeth continued, coolly, "It was a case of 'The wicked flee, When no man pursueth,' is it not, my love? Well, he has solved the problem for Mrs. Head and her lawyers. And you have said all along, haven't you, dear love, that you would not be called upon to testify in court." She paused and looked across at Hannah again. "Dear love, there is no occasion to reproach yourself. One does not mourn such a loss. You yourself have assured me that he was on the path to destruction—of himself and others. Thankfully he has taken no others with him."

Hannah looked up to meet her eyes. Elizabeth's blue eyes usually gazed out at the world with a mild benevolence tinged with amusement. But at a few times in their years together she had seen them as they were now—bold and uncompromising. This was the Elizabeth who dwelt sometimes behind the disarming facade of an amiable if eccentric spinster. She sighed and capitulated. "All right, Liz."

∿ ∿ ∿ ∿ ∿

Hugh told Daisy, "Well, that's over with. The coroner says it was suicide. He drank a lot and there is no evidence that anyone else had anything to do with it. The people at the lodging house knew nothing about him. He kept to himself and it was two days before they noticed he was not about. We can wash our hands of the whole thing. About his claim? The judge has thrown it out of court. The fellow was represented by Jake Turner, the biggest shyster in town. He petitioned the court to dismiss the challenge, since his client was dead and he could no longer represent him. I suppose Turner took the fellow's money, whatever he had, and now he doesn't want anything more to do with the case. He is after bigger fish. You realize, Daisy, that this is only a beginning. We're going to be deluged with all sorts of claims against the estate—though I hope none as crackpot as this one. It's going to be years before this matter is closed."

They were seated on the glider on the side porch of the Sixteenth Street house, among the big ferns. Daisy looked sideways at him. "Madame Aurora was right after all."

He looked at her blankly. "Madame Aurora? About what?"

"You remember, she said there was no point to her saying she would go into court to testify because it wouldn't be necessary."

"Oh, yes. Well, I suppose so. But how could she have foreseen that he was going to commit suicide?"

Daisy glanced at him again. "You'll have to ask her."

∿ ∿ ∿ ∿ ∿

The newspapers forgot the claimant to the Head Estate almost as soon as he was buried. There were other more important lawsuits coming into the courts involving the Colonel's affairs. A small item in *The Washington Post* was almost overlooked by many readers. Mrs. Head, it said, was going abroad for an extended stay.

It was Madame Aurora, Daisy told Nell, who had persuaded her aunt to go abroad, pointing out that there was no reason for her to linger in Washington through the winter season, when she would not be entertaining. Some months out of the country would dull people's memory of the sensational events of the summer.

At first Daisy was in despair. "But, Nell, what are we going to do? I can't be away from you all that time. I shall have to go with her. Aunt Edie will never go abroad without me. She is already talking about how much I shall enjoy London and Paris and Rome—about what a wonderful thing this will be for me— broaden my mind and refine my social graces. And when we get back she can announce my engagement to Hugh. Then I can settle down to the serious business of life as Hugh's wife and provide her with a family she can call her own."

Nell asked, unhappy. "What did you say when she said that?"

"What could I say, Nell. There is no use my saying I won't marry Hugh. She won't believe it any more than he does. She would put it down to a piece of girlish waywardness that will be cured by my travels abroad. She was surprised that I wasn't more enthusiastic when she announced this to me. She thinks it is because I don't want to be separated from Hugh for so long. But she also thinks that it is a case of absence making the heart grow fonder."

But the next day when they met they each rushed to the other elated with a piece of joyful news to share. Facing each other's eagerness, they stopped, stared at each other and spoke at the same time.

"Daisy, Miss Beaufort has just told me something —"

"Nell, honey, guess what Aunt Edie told me this morning —"

They both stopped and laughed and Nell said, "You go first."

"It's Madame Aurora's idea. Aunt Edie is going abroad with her and Miss Beaufort. I don't have to go. I can't imagine what Madame Aurora said to her, but she is quite happy about it— just eager to get everything arranged."

"And Miss Beaufort told me that we—you and I can live in their house while they are gone. She said your aunt is closing up that big mausoleum on Sixteenth Street, so you would have to have somewhere to live. Oh, Daisy, how lovely it will be!"

But Daisy's elation seemed tempered by some reservation. "It'll not be just us, Nell. My cousin Mattie Rawles from the Eastern Shore will live there with us."

"Daisy!"

There was a little smile on Daisy's face. "It's part of the price we have to pay, honey. You don't suppose for a moment that Aunt Edie would let me live in a house alone with just another girl without a chaperone? Why, we'd both lose our reputations! What would the young men think who came courting, if we didn't have a duenna?" Daisy put her arm through Nell's as they walked along. "It won't be so bad, honey. Cousin Mattie is a nice old thing. She'll do the housekeeping and besides she's a spinster and old and needs a home. See what happens to you if you don't get a husband?"

"Daisy, shut up!"

Daisy sighed. "I have another piece of news to tell you. I haven't told anyone else. I can't really—certainly not Aunt Edie. She'd be mortified."

Nell looked down at her at her side. "What is it, Daisy?"

"Don't look so uneasy." Her eyes were bright as she looked up at Nell. "I've got an assignment with Leslie's *Illustrated Weekly* to write a column about what's going on in Washington. Nell, just think of it! No, you can't kiss me out here on the street!"

ᴧ ᴧ ᴧ ᴧ ᴧ

The street lamp shone into the corner of their bedroom. Usually Hannah adjusted the curtain so that it would block the square of light from the street lamp on the wall. But tonight she had not thought to do so and when she was at last in bed beside Elizabeth and had made a move to get up for it, Elizabeth had held her down.

"It doesn't matter, dear love. We can pretend it is the moon. Do you remember, sweetheart, the cottage at the seminary when, as you said, you came to find me and we slept together for the first time? There was a moon then, a fine clear moon, and we did not need a lamp to see our way down from the Principal's residence to our cottage."

Hannah sank more deeply down into the bed, clasping her arms around Elizabeth's thin, bony body.

Elizabeth went on in her ear, "Ah, of course you do remember, dear heart. Perhaps you are right, that there was some magic, some miraculous force that brought you to me." she felt Hannah's hands telling her that this was Hannah's certain belief. "The Greeks, you know, explained such things by the actions of their gods and goddesses—most capricious beings who could be friend or foe at a whim. But you say that our meeting could not have been such a caprice. Well, then, it was heaven that guided you to me. Even the Greeks speak of heaven sometimes, as always beneficient."

She felt Hannah's breath against her throat, as Hannah spoke.

"Yes, heaven," said Elizabeth firmly, pressing closer to her, "Heaven, where we are now."

The End

Publications of
THE NAIAD PRESS, INC.
P.O. Box 10543 • Tallahassee, Florida 32302
Mail orders welcome. Please include 15% postage.

Toothpick House by Lee Lynch. A novel. 264 pp.
ISBN 0-930044-45-2 $7.95

Madame Aurora by Sarah Aldridge. A novel. 256 pp.
ISBN 0-930044-44-4 $7.95

Curious Wine by Katherine V. Forrest. A novel. 176 pp.
ISBN 0-930044-43-6 $7.50

Black Lesbian in White America. Short stories, essays,
autobiography. 144 pp. ISBN 0-930044-41-X $7.50

Contract with the World by Jane Rule. A novel. 340 pp.
ISBN 0-930044-28-2 $7.95

Yantras of Womanlove by Tee A. Corinne. Photographs. 64 pp.
ISBN 0-930044-30-4 $6.95

Mrs. Porter's Letter by Vicki P. McConnell. A mystery novel.
224 pp. ISBN 0-930044-29-0 $6.95

To the Cleveland Station by Carol Anne Douglas. A novel.
192 pp. ISBN 0-930044-27-4 $6.95

The Nesting Place by Sarah Aldridge. A novel. 224 pp.
ISBN 0-930044-26-6 $6.95

This Is Not for You by Jane Rule. A novel. 284 pp.
ISBN 0-930044-25-8 $7.95

Faultline by Sheila Ortiz Taylor. A novel. 140 pp.
ISBN 0-930044-24-X $6.95

The Lesbian in Literature by Barbara Grier. 3d ed.
Foreword by Maida Tilchen. A comprehensive bibliography.
240 pp. ISBN 0-930044-23-1 ind. $7.95
inst. $10.00

Anna's Country by Elizabeth Lang. A novel. 208 pp.
ISBN 0-930044-19-3 $6.95

Lesbian Writer: Collected Work of Claudia Scott
edited by Frances Hanckel and Susan Windle. Poetry. 128 pp.
ISBN 0-930044-22-3 $4.50

Prism by Valerie Taylor. A novel. 158 pp.
ISBN 0-930044-18-5 $6.95

Black Lesbians: An Annotated Bibliography compiled by
JR Roberts. Foreword by Barbara Smith. 112 pp.
ISBN 0-930044-21-5 ind. $5.95
inst. $8.00

The Marquise and the Novice by Victoria Ramstetter.
  A novel. 108 pp. ISBN 0-930044-16-9 $4.95

Labiaflowers by Tee A. Corinne. 40 pp.
  ISBN 0-930044-20-7 $3.95

Outlander by Jane Rule. Short stories, essays. 207 pp.
  ISBN 0-930044-17-7 $6.95

Sapphistry: The Book of Lesbian Sexuality by Pat Califia.
  2nd edition, revised. 195 pp. ISBN 0-930044-47-9 $7.95

The Black and White of It by Ann Allen Shockley.
  Short stories. 112 pp. ISBN 0-930044-15-0 $5.95

All True Lovers by Sarah Aldridge. A novel. 292 pp.
  ISBN 0-930044-10-X $6.95

The Muse of the Violets by Renee Vivien. Poetry. 84 pp.
  ISBN 0-930044-07-X $4.00

A Woman Appeared to Me by Renee Vivien. Translated by
  Jeannette H. Foster. A novel. xxxi, 65 pp.
  ISBN 0-930044-06-1 $5.00

Cytherea's Breath by Sarah Aldridge. A novel. 240 pp.
  ISBN 0-930044-02-9 $6.95

Tottie by Sarah Aldridge. A novel. 181 pp.
  ISBN 0-930044-01-0 $5.95

The Latecomer by Sarah Aldridge. A novel. 107 pp.
  ISBN 0-930044-00-2 $5.00

VOLUTE BOOKS

Journey to Fulfillment	by Valerie Taylor	$3.95
A World without Men	by Valerie Taylor	$3.95
Return to Lesbos	by Valerie Taylor	$3.95
Desert of the Heart	by Jane Rule	$3.95
Odd Girl Out	by Ann Bannon	$3.95
I Am a Woman	by Ann Bannon	$3.95
Women in the Shadows	by Ann Bannon	$3.95
Journey to a Woman	by Ann Bannon	$3.95
Beebo Brinker	by Ann Bannon	$3.95

Naiad Press, Inc. and its imprint Volute Books (inexpensive mass market paperbacks appear in Volute Books) may always be purchased by mail as well as in your local bookstores.